Also by James Yorkston

It's Lovely to Be Here (2011)
Three Craws (2016)

Selected Discography:

Moving Up Country (2002)
Just Beyond the River (2004)
The Year of the Leopard (2006)
Roaring the Gospel (2007)
When the Haar Rolls In (2008)
Folk Songs (2009)
I Was a Cat from a Book (2012)
The Cellardyke Recording and Wassailing Society (2014)
The Route to the Harmonium (2019)
The Wide, Wide River (2021)

With Yorkston/Thorne/Khan
Everything Sacred (2016)
Neuk Wight Delhi All-Stars (2017)
Navarasa: Nine Emotions (2020)

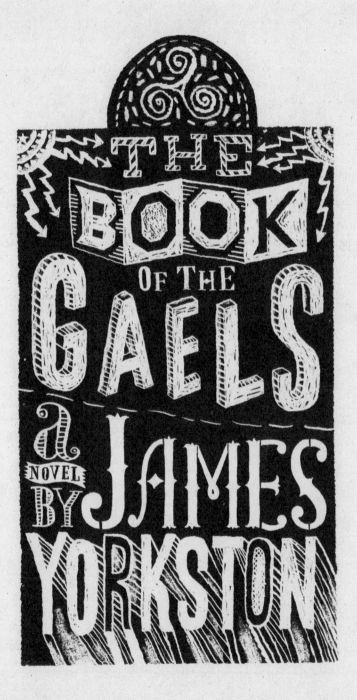

THE
BOOK
OF THE
GAELS

A
NOVEL
BY JAMES
YORKSTON

First published in 2022 by Oldcastle Books,
Harpenden, Herts, UK
www.oldcastlebooks.co.uk

A CIP catalogue record for this book is available from the British Library.

ISBN:
978-0-85730-518-3 (Paperback)
978-0-85730-519-0 (Ebook)

Typeset 11.25 on 13.7pt Adobe Garamond
by Avocet Typeset, Bideford, Devon, UK
Printed and bound in the UK by Clays Ltd, Elcograf S.p.A.

And where was God when you needed him?
Swimming, rolling with the devil?
Grabbing at flailing legs?

(Extract from *The Book of the Gaels* by Fraser Donald McLeod)

This is how I remember it:

1

Creagh, West Cork, 1975

DUE TO THE PROXIMITY of the house to the lough, or perhaps more accurately, the proximity of the house to the cess pit, there was always an army of flies around, and they were more often in the house than out. I'd say the constant rain was an irritation for them, and here inside they'd find enough scraps and scrapes of food to get by. We'd watch them squadron around the house, up and down the staircase, in and out of rooms, groups of twenty or so, sometimes interacting with smaller groups, buzzing, conversing. We'd be sitting there, my wee brother Paul and me, commentating on their battle manoeuvres, the flies from upstairs being the rotten Jerrys, and our brave Scottish brigade gallantly guarding the foot, the exit to outside. What helped our fantastic little game was that on occasion a fly would all of a sudden drop out of the air, dead. It'd lie beside us, give us a last shimmy, a shake of the legs and be still.

We discussed when it had last been to Confession. Would its soul be clean? *Bless me, fly-father, for I have sinned. It has been two long minutes since my last confession. In that time, I have landed on an apple and wandered around a bit before taking off again for the big light, you know, the one in the kitchen...*

Once, a fly death-valleyed in Paul's hair, and sensing it wasn't on the hallowed ground of the window sill or the staircase, or the sink or the fruit bowl, or a shoe or drink, it fuzzled for a good minute longer than we were used to. Paul was screaming *Get it off! Get it off!* And I was dancing around him like a puppet master, invisible strings to Paul's head, scared to touch him, scared to see the fly. When the buzzing stopped, Paul sat on the stairs weeping and I, bravely, looked through his hair and removed most of the fly.

Is it all gone?

It is.

It wasn't, but the most of it was. I think maybe I lost a leg with the combing, and maybe a wing, but nothing one wouldn't get riding down the path outside on a pony or a bicycle.

Once the bodies were dead for sure, safe, still, we'd pick them up by shuffling them on to pieces of paper using one of our father's old books, until we had a bunch, twenty or so, then we'd carefully carry them to the top of the stair. We'd position ourselves and wait, waiting for the next battalion of flies to emerge from below. When they arrived, or when we had become bored, we'd throw the entire lot of carcasses into the air and down the stairwell, shouting *Attack! Attack!* And *Hiawatha!*

I have no idea what the other flies thought, if anything. Seeing their dead cousins springing briefly back into life then falling like a stone once more on to the ribbed stair carpet below.

Next time we scooped them up, they'd be missing legs, half their bodies, wings… Where did it go, all this excess?

Come supper, I'd stir my soup with caution.

2

FATHER WOULD STAY in his room this whole time, typing away on his gun-metal typewriter. He'd feed us, come the evening, and in the morning, but during the day we were more or less free to roam.

We'd have piled downstairs at first light – we wouldn't know the time, but the dark wooden mantel clock would pitch in at some point and warn us: *five, six, seven…* and as the morning wore on, the *eight, nine* and *ten*. And if he wasn't up by then, well, we wouldn't expect him. We'd grab ourselves whatever bread there was and shriek through it with a blunt butter knife, use the same knife to cover it with butter and dunk into the jam pot. We couldn't reach a tap for a drink, unless we drank from the bath taps, which we did, on occasion. And if we were making too much noise, we'd sometimes hear the creaks of the wooden ceiling and floorboards above and we'd freeze –

And if there was silence that followed, we could relax.

But if there were the mighty clumps of father making his way downstairs barefoot, we'd panic and reach for anything that looked respectable, little there was in that darkened kitchen. A postcard. A hairbrush.

We'd push the food into the middle of the table, an island, untouched by our young hands and watch, wait for the internal stable door to creak open.

And there he'd emerge, reddened feet, gnarled nails, eyes glazed, hair slanting like the roof of a collapsed shed. If we kept quiet, we were invisible, sometimes, and he'd pass us by without even an acknowledgement, not even a look. He'd pass through the kitchen, into the tiny vertical coffin lavatory cupboard and release a long stream of pish that seemed to go on forever. Paul and me would stare at each other, counting – *thirteen, fourteen, fifteen* – whilst tidying more, finishing any distilled bath water, dabbing up crumbs, straightening pyjama jackets.

We would learn the subtleties. If he went to wash his hands, he could be getting up and we could be in trouble, for something. For eating the food, maybe. Or waking him. But if he just came straight through, with no hand-wash, that was him, going back to bed. We'd sit bolt upright, eyes locked, don't follow his movement – and he'd be out, out of the kitchen, flicking the door closed behind him and creaking up the wooden stairs.

We'd leave it a minute then that'd be us, breathing out, reaching for the bread, having our fill then cleaning the butter. If we'd eaten too much jam, if the jar was looking empty, we'd take it to the bathroom and mix in some bath water, put the lid on and shake it up. Before too long the jam would be a watery soup, but father never seemed to notice. We would, of course, but the taste of the sugar was still there and if the bread was stale, the water would help that too.

*

Mid-morning, before lunch, we'd once more begin to hear mutterings and stretches, floorboards strained, bed springs. By that time, we were braver, making more noise, killing more soldiers, clashing more swords – the swords being sticks, of course, or merely long grass. Then, most days, a slow, gradual clatter of keys as he pushed the ancient metal typewriter through its paces. What he was writing we did not know, didn't understand how this machine could communicate, though he'd on occasion show us the spidery signs, squares and circles, the endless black/grey letters snaking across the page. We could read a bit, of course we could, but whatever father was writing, well, that took a different kind of reading.

You know, his words made no sense at all.

On the good days he'd bring us in and shout with joy – *Joseph! Paul! Will you come and see this now!* – and we'd stop whatever we were doing and cautiously troop up the stairs; he'd be dressed then, mostly, or half dressed, but trousers on, vest too, a shirt maybe, his thick woollen jumper from autumn to spring's end – and he'd wave a sheet of paper in front of us. Six lines, it'd have, sometimes a little more. The lettering stuck in the middle of the page, as if shaken. He'd clip it to the other ones, the other patterns we'd seen and he'd be joyous. We were too, but we were also cautious, as surely as night came after day his moments of joy would be followed by long stretches of black, black mood. *Come on, come on, get ready and we'll take this to town and post it off. Post it away.*

Would we make it? We did, sometimes. Mostly, maybe. But there were enough days when the walk would kill him of his enthusiasm. The three miles or so – if no one stopped to pick us up – enough for the hatred of his scribbles, their delicate bridges and open-hearted lunges of faith – well, he'd go quiet, or start muttering to himself, or growling, swearing through clenched teeth, until we'd either turn around there and then – and that may be considered a good day – or he'd rip the whole thing up, the whole envelope, the entire package of words, the last month's clattering of keys – distributed amongst the hedgerows. Left to soak in the inevitable rains or perhaps picked up by other curious walkers, the only final audience to his work. And what would they make of it all? *That Scottish loon from down below*, perhaps.

Paul and me would talk to father then, before his mood could change. And we'd get the best of him – for this was the best of him, when he was full of bright and wit. I think there was a part of him too who knew this journey into town was walking on shoogly ground, and he needed the suspension of cruel reality so he'd have the confidence and strength to complete, to finalise, to walk into the Post Office and send the damn thing off.

Because many times, yep, many times we'd get into town and walk straight by that Post Office, with its peculiar name: *Oifig an*

Phoist. Paul and me would look at each other with knowing eyes and perhaps hold hands. We'd see where father would go, we'd know where he'd go and sometimes the bar would take him and sometimes not. Sometimes he'd take a pint, us waiting outside in the light, barely able to see him in amongst the stour and surroundings of other men, these ones much older than *father*.

And there'd be times when he wouldn't be seen for hours – Paul and me playing with street-twigs in a puddle over the road, or running circles around the square, our stomachs calling out but not enough to poke our heads into the gloom. We'd keep an eye out, of course, to see if he'd emerge.

But if the drink was his curse, it was also his crutch and companion, urging him on, encouraging him, strengthening him, easing him in to the Post Office – and we'd spy and drop our game, running straight over and watching – he'd wait, a queue of conversations, his sole Scottish voice in amongst the Irish, not a place to be in a hurry – and we'd wish these people quiet, hurry them up. He needed his confidence. And if he reached the front of the queue – that was it. We were away. His words, on a page, wrapped in a brown paper envelope, would be handed over to old Mr Walsh and then they'd be off and then we'd be off. He'd turn to look for us – forgotten, we were sure, until that moment – and he'd smile. He'd walk over, bend down and pick us up, both together. *Daddy's done his work now. C'mon, we'll go home.*

Then, we'd walk by the bakers, seldom anywhere else, and pick up yesterday's bread. We didn't mind and neither did father. *It's good for their teeth* he'd tell the baker, who'd wink at us and on occasion, rarely, but I remember it so it's worth mentioning – on occasion the baker man would give us a small ball of fresh dough each. We'd suck on it, chewing slowly, the mysterious sour taste and spider web texture sticking to our teeth, refusing to leave our teeth, eventually leaving our mouths tasting something *rotten*.

The walk home would be ok. The tension had gone. He was a realist, in that sense, my father. He couldn't stop the clock now, could he? Sometimes he'd laugh to himself, but this lack of confidence, this despair was a very different beast to what he'd experience *before* the posting. Then, he'd berate himself, curse his mindset and his foolish ideas. Now, he'd be laughing *at* himself, in the way one would laugh at a drunken man making a fool of himself at a wedding... Now, all we could do was wait and enjoy the high spirits, we'd bounce and skip down the road, the journey home taking a fifth of the walk into town, the sun seemingly always out, or at least the rain warm, we'd chase, hide and seek, sing songs.

And not one of us would want to get home. In my mind, I'd see home as black, dark green, damp, cold, close, quiet, stone, worrying, sad. We did not want to be *there*. Here, outside, the fields were breathing, the grass was showing off its colouring, the plain pale green to deep, lush, almost turquoise – a delight to our gloom-squandered eyes. I'd see Paul's eyes alight in the strong sun, see his smile, that beaming smile...

We'd follow a wren as it darted along the hedgerow. We'd follow the curve of the sun as it arched overhead. We'd pick out beasts and faces from the high, thin clouds, and maybe, if we were lucky, father would mention our mother... It would be rare, but a word – or a sentence – then we'd bolt ourselves to sense, concentrate utterly, keep it, memorise it. *She loved the song-birds.* Stack it up with our other words, our other clues, other shades and colours that added up to our own personal imagined portraits. We couldn't ask, we knew that. If we went to the well, the well would dry up. We just had to wait.

A clod of peat seems
an easy cut
and a simple stack.
I carry
a different kind of weight.
I could work between these fine fellows for
sixteen summer weeks
and they still would not know.

We talk rot
and laugh at local misfortune.
I carefully count through my coins
whilst
they scatter their own on rough wooden boards.

At some point I shall make a show of leaving
as though I've somewhere to go
I shall put on my coat and say my goodbyes
And slowly shuffle next door.

(Extract from *The Book of the Gaels* by Fraser Donald McLeod)

3

WE'D BEEN BACK here at Creagh almost a year. The house had belonged to mother. But once mother had gone… well, father hadn't settled here. Too many memories, I suppose, and he'd hauled us all back to Scotland. But then he hadn't settled in Scotland, either. So now we were here again, in amongst those memories that had chased him away the first time.

We hardly knew anyone, and father wasn't exactly encouraging visitors. If they were relations or friends of my mother, my father could barely look them in the eye. They seemed ok to us. We'd peek at them, round the corner, or out of the window, and we'd maybe get a wave or a grin, but father would only be defensive and blistery, whatever their good intentions. He'd close the door on them as soon as he could.

They stopped coming, eventually. Can you blame them?

But the local priest never gave up. There'd be a knock on the door which would disturb my father from his room, he'd slow his way down the stairs, pulling the straps of his braces over his white grey shirt, Paul and me moving out of his way, but watching in horror as his un-socked rock-feet crushed our collection of flies. Father would swing the door open and there would be the priest, nodding his head and offering a handshake.

Eventually, after a dozen such visits of politeness and pleasantry, this priest fellow was invited in. He stayed for the afternoon and sat by the window, whispering away to father.

Hours later, they'd emerged, my father red-faced, but calm. He looked at me and nodded, before showing the priest out.

*

That evening, my father was quieter than usual, if that was even possible. A good quiet, though. It was peaceful. The fire was lit and we sat snuggled up to him, me reading a book, Paul driving a matchbox as if it were a car, over and up the back of the chair, time and time again.

*

Next day, the priest came back. And this time he brought a nun with him. Paul and me scarpered in an instant.

We hid close by in the cupboard below the stair, listening in and hearing only a low murmur of the priest, an occasional squawk of the nun, the slow stove boiling of the water – and how my father would be hating to use the fuel to boil that water – then waiting, as they drank their lukewarm grey black green tea. The ritual lasted a good chunk of the afternoon, Paul and me getting restless but too curious to leave, too scared to misbehave, to risk any wrath, especially in front of a nun, with her thick black glasses and wavering smile. Eventually we were called in, gently at first, *Paul – Joseph – Joseph, bring your brother here...* but we did not move, which led to father opening the slatted green door and heaving us out. *Don't be scared of these lot*, he whispered, then introduced us – *Joseph, Paul, this is Sister Moira, and of course Father Magee...* Sister Moira smiled. *Well hello, boys. We'll be delighted to have you with us at the school, all the way from Scotland so – perhaps there'll be something you can teach us!*

School? I looked at father, who smiled – almost – back at me. *Ok, boys – Away back and play now...*

And we fled – *School! With nuns! No way... You heard! You heard! But who would look after the flies? What about father, what about... lunch, what about...*

Outside the door, we heard Sister Moira speak to my father – *You've made the right decision, Mr McLeod. We'll take care of them. You have my word. Sinéad was a beautiful young woman, and my heart goes out to yourself and these children of hers.*

*

Us saying our goodbyes, my father closing first the outer door, with its glass-paned panels and then the inner door, the door that shut out all the light. Shutting them right out outside, out of our world, this world. As our eyes adjusted, my father stood scratching his chin.

The nuns. They're going to teach you… and maybe feed you, too.

Feed us!?

A-ha. That's what they promised.

I smiled at Paul, and him at me.

I attempt these lines
in hope they will somehow reply,
telling me:

'And this is how you will live.
This is the path that will lead you through,
here is the answer you were seeking.'

But for now, they are achingly quiet.

Wounded,
or shy,
perhaps.

I look over my shoulder
far too often.

4

THE RAIN CAME that evening, and it brought us outside. Father appeared, grinning – *Come on!* – Paul and me looked at each other and prepared for the onslaught that awaited. As father pulled on his boots, we added layer upon layer, all our jumpers and shirts, followed by the big woollen beany hats that Mrs Cronin from up the lane had knitted us, our scarves, and finally our coats. We knew what'd be up and sure enough, within moments father had us leaving the house and walking outside, him striding quickly ahead, then returning and grabbing my own hand, Paul holding my other and – off we went, in procession, down to the lough. We'd learnt not to grumble, for this would be a happy time for us all. Father couldn't complain about the weather, after all it was him who was dragging us now right into the heart of it. We began the slow freeze and curse the lack of second trousers or be grateful we remembered *all* our socks. Past the farms, sensible dogs pricking up their ears and seeing us approach, but them being keen on being dry and barking only, not charging towards us. Father picked up a long stick anyway, just to wave, beckon with. We continued on, father's speed, us slipping behind him on the once-tarmacked road, long now defeated by grasses and wildflowers. We slipped into the forest, offering a small degree of cover but nothing really, almost bigger raindrops now, collecting on the canopy and falling far down on to us.

Whack! Right on the nose.

Look down, watch my step, avoid the sticks, the slips, passing occasional ruined buildings, ancient tracks, heavily mossed walls…

…and finally out, out of the forest and by the lough, the rain now tipping upon us and us – well, my father – hysterical with the noise – at least, I've always thought it was the noise, the beating of the rain upon the lough, the lough surrounded by forests and mountains on each side and the roar of the falling weather reverberating all around. There was a car there too, parked a good few stones' throw away, but they had a motor running and father looked to them anxiously, slipping his face from them to the lough, them to the lough, until they turned their motor off and he relaxed *There you go* and concentrated on the lough.

He was hypnotised, staring out there. There was nothing else to hear, nothing else to think about, just the enormity of the body of water itself and the huge, vacuumed swell of the rainfall. The incessant downpour, constantly slapping our backs, felt like a massage, more distraction from real life, more putting us firmly *here* in the *now*.

The wet began to trickle through my defences and down my neck. One tiny river, then another. Reach my tightened waistband and circle around, tickling. I'd ignore it, best I could.

Looking up at father, his eyes were wide, occasionally wiped by a naked hand, he was inviting the weather, challenging, revelling, swimming in it. His jaw was slammed shut, slightly shaking, steam piling out of his nostrils like a bull, blinking his eyes as if this dwam was delivering some magical, powerful charm. Shaking himself from a momentary slumber then back, staring once more, eyes darting left and right but always, always returning straight down the line, forwards, as far as the eye could see, a mile or so across into the inlet where this giant, deep lough met the Irish Sea.

5

THAT FIRST SCHOOL day, Paul and me were picked up by Seamus, the oldest boy from the farm that rode next to my father's scant bit of land. A year on me at least, I suppose he was eleven or twelve, Seamus was growing, building himself into a bull of a man, taking on complete farm work for years now, as is the way, but still, to his annoyance, stuck with us youngsters.

The walk to this new school was short, a few hundred yards up the lane just, a sense of dread but curiosity – and joy at being outside, let's not forget that, the joy of having escaped the house, the knots of tension that so seemed to follow my father around.

Seamus walked as quickly as his long hob-nailed thick leather boots would take him, and me, I struggled to keep up. Paul, well, he gave me his hand and I can only guess it was for the help with the slight hill and maybe for the comfort of the familiar.

Slow down, Joseph, slow down.

He stumbled over and again and over once more as we passed bramble bushes loaded with berries, fields with horses, mostly, plenty for the eyes to see. I tried to keep up with Seamus, but it wasn't long before the school was within view and then we could relax, for the final walk was just a short ease along the road.

The school building never really grew. In the distance it looked small, like a shell of a giant snail or such, but upon approach, although the ground around it, the fields and trees all swelled to their accepted, predicted size, the school struggled to keep up and when we arrived it was almost as tiny as when we began. Seamus waited for us at the doorway and finally, when we were right there, he chapped on the door. We received an *enter now* and Seamus darted in, no looking back, no welcoming usher. I looked at Paul, himself leaning, unconsciously dragging us in the direction of home, then turned and gently encouraged him in.

*

And if I thought the house, our house, was dark and small and damp and cold, then, well, I was ignorant of how much stronger all those features could become. For here, I'd say, half the size of the building itself was the thick and width of the stone, stone which looks as though it'd come from a far grander building, perhaps a large church or cathedral even, but now blocked down here, as though it'd rolled from a cart and it'd been decided to just leave it and build.

*

There is a window, though it too is small, of course.

With the dankness of the room cleared, my eyes picked out a half-dozen pairs of eyes, seated but turned towards us and there, in the front, a tall, wide nun, not the nun who visited us.

In you come now, come now – sit.

She is larger and taller than the friendly nun of our living room, though wearing the same shapeless brown costume.

She points, with a stick, to two small chairs behind two small desks, right at the very back of the room.

Seamus has taken his place at the front of us all, close to the lady, the nun. He has made it clear to all concerned that he was not *with us*.

And the holy lady, she speaks:

Now. We have two new additions. They are from Scotland…

The faces turn again, to re-view, re-evaluate these *Scotland* creatures.

…But their mother was from here and they are very welcome.

A silence, as our eyes adjust and we're rated, graded, on our appearance, our clothing, our hair. The brown eyes, brown haired bodies looking at us turn, one by one, back around to face the

22

front, face the nun. I recognise a few, from running in the fields, passing the farms…

Now, Joseph, and Paul. Do your best to listen and catch up. We are discussing the Annunciation.

The what?

The final peering head returns to the nun and then the nun is off, speaking of some holy event that we do not understand. Seated and still, our bodies slowly cool even further as the creeping damp of the building crawls up our legs and into our backs, pushing ice between our skin and our meagre clothing.

*

It's a struggle to concentrate when there is nothing to concentrate on but the dark and the imperceptible lulling of the religious language, but if we veer off, if our eyelids droop or we stare at the window to outside that teases us, the nun will slam the stick against her table and call out *Paul!* Or *Joseph! Sit up!* And we'll get the shock of our lives and sit bolt upright.

And those moments, although short, are a relief, as they'll be the first words we understand.

The shaft of sunlight pours in like a straight, powerful waterfall, the tiny dancing specks of dust being the salmon. The stour is such that the air looks thicker than I'm used to, and it's no surprise that I imagine my breathing is becoming slowly slightly more audible, though not noisy, more a whispered pull. The dust floats harmlessly, ignoring the mantra of the nun, on occasion landing on one of the girls, who is sitting right in the stream of sunlight. The girl will turn and glare at the window, infuriated no doubt by the heat of the sun, the same way we're shivering through the lack of it. From her, my eyes move to the other children, carefully, subtly. We're clearly of similar stock. There are no riches here, no jumpers new or fitting, no shirts clean, no shoes not worn for a thousand days before by older siblings or other children altogether.

On occasion the nun's voice will rise in tone slightly and the class will join in the talking, reciting with the nun. This will be the prayer, I guess, and I mouth along *A waggy waggy. A log nog bog. A diggedy dog.* Paul stares at me, perhaps confused, worried that he's the only one there who cannot speak this holy tongue, this long tumble of words, perhaps panicking he's lost his hearing or his sanity. I widen my eyes at him and exaggerate my speech slightly, just enough for him to hear and then he gets it and joins in *A winga rach wock whan. A ligger lock bong.* We smile, and I almost laugh, but the fear of *The Nun* keeps me stable.

Throughout, there's a slow, steady rustle, the children's feet occasionally, not in a rhythm, but between them all a constant, an occasional rub of soles of feet, edges of feet on loose Linoleum. My mind wanders down and I see the results of the rubbing, the different shaped scars, the horseshoe, the wave, the common-or-garden *scuff*. My desk is riddled with scratches and markers, graffiti, names. I idly move my thumbnail up and down a carving of a snake. God's own enemies, snakes. I wonder how it got in here.

Lunch. Come on, lunch.

There's no clock, but by the way the sunlight is creeping through the window, the angle of the shaft changing and then disappearing, almost, we all know it's past lunchtime. My stomach complains. Soon others join in, the thought of lack of food placed in their heads by my own internal rumblings, perhaps. Eventually, the nun slowly ends her business, lowers her stick, closes her imposing black leather Bible, and declares – *Now. Food.*

Still they wait. Still our classmates sit, as motionless as herons, awaiting their catch.

Grace first – and everyone stands. We leap up. We're hidden now, behind the heads so our murmur is less important.

As quickly as they stood, they sit. We collapse after them, anxious not to be the cause of any delay.

Now. Begin.

But where's the food? Begin what? The other children are all off, hands diving straight to the bags between their feet, emerging with sandwiches or hunks of bread, occasional bits of fruit. Paul and me look at each other in panic. *We have no food.* We've sat through the coarseness of the morning, so where is our reward?

You two. Come to the front.

No one stops eating as she beckons us forward. Paul reaches for my hand and I take it. I am the elder, I pass down the comfort, though there is none in me. I push out my chest, adding six months and adult bravery to my stature. We creep through the desks and emerge in the square foot of space in front of the nun.

No food, is it?

We are motionless but our eyes, betraying our hunger by glancing from her own to her case to the stick to the *What happens next?*

Eventually, I reply – *No, Miss.*

I am not a Miss. I am a Sister.

No, Sister. We have no food.

She grimaces. She looks neither happy nor satisfied.

God will provide.

I don't know what that means and I don't know if she's expecting an answer, but then –

Sit down now –

And she nods towards our chairs, empty of hand, empty of stomach. But I'm staring at her, my mouth creeping open as if to talk, or better, eat – I almost raise an arm to point, to demonstrate that the others are eating and we were told…

Go on! Close your mouth before the devil gets in and settles inside you. Sit!

We have no options. For now, anyhow. We turn and make our way back through, Paul crying, just a little. Sobbing. As we pass an anonymous table a younger girl rips off a bit of her crust and quietly hands it to me. The nun makes a noise – *Huh.*

I give her no option to tell us off or take the food. Quickly, I bite it in two and give half to Paul who shoves it in his mouth, quietening the crying. Two small mouthfuls of bread.

We sit back down and watch, wait, listen, our stomachs still churning, insulted as they were by the meagre offering of the crust. The nun removes a brown paper bag from her satchel and slowly, precisely, irritatingly, nibbles away at a large cheese sandwich. Paul is watching her, quietly sobbing.

*

The afternoon is a long, perpetual drag and in my mind, I'm building up the strongest case I can for not ever returning. The woman is a witch. The place is colder and damper than our own. There's no light. The floor is just flapping, filthy lino, worn down with dirt. There's no lavatory and even if there were, no one would be brave enough to ask. Paul has stopped crying and is just staring at the nun. Later, he tells me that in his mind she was being bombarded by one of our squadrons of flies.

At the end of the afternoon we all stand. They recite some speech, and then we leave. Everyone pushes past us and such is the desire to escape into the sunshine, by the time we're out the clutch of pupils has almost disappeared, footfall audible, running and screaming, escaping. All that remains is the girl who fed us. She's standing a good ten yards from the school, and not *waiting* as such, but there, and well, perhaps *waiting*.

Paul and me are too scared to talk, despite us being outside and the nun being within. We've been hypnotised by the cold and the drudgery. Paul's shivering, embracing himself, hopping

I need to pee…

And he runs straight up the hedgerow, past the waiting girl, to the nearest gate post where he does his business, quickly and unashamed.

As I reach where the girl is standing, she turns and looks toward me –

Thank you for the food.

She smiles.

Where's Scotland? Is it near Kerry? My father's been to Kerry, for the market.

But right now, Scotland seems far away.

It's...

Scotland plays in my head like an old film, the memories thinning and refining themselves, until they become streamlined, losing detail on each play, just the basics, the outline, the echo...

It's good. It's warm.

Warm?

I nod.

I'm Grace. Who are you?

My name's Joseph.

Paul returns. His head is jumping, interrupting. *That stupid old woman.*

A hand shoots up to the girl Grace's face, shocked.

There was NO food. That stupid old woman.

He's stomping and almost in tears again. Clenched fists, angered. He's screwed his face up, making it look as tight and contorted as he possibly can.

I turn to look, make sure the nun hasn't heard, a whack around the head could possibly be expected from that stick of hers. Grace leans forward, neck extended, head as close as it can go without moving her feet, crunches her eyes and spits out -

Don't say that, or you'll not go to Heaven.

Then – *C'mon.*

We turn and see the door opening, the first signs of the nun emerging. Grace grabs my hand and pulls me away, up the path towards home.

If she gets you, she'll ask you everything she said and invite herself inside to your house and worry your mother and make her eat everything in there, if there's any cake or tea or milk she'll have it, then there'll be trouble when she goes. Do you have cake in Scotland?

I nod, though we seldom did.

Despite her hurry, despite her pull and interest, Paul is way ahead of us, running home, his body hurtling down the middle of the path, no looking back. *See you* I say and disjoin hands, sprinting and overtaking her, before quickly getting beside Paul, keeping his speed going, keeping the run alive.

I turn and Grace's jogging behind us, but not for us, just away from the nun, I see that. It's clear why the other children got out so quickly, it was a head-start away.

Here are the dragonfly
you loved.

'This! This is why we're here!'
The long, hidden pond,
the still, the warmth around it…

It is ours alone,
for now.

But watch your step
for the moss on the water
can be deceptive.

6

*B*UT THERE WAS *no food, father...*
What do you mean no food! For sure, there was!

We're in his study. We crashed into the house and hurled up the stairs, racketing, Paul crying, then forgetting to cry, what with his own fury, then remembering and crying once more.

We didn't even knock on his door, poor man. He got some shock.

What the fuck?

That stops us cold, that word does, and he's staring, our eyes readjusting to the more familiar darkened room. He's sat at the typewriter beast, but body turned in our direction. His feet are still with the work, the dwam of the paper – that's where he wants to be right now.

What do you mean there was no food!?

It – there – everyone else...

He looks furious. Paul lets go – *There wasn't anything else for us, everyone ate except us, it was colder than here, not better, there was no food at all and no one even LOOKED at us and the nun just spoke a nonsense over and over and it smelled like an old loo...*

My father laughed. But then he began shaking his head, back and forth, and the smile went, quick. *Is this true Joseph? About the food, I mean?*

I nod. *We haven't eaten, Father. Not at all today.*

He takes one of his enormous rough hands and drags it slowly from his forehead down to his neck and again, rubbing his ears, once each. Silence, the hands to hips, he looks at the paper looking at him, admits defeat and swings his thick legs towards us, before standing. *Ok Come downstairs and we'll see what there is. And boys?*

Paul is hopping, anxious to get down the stairs.

Don't charge in on me like that, eh? Don't do that.

Yes, father. And Paul's off. I wait for father and wonder why doesn't he open the curtains? It's so dark in here. There's a tiny electric lamp burring away in the corner, but the curtains would be better open, surely, he must know that? I'm ushered out and down I go, quickly, three steps at a time.

*

There's a single thick crust. Father divides it into two and pours some watery jam over it. We wolf it down in silence. We poke up the crumbs and lick the plate. Father pours us a jug of water each and that chases down our feast.

Don't worry. I'll sort it.

He says. Then, to himself:

I'll sort it.

*

Soon after, the sun still high, we're off, walking the mile or so towards the convent. There's a push in my father's step, he's keen to get this dealt with straightaway. It's a tall, impressive, foreboding building, cathedral huge – *How many nuns can fit inside there?*

Father doesn't want us inside, fortunately, for I remember the one time we were in, being confronted by corridors of portraits of stiff, holy, fearsome old ladies, staring miserably down, drilling their stares into those fortunate enough to be young and alive.

Wait.

He opens the entrance door and disappears. Paul immediately turns and runs towards the *Broken-Down Tree*, a place we'd discovered on a previous visit. He climbs aboard this long, horizontal fir tree and using his weight begins to shake the trunk, the branches. Midges and beasts jump off from all sides and I jump on behind.

31

Before long, the two of us deep into a game of *Pirates and Nuns*, where us brave pirates push the nuns from the boat with our legs, the boat thrusting forwards into a choppy ocean *Watch out! Another one, another one!* And we kick her away, the sharks grabbing her feet and pulling her under. Every time she falls, we recite the same quick prayer, before it descends into a mere mumble – *Glory be to the Father, and to the belllubedyblub...* Soon, we're deep in the ocean, shrieking, the waves throwing us back and side, me grabbing Paul, Paul holding on and swaying his body in circles, causing the boat to rock, the tree to shake, the laughs to shout. *Where shall we go?* And *Watch out for the sharks!* And *Watch out for the nuns!* And – *We'll go for the ocean! We'll go for Scotland!* and –

And before we know it, there's a real nun, right there beside us. I spy her one second before she speaks, but she speaks anyway and she is not happy.

You two. Keep the noise down immediately. This is the garden of the House of God, not some... not some playpark.

The waters calm, instantly. Paul freezes still, arms locked against a tributary branch, itself which is daring to continue its shudder, regardless of the anger of the audience. I, as the elder, turn and face her, await the word of the holy lady:

Now. Climb down from there and say two Hail Marys. Pull yourselves together and wait for your father in silence.

She adds a long, disapproving stare, her eyes grating us up and down, waits for our dismount then turns and leaves, her brown hem catching the damp of the longer grass.

Hail Mary.

I say. Paul replies –

Hail Mary.

But as the nun is now out of earshot, we leave it there.

*

We sit on some rocks. Paul has a pinecone that he's idly pushing backwards and forth, backwards and forth across his thigh. I watch and count the seeds that pop out, then roll down off of him on to the pathway.

*

We're walking too quickly for him to be happy.

Softly – *Did you lie to me?*

He's lumbering forwards, one of us in each hand, being dragged behind him, away, away from our perch.

As soon as we're out of earshot of the nunnery –

Did you lie to me? Did you get food?

What? No, father.

He's in a fury. Face red, teeth clammed, looking at us in turn, jagging his arms forward, which pulls us, hurts us, rips at our shoulders.

She said she made you food and that you ate it well enough.

Paul is crying. I'm not, but I would be if I had an elder brother, for sure – *Father, we didn't have any food, I swear to God, I swear, I swear to mama…*

Don't bring your mother into this!

And he slaps my head, not hard, but enough, then stops us all walking. We're out of eyeshot of the nuns now. He kneels on the floor and brings us directly to his eye line. He's studying us, looking for non-truths, for deception.

She said – Sister Kathleen said – She said that you'd eaten the food they'd made for you. A big white sandwich. They brought in the nun who made the thing. She was almost in tears, crying about cheese of all things. Boys, I lost my temper in there and I bawled at them. Tell me. Are you lying? Did you eat that food?

We shake our heads wildly. Paul's tears hit my cheek and I begin to cry, but I have to say –

There was nothing for us, father. She – the nun – she ate food, the boys and girls ate food, but all we got was a crust from another girl, that was it…

A crust? You told me you'd had nothing!

A glimpse of our guilt, a hint of deception

It was…

Paul now –

…Da', we didn't eat. A mouthful of crust of bread was all. From a little girl NOT from the nun…

…the nun said 'God will provide' then she ate the sandwich…

…we had nothing. Nothing.

My father is breathing heavy, furious, but he believes us. He's straining inside, desperate to lash out or throttle. Not us though, I know that.

These fucking nuns…

Twice now, twice now we've heard that. It shocks Paul and me to quiet.

Ten, twenty deep breaths, slowing as they go, gradually calming, coming to.

Ok lads. You boys and me – keep on telling the truth and we'll all be ok. We'll all be ok.

Father picks Paul up and places him high on his shoulders, brings Paul's hands down over his face, briefly kissing them and begins the silent walk home.

*

The next morning there's a knock at the door and the nun – Sister Kathleen, we know – is standing, expectant and defiant.

She's gurning, almost. Not smiling or grinning. She has moved her lips into a joyful position, but her eyes are dead with anger.

My father slowly looks her up and down, giving her a clear warning then pats us out of the door. As we get out of earshot, as we hear him closing our homely front door, Sister Kathleen asks –

So. Are you two greedy little pigs ready for school?

*

We got fed that day. At lunch, we were called to the front and presented with that grand-looking sandwich. Sister Kathleen opened it up, to see what was inside, teased us with the delay, the hunger, the fear of the thievery, but she handed it over – pointedly to Paul, who presented it to me. I ripped it in two right there and then in front of her and returned Paul the bigger half. As we walked back to our chairs the other children would watch, some with envy I guess, as their own food looked scant, but we were fed and that's what mattered to me. Young Grace smiled, Paul smiled and so did I.

And, that afternoon, God's word sounded better with a full tummy.

Upon our walk from school, laughing and chatting with young Grace, our new friend and co-conspirator/chief whisperer in the Battle against Nuns and Boredom, father was awaiting. He looked agitated. But something else, too. Like, he looked surprised. *Happy*, almost.

I've some news, boys. We've to go to Dublin.

To Dublin?

You heard me. First thing tomorrow.

And in his hand, he was holding a small, folded piece of paper.

These wonders,
these grass held
over-high cliffs,
frame mountains of water.

If we dare look below, we see
rocks that would crush you or I
being played with
as though
cat with mouse.

7

THAT NIGHT, I sleep, and I dream, I dream of the great lough once more. Father taught us to swim, slowly, over the years, but we've always been in it, first crabbing, with our tiny little nets, paddling just, but then down, crawling, scraping our bellies along the bottom coming up all scratched and raw-lined from the rocks and the barnacles and the salt, the salt for the sea gets in to this particular bit of water... We'd never have floats, or armbands – sure, we'd see tourists with both – but father would say *They won't help you, if you don't have them...* so we'd carry on, almost a struggle at times, warmer in the summer, but in the summer seeing so many children on their boats and us not allowed *until you can swim from one side to the other* which seemed a lot to ask, but finally, when I probably could swim half of it, and I could venture out a good stone's throw from the shore, then father would relax and let me explore, dive down under, pop back up a full twenty seconds later... Paul was behind me with HIS swimming, but then why wouldn't he be, with him being younger and soon the tourists would speak to father *He's a fine swimmer* and father would grin, almost, at these city dwellers with their inflated lifebelts. He'd say it to them, too – *They won't help you, if you don't have them...*

8

WE FELL INTO the church, that was my memory of it, I certainly didn't hear any crashing or thunderous shoulder charge, but then father was cursing and the rain was pelting and I was keeping my ears pretty quiet. So, we fell into the church, or the porch, anyhow.

We'd been walking for most of the day, father had stuck his thumb out and we'd got a lift, but we'd ended up going north into Kerry, the driver, a farmer, just wanting the company and eventually telling my father *Kerry is a better place than Dublin sure* and father losing his rag and us getting booted out of the car, a stinking old, long estate that had no doubt carried plenty of livestock in its time. Paul and me had been playing a game in the back, the game being *What died in here?* Guessing what could have caused such a tumultuous stink; the winner, at the moment of our ejection, the winner was *a mouse in a cat in the stomach of an old cow in Sister Kathleen's habit*. But it was a hollow victory, for soon we were out, in the rain, and even though the farmer said – *Get back in the car you fool, the rain will soak you* – Well, even though he said that, father had hammered the car with an angry *thump*, father's leather suitcase slamming down against the windscreen and that was enough – and now we were alone, out in the rain and the cold.

We had to walk. The sensible thing, looking back, would have been to hitch back the way we came, but father reckoned the side roads were for the best, although surely he should have known, as I knew, as Paul knew, even, the side roads would not be going in any sort of straight line at all and there'd be few vehicles upon them other than more farmers and perhaps the odd holidaymaker out for a spin, but no chance of a one-off lift to Dublin, or Cork, where father told us he was aiming we'd get to first, to spend the night.

The night seemed close now, with Cork considerably further.

My father tried to keep us strong. Paul got a lift on his back every now and then. I walked, then jogged, walked, then jogged along, to keep up.

We'd keep our eyes open, for the ditches, the high branches from the uncut bushes, the speed of father's gallop; but our ears, too, for the words – the *Jesus!*, the *Bastard*, the *C'mon!* –whenever a car went by without picking us up… and who would pick us up? One man, two children and a lot of wet… And risk maybe.

Sure, who were they standing out in the cold, and what were they doing out here?

And soon the dark came and between the clouds the stars blurred out, and my father, he said, used them to navigate. Through the fields, of all the places, as who would see us to pick us up and rescue in a field? And the wet from the hay or the leaves of the crop, soaking upwards, the rain soaking downwards. Paul was in some kind of sleep on father's back, head bouncing up and down against his shoulders, and me, I was struggling behind now, following their silhouette through the blue-black gloom, mind closing down, my legs complaining, my arms falling, not even the energy to hold them still.

Until – dead stop, arriving at a doorway. A glass door, leading to a small porch, then behind, a few feet – a church. I'd not even seen it approach. Just another dark shape on the horizon that wasn't father's back. I was delighted though. Soaked through and delighted. My woollen trousers had given up on any waterproofing an hour back, a dozen whole fields back. This was something, some hope. This was anything.

The door was open and we were in.

And at first, this small glass room was relief, it was the dropping of the wind, the ears re-setting, the stationary muscles relaxing, but then soon, it was replaced with new – the cold brought to life by the lack of our movement, the chattering of someone's teeth – my own, it seemed – then Paul, whining, father stomping his thick leather shoes up and down, up and down. The wind was still there, of course, battering the door an inch or so open and closed, open and closed, as if a beast was outside, repeatedly trying to enter…

…and my clothes, well, they recovered from the wind pulling, forcing them in all directions and resigned themselves to falling flat on my skin, forcing the cold and the wet upon me. Through the gloom, I could see father looking at me and shaking his head. For a moment, there seemed to be a questioning visible, perhaps his younger self wondering what the heck to do and resorting to asking little ol' me, as if I would have the answer. For the answer, surely, was not to remain in this small wind-buffeted glass rectangle, with only a door mat for comfort.

I didn't pray. Paul wouldn't have, either. He was still half asleep, exhausted. And I doubt father did. But there was a mighty gust of wind, followed by a click, a tiny almost imperceptible click, and the internal door to the church itself slowly peeled open. I looked down, to the black of the floor, as if searching for a mouse that'd ventured through to allow us entry, but there was no such mouse, of course. Back up, and father's reaching for the handle and levering the door open the rest of the way. We go through to the church proper and push the door shut.

*

More silence, an immediate escape from the storm, the rain on the windows, those speckled windows glowing like horizontal gravestones, a peeled grey light barely making it inside, but marking the walls, the structure, the space that we are in.

And it is warmer, perhaps. No, not warmer, but – less wind battered. I wonder if anyone lives here, any priest or watchman or tramp or – anyone with a welcome? A warm drink. A bowl of anything to eat. An apple. Whatever.

Father is standing by Paul, who I can just make out half sitting, half lying on a pew. I see the motion between them. I walk closer and make out the undressing. Father hands me Paul's coat, now thrice its usual weight with the waterlogging.

Here. Squeeze it. Try and get most of the water out.

And I take it and shake it up and down, pull it towards me, pull it close, water dripping on to the floor, but on to me, too –

No, don't do it on yourself, don't be an eejit – on the floor, look –

And he takes an arm and in the grey light, he slowly coils it into a snake shape, twisting it around and around, from snake to spring, dripping on to the floor, then back to me –

Do your best –

He turns to Paul again and feels, then removes the rest of his clothes, one by one, jumper, shirt, vest, trousers, underwear, peeling out as much of the wet as he can. Paul is shivering, but what else could father have done?

Joseph, try and find something for him to wear – go on –

What, father?

I don't know – anything. A… what are they called – a cloak – a gown. A sheet. Anything.

I play blind man's buff in the dark, aching from pew to pew, glad now to be moving for it is keeping me from freezing, but finding nothing organic, or material, until I reach the altar –

Father –

What is it?

Can I go on to the altar?

Of course, you can.

Is it not holy?

It's a slab of old stone, Joseph, if that. Come on now – Paul's cold.

I don't doubt that.

And I climb, feeling the steps with my hand, making sure I don't make a mess of it and trip and graze a knee.

I reach the altar. My head height, almost. Something flecks against me and I recoil, a split second later a clatter on the floor as a whatever it was reaches ground level.

Ah!

Jesus, Joseph, what was that?

I don't, I don't know father… It was on the altar…

It'll be a candlestick, maybe. Pick it up. Bring it over.

I feel around on the floor – a horrible job in this near dark, what if it was *a rat* that fell off – an angry rat with big teeth, now awaiting its revenge…

C'mon, Joseph.

It's there, the candlestick. I pick it up, a cold metal, and hear another slight dunt, which I presume rightly to be the candle itself, falling out. That has a very different feel, of course, the wax warmer than the holder. I bring them up and carry them over to father.

Here – here.

A hand comes out of the dark and plucks my winnings. I don't know what to do, continue the hunt for clothing or wait, so I wait and that's the right decision, for a fumble later the device is handed back to me – *Hold it still now – on the holder, not the stick, that's it…*

And I hold it, as asked, important. Paul lightly snuffling now, almost asleep but shivering, and then – within a moment – there's a spark of light and I'm blinded momentarily. I can see father's hand, cuffing the match, being brought toward me – the sudden glow of it surprises me still and I back off, then hold the candle forwards, forwards and still, letting father bring the match closer and finally on the wick, and then, the candle slowly takes to life.

And with this new light, I can see that father has his huge coat off and that Paul is now almost asleep within that coat. How I long for that particular warmth.

See if you can find some more, will you?

More what?

More candles! There should be at least one other of them on the altar. These things come in pairs, you know.

He's smiling, I can see, and I'm off, though the light of the candle has re-set my eyes and a golden-red blur mocks my attempts to avoid the pews.

*

I'm laid down flat, wrapped in an altar cloth and wearing an altar boy's cassock. A dressing gown, almost. I removed the beading around the waist, the rope-knot digging into me. Father has squeezed most of the water out of my clothes and they're hanging, not drying, but not chilling me either. I'm struggling to keep an eye open and am, on occasion, asking father if he needs any further help, but he's lowing me to sleep now – *Just rest, rest* – and finally he walks over toward me, places his huge fat hand on my face and gently pulls my eyelids down.

Sleep,
Sinéad,
sleep.
and be aware of my love.

And if you should dream, then dream of us,
entwined.

Not the panic,
nor the fall,
nor the loss

Let me deal with those.

I tell myself – that was the only moment in your life
you were ever alone.

As if that would be enough.

Oh, sleep,
Sinéad,
sleep,
And be aware of my love.

9

THE NIGHT BROUGHT many things, including, on occasion, deep, dream-filled slumber, but also the vacuum and clatter of a storm, the hurling of the rain on the window, sounding more like tiny pebbles than drops of water. I slept, on and off, but the pew was not encouraging, though at least it was not the stone cold of the floor, and it was blissfully dry. As the dawn arrived, I managed to squeeze my eyes closed and not think about hunger or what the day would bring.

So when the door finally opened, the door we'd entered through, I was still down, asleep, almost. I suppose I may have heard the rattle of the door, but there'd been so many rattles through the night, why would this one be different? But it was –

Well. Now then. What have we here?

I open my eyes to see father springing up, but now wearing his dry night-clothing: priest's robes, and them a ridiculous bright purple and gold, so obvious in the light, as glaring now as they were hidden by the dark just a few hours ago.

Is that you're wearing… Is that you're wearing my Easter vestments!? Well well!

My father, who'd clearly been deep asleep, spluttered into life –

Ah I'm sorry, Father, we were caught – we were caught in the rain –

And he gestures to Paul, to me and to Paul again, the youngster surely brokering the most sympathy. And Paul, waking then, looks at father and squeaks out *Where are we? My back hurts. I'm hungry.*

We didn't break in – the door – the door was open…

I look to the priest, to see what divine intervention to our morning this will be – he gestures with his hands, in that typical

45

pose of Christ showing the wounds on his palms, and says – *You are all welcome here in God's church, my children. But – I'd ask you return the garments, if you please… Ah no – come on, come on now – the candles! You've used up the altar candles, oh I must say…*

I'm sorry, Father, there was no light and the children – again he gestures to us, for it is our fault, we are to blame – *We needed… the warmth. The light.*

The priest, he smiles. He walks to my father and embraces him for a good long time, not a minute, but over the usual politeness, surely.

Don't you worry. There are plenty more, my child. Now – I have to get ready for the Mass. You'll be staying for the Mass, surely?

My heart jumped. God, I hope not… But –

We will. And Father?

Yes, son?

There's one more thing –

My father gestures down to where he'd been sleeping, just another pew, same as my own. Beside it, on the floor, standing upright, a long green bottle with a coloured label. I can't quite make out what it says –

I'm sorry. I was cold.

Heh. My, my. Well, never mind. I'm sure you'll be attending confession after the Mass, won't you, my son?

*

We dressed quickly. Our clothes were still wet, still cold, but now stank of church damp. Father clambering out of the priest costume was a sight, looking grand and gentry at the start, then confused along the way – waving his arms to escape, but looking like he was wearing a ghost costume – then the battered woollen trousers and stained undervest coming into view, clothing that announced who he really was.

You can keep those cassocks on, boys, if you'd like to try at serving on the altar?

But father grinned – *No lads, take them off. Give them back to Father – Father?*

Father Thomas. Fair enough. You can't blame a man for trying, can you? Now. Give me a hand straightening up this altar, will you? Seems there's been a bit of commotion here...

*

The church slowly began to fill. We sat tight in the back row, watching, farmers in their best clothes, mostly, I'd say, a lot of old women, fewer old men, some children around our age, always curious to see them, to see how well trained they'd been, how silent they were. One boy, maybe twelve years old, was wearing a tie. I felt my own neck. It felt better, my shirt loose.

The congregation seemed to like this priest, there was an attention towards him that I'd never seen back to the few times we'd attended Mass... but I wasn't filled with the Holy Spirit, it was still the hunger pangs. Paul was clutching his stomach and rocking back and forth, father's hand on his head, lightly rubbing. I wonder what father was planning. Where we were going to go? All these people must mean some route to civilisation, perhaps some buttered toast...

There were no songs, which was a shame, as I always enjoyed the songs, the comforting drone of the crowd.

Paul was peering up, at me, then the priest, at father, then those around us. I was wondering what he was looking for, but then it all became clear. At the word of the priest, the whole lot of them stood up as one and began to file to the front of the church. We'd seen this before of course, it was where the people went for the little white biscuits – and Paul, well, he jumped off father's lap as quick as a midge and joined that queue. Father made to grab at him, then relaxed, slopped back and grinned. Father then motioned me over, a glint in his eye and both me and him joined the parade, shuffling slowly to Father Thomas. As Paul reached the top of the queue, he stepped forward to Father Thomas, and copying an action he'd seen many times, he stuck his tongue out at the priest. Perhaps a little more vulgar looking than normal, but no matter. Father Thomas looked at my father and said loudly *He's a little young for his communion, is he not?* And my father, with not a skip, replied – *We were in Spain, Father. It's done a little younger there.*

I have no recollection of being in Spain.

Spain was it?

Looking directly at my father, a slight raising of the eyebrows?

It was, Father.

Well then. Spain it is.

And I don't know what he gave to Paul, but when it came to my turn, there was a tremendous little pile of white discs pushed on to my tongue and into my mouth. I chewed, chewed and swallowed and made my way back to our seats, where Paul was waiting. There was still the remainder of a queue and Paul whispered *Can I go up again, father?* But a hand on his shoulder said *No.*

The Mass went quiet then. I couldn't hear anybody else chewing.

10

WE WAITED. WE waited until the last of the parishioners had gone, an old lady hanging back for a word with Father Thomas, then talking about her sisters in purgatory and special Masses and *had there been any word from Dublin?* And finally, when she departed, my father approached Father Thomas and spoke – *Thank you, Father. I appreciate what you did.*

And what was that, my son?

Let us stay. Didn't kick us out. Gave us… bread.

The sacrament? That's not bread, my son, that's the body of Christ as sure as you and I live and breathe.

And then he smiled – *And I guess I'm thankful you didn't find it last night and eat it all yourself!*

My father laughed – *I guess we never found it* – then blinked his eyes – *Father… Would you be able…*

Is it money you're after now?

No – No, Father. I don't beg. We're not beggars. I have a wage waiting me in Dublin. I'm a writer, you see. I need to see my – my publisher.

A writer? Well, you'll need all of God's help for that, my son. Here – it's not the smutty stuff, is it? I've no time for that.

My father grinned – *No. It's – It's poetry.*

Poetry?

Father, barely – *Yes*

Ha! Well, you'll need God and beyond then to help you!

I don't – I don't need anything, Father – Just a point to the road to Dublin. We got in all sorts of bother yesterday, ended up here, as your…

Guests?

Guests, Father, yes. Thank you.

49

Well don't you worry. I'll give you and these young lads a lift to the main road and you can try your luck easily enough down there. But before we go –

Yes, Father?

Would you agree that God was looking out for you last night? Granting you shelter in this modest building?

Perhaps, Father, perhaps.

*

I fall behind, just a few steps, just to pee. I've waited until there's a bend in the lane, for privacy. Father strides on, Paul galloping beside him, the sole on his left foot beginning to flap just a little.

It's tall grass, mostly, that I'm peeing on. Wildflowers, the buzz of insects. I watch as a fly – just a common black fly – dizzily crashes into a waterlogged and very visible spider's web. I'm stuck here, now, mid-flow, so watch on. The fly must realise – instinct, you know – for his energy goes from placid buzz or hum to full-speed panic *get me out of here* mode and I think how much energy he must be expending... A spider comes out of his hiding place, quickly looking to see the fuss, and within a second, he's on top of the fly, preening his legs, sharpening his teeth. The fly is not giving up though, no, any thought of tomorrow gone for the little fellow and I think *I could save him, right now, with a twig, perhaps* but instead I stand back and watch, my pee finished. The fly is doomed, I think, I zip up and make to leave – but – suddenly – as if a motor car has got started, the big black ink splot of a fly has gone and is airborne again – this time with even less grace than before, and I think it must be the exhaustion, but no – he veers toward me and I jump back and see, quite clearly – that the spider is on the fly's back. Now, who knows what the spider is thinking now? There'll have been a lot of energy gone into making that web and now he's flying away on top of his dinner. I'm guessing the fly will collapse somewhere and the spider will finish him off and soon enough the fly crash lands into the other side of the lane, another layer of tall grass and wildflower. I peer over, carefully, should it rise, but cannot spot them, fallen now as they are in the wet of the grass. I stay for a moment, then hear Father calling *Joseph! Come on now!* And rush back to keep up.

*

As the road curved downwards, the verges closed in, and drops of the ever-present moisture began to dipple on to our heads, necks, cheeks. Caught on the leaves above, pooling, weighing down and depositing, on repeat. The air warms, close, the wet a comfort now, cooling us down this far into our walk. I wonder if father knows the way. We're not on a main road, no, more an aside that seemed to be roughly going in the right direction, but then, these side roads bend and double back on themselves without warning and we could be heading back homewards for all father knew. A maze of hedges and fields. I begin to count gates, looking out for peculiarities, should I be able to say *Father, we've been this way* – as if such knowledge would have any worth other than the chance of a skelp, a light skelp at this time of day, but in a few hours… well, I'd be keeping my mouth shut then.

Paul is riding on father's back again. I envy him. My father commanding, over and over – *Keep your back straight, Paul. C'mon now, straighten the back, or else your weight shifts and it's harder to carry…* It suits me, in a way, as it slows father, whether he realises it or not, which makes it easier for me to keep up.

A steep, wet decline and I worry about father slipping and dropping Paul on to his head… I watch father's leather soles, sure and careful, from his feet, sloshing in the wet gravel, his suitcase, slapping against his side, up to Paul. Slowly, a bright yellow appears, breaking through the green of the leaves, an artificial, too bright yellow, then voices – I peek to see, I strain to hear, but nothing, just a ramble, until we turn a final corner and ahead there are half a dozen strangers, of course, gathered around a shrine of some sort.

As we approach, they turn, quieten and await us, smiling.

These shrines crop up everywhere, and although I do not believe, for father would not allow *that*, I always avert my eyes, should the Blessed Virgin wink at me or offer an arm of friendship or bleed from her heart or get into my sleep... They attract the tourists, the parishioners, the priests holding real, genuine Masses on the roadsides... My father has no time for it though, so we usually escape that particular waste of an afternoon.

Hello

One of the ladies, she must be eighty, or sixty perhaps, is slightly bowing to father, to us. I can't place them. They have peculiar foreign faces. Father lifts Paul down from his shoulders and they crow around him, *aahing* and *oohing*. As I arrive at the rear, the ladies approach one by one and make to greet me in a mock, grown-up to grown-up way. I'm too old to hide behind father's trousers, but I stand stock still, embarrassed at this parade of admiring grannies.

Do you know who... statue?

One of the ladies is addressing father, in halting, precise English – *Eh?*

Umm... Who is this?

Ah! This is who they call Mary. The Blessed Virgin Mary...

And she turns and gabbles to the rest in a language I do not understand, who, in reply *Umm!* And *Aah!* as appropriate.

Paul is staring. One of the ladies has a half-bitten sandwich in her hand and Paul has fixed on it. I watch him, should he grab...

The lady spots, she realises, and she says something to father, who replies with a grunt. A grunt that is taken to mean – *Sure, please do rip your sandwich in half and offer to my son* – for that is what happens and Paul grabs it from her and shoves it into his mouth whole, before the little people can take it, or more likely, me. Paul turns and looks at me, his cheeks puffed out and makes a curious, high-pitched, excited noise, glee, delight, his eyes wide open, a huge grin on his swollen mouth.

The grannies seem shocked at his lack of table manners, his speed, his gusto and my reaction, for I had leaned forward involuntarily, as if to catch any crumbs, and now my face is one of betrayal and disappointment. Father too, even his body was half-turned, his hand pawed out towards Paul, as if he also was expecting a shared third of this tiny half-sandwich…

There's a silence now, as we watch Paul slowly, very slowly, munch and chew his way through the food. He needs a drink, of course, to wash it down, but we just stare in wonderment.

Father turns to me and raises his eyebrows, an apology, a shrug, a *What could I do?*

We turn then to the grannies, our part in their play. *Sorry about that.*

They're looking at us in a different way now, up and down, up and down, our trousers, our broken-down shoes, our general thinning wariness, my father's sunken eyes and then – then their bags open and out from within comes more food – bright white bread, crusts off, peculiar colours within. They hand them over, one by one, my father passing on to me and me staring for an instant at this peculiar orange-coloured filling, not carrot, sniffing – fish! – and nibbling, then eating, quickly, slowly, quickly, slowly, remember to chew – and there's another sandwich awaiting me and, I bet, another after that. I'm in some kind of heaven. I turn and look at the Blessed Virgin, who is smiling down toward me.

When we first met
your eyes were open and kind.
We spoke of
Art, Music, and Photography,
the big things, you know?
Safe in conversation with another who would understand.
And the fury of the real world? – Shh! Forget that!
I mentioned
I wanted to be a poet -
'I AM a poet!'
and you laughed
for you knew
every tickle, every joy
that laugh would bring me.
'Come with me, poet,
for I know a place
of such beauty
the words will fall from you
like dew drops
stretching awake on a spring morning.'

11

WE SIT, WE lean against the wall, my father's cheeks flushed with the kindness and explaining now about the shrine. *There was an apparition here* – but the lady, the one lady who can understand English doesn't know that word, so my father says *a ghost, a spook* – before finally lifting his arms and making a childish ghost sound. *Ah, ah,* replies the woman, who turns and explains, though I think my father's theatrics had purveyed the general gist.

He's making it up, of course. He doesn't know one shrine from the other, he glances at them all with the same disinterest, but after feeding us, well, he feels he owes, perhaps, or is just full of the energy, or maybe expecting more food, if we remain, long enough.

The lady who can speak English asks about the forested hill we are standing beside – *And what is hill?*

Eh?

Is... a holy hill?

Eh? Nah – it's just –

Her face drops and she raises her arms slightly, gesturing towards Our Lady. And father realises, quickly, that this is to be a holy hill, after all –

Yes – this IS a holy hill. This is St Patrick's hill. His very own hill. Snakes, you know? There's no snakes in Ireland, and no snakes on this hill. No snakes.

Her eyes light up once more and she passes on the word of father, my father nodding a *No* and doing snake shapes with his arms. He turns to us – *There are no snakes, are there boys, not here?* – I shake my head. I hope there's not, anyway. Snakes! I don't need those in my worries.

Before long, we've all pushed through a clearing and on to a reasonably official-looking pathway, walking up, up the hill. It's steep. Paul has rushed off and is bashing at leaves with a thin stick, shouting *Bam! Baya! Waa!* Father is talking away, affecting a light Irish accent, though I doubt these ladies would know the difference – *And sure, this is where the early settlers set themselves up to keep an eye out for Vikings.*

Vi – Vikings?

Yeah – you know – and he makes horn shapes with his fingers. She translates, I suspect, that the early Irish were scared of bulls.

I run off, upwards into the forest, the hill, to horse around with Paul, finding a broken-down dwelling, scattered litter, beer bottles... I hope father doesn't spy this spot and consider it a suitable place to stay. I almost stand in front of it and wave him on, but they pass by, slowly, grinding their way to the top.

Joseph! Look at this – Paul calls me over and shows me a layer of broken glass, fear in his eyes – *We shouldn't be around here. There's thistles. Thistles and all sorts.*

I spy a shred of cloth, army green, been used for who knows what. There's a smell, too, and flies, discarded newspapers... I peek my neck around a broken-down corner and it's all grass, but in the corner, along the edge, the grass has been flattened smooth, leaving a body-shaped dent.

This isn't a place of joy. I look for a moment, then call Paul – *C'mon, we need to go.* We climb out and run back up to catch the safety of father's outstretched hands.

*

A what? A farmer? No. I'm a writer. We're off to Dublin. To meet... to meet my publisher. Yep. The suitcase? Poems...

*

No. No. She died. It's just us. Just us, now.

*

We reach the top, eventually. The ladies are exhausted, Paul and me too, and although the weather is holding, it's only just. The ever-present threat of rain is here and there is almost no view whatsoever, just a great, thick, wet grey.

The ladies are curled into a group. Our friend arises and we're handed some sandwiches, but only three half-slices now, the supplies running low, the ladies being careful. Who'd want to be hungry, after all?

We're sat outwith. A few feet along. We cannot eavesdrop anyway, though they can to a degree.

My sandwich is carrot. Paul's too. After the luxury of the orange fish, this is a climbdown.

Dada, this is just… carrot.

Shh now, don't complain. Look – And whispers – *I think these ladies may give us a lift on to Cork City. Let's keep our peace. The main lady – Mrs Tanaka, she told me, I think – mentioned it, seems to be discussing it with the others… You boys need to raise your charm levels, now…*

We peer round at them to find them peering round at us. We quickly turn back. *Damn. Just… just ignore them. C'mon. Eat up, boys.*

We finish our food in a moment. Father looks this way, then that, then up, up into the clouds. Anywhere but to the ladies, our ladies of the sacred journey to Cork. Finally, he pats Paul on the shoulder and gets up, slowly walking back toward them – *Now then, shall we make our way down again? It seems as though it may rain. Any moment, actually.*

*

They can't leave us in the rain, no. It's creeping into dark now, too. They can't leave us in the dark and the rain, can they?

Their van is small though, and it is full of old people necessities. Handbags. Umbrellas. Cushions. I look up at my father and curse his size. Myself and Paul could easily squeeze in…

They push, shove their way in amongst, tired now, wet old

grannies, their mysterious language sharp and spitting. *Whose stupid idea was it to climb the hill? Why have we got these… hitch-hikers?* Perhaps.

But father knows the stakes are high and he encourages us forwards – *C'mon, boys* – until we're almost in the queue for the van itself.

But the ladies aren't for opening, not for shifting over. I mean, they probably think we have a perfectly good home to go to – and we do – but I don't know how many miles away it is and even where those miles even begin. In this weather, that broken-down horror house on the hillside seems inviting, almost. At least we'd be out of the wind…

But the door slams shut, without us. A quick sliding *chunk*. No discussion. Our leading friend is leaning out of the front passenger side and is hurrying her goodbyes – *Tank you, tank you* – as we stand, the wet from the sky to our heads to our noses to the drop to the jacket, the trouser, the shoe and the floor, then on its way to the nearest lough.

My father, resigned, raises his cap and bows. He snorts, smiles and says, quietly – *Thank you.* Then – *Wave boys. C'mon now, wave –*

And we do that, Paul and me. We wave at the misted-up windows, until father turns us around and we begin the walk back to the relative shelter of an overhanging tree.

He's studying the floor. Looking at us, his footsteps. Wondering… Do we try and find the church? Just keep on walking – he looks above and around, spying occasional glimpses of light, two, three miles away in the distance, but signs of life, and perhaps somewhere to aim for, even if a welcome isn't a given.

And the van's engine turns over and our clasp to humanity is weakening.

And it turns over once more.

But it doesn't take.

My father stops looking, he's listening now, but not watching, not obviously…

It turns again, but… it's not starting. The engine won't start.

And again, then silence. My father waits, one, two, three – looks down at us, looking up at him, then –

Fuck it.

And he runs the thirty feet back to the van, whacking the bonnet upon arrival and making *raise it! Raise it!* motions.

He said 'Fuck it'.

I look to Paul.

Did you hear him?

I nod. *Fuck it.*

Fuck it.

Now, I don't know what my father knows about engines, but we run over to be with him and he's soon peeling a silver stick out of somewhere and wiping it clean, or dry perhaps with his shirt, then planting it back in the engine and saying – *Go on, go on – again – again* – But, no, there's nothing, no spark of life…

Fuck it.

We peel back a few yards, clinging to each other.

We'll need – we'll need – and he's scouring the roadside, looking for who knows what until – he spies the road falling slightly maybe fifty yards away.

That'll do, that'll do –

And he slams the bonnet down, calling the driver out – she has discarded her waterproof and is reluctant, but she squeezes over on to the front passenger side, now sharing a seat with our English-speaking friend – *Boys, boys – help me – help me push the van, eh? As much as you can* – and he's half in the cab, half out, shoving at this metal hulk, a good few tonnes surely, as if Paul and me can do that… But we heave and hope and hope and, of course, go nowhere.

Eventually the ladies figure out what is going on and the door slides open once more, Mrs Tanaka climbing out too and between her and my father and two or three of the others, the van slowly begins to shift forwards. *More, more – c'mon* – my father encourages and we heave, we grunt, Paul and me providing more noise than use, but showing our efforts – *O, just a bit further* – and then we hit the slope, and the van begins to move itself, not too fast, but picking up speed, losing Paul and me and two or three of the grannies, until it's just the remaining passengers left in and father jumping into the driving seat and pulling the door closed behind him. He drops out of sight and there's nothing but us, the rain and the bewildered, panting grannies, but then… a cough, a stutter and we hear the van's engine, churning into life. Paul grabs my sleeve – *Joseph, look!* – and we can see a cloud of diesel smoke, thicker and bluer than the grey of the rain, rising above the bush-green sides of the lane. *C'mon then,* I say, and we run over, the grannies following suit, animated, excited now.

We turn the corner and father's standing half in, half out of the driver's seat, one foot revving the engine in display, keeping it going. The grannies pile in the side door and Paul and me wait, unsure, until father gestures, silently – *GET IN* – his mouth wide, his eyes pointing, his head nudging – then, out loud – *Get in boys, any way you can* – and I jump-dive into the back, the door sliding shut behind me in an instant, to the close, the warmth, the relative quiet of the inside. But where's Paul? *Wait! Wait!* A second later he's through father's door, then on father's knee. *Ok? All in then? Then we're off.*

These two –
Real, precise,
and –
Ours.
(Well, you wanted answers!)
What shall we do with them?
We shall fill them to the brim
with our love
and our hope.
Never let them believe
even for a moment
That they are not
The spark of the light of our every morning.

(Be they brats OR saints – for who knows what YOUR family brings.)

12

THERE'D BEEN A misunderstanding, or plenty of them. For the ladies weren't staying in Cork City at all, but in the small town of Schull, in the county of Cork, and Mrs Tanaka had figured out we were driving the wrong way somehow, so Father had to turn us back around, from the outskirts of our destination, cursing.

When we finally arrived at their dwelling, a small, private hotel, right on the bay in Schull itself, two of the kindly elderlies agreed to share a room and give our small family a room of its own for the night. *But just for night*, Mrs Tanaka almost pleaded. And my father, he nodded, apologetically *We're very grateful, we really are.* She'd smiled a little and closed her door, the accompanying sound of a shifting lock immediate. Father, hand on his hips, exhaled loudly then directed us through to our room.

And we three, we three climbed on to the wide double bed and slept, immediately, Paul clinging on to father, whose eyes had shut the second his head came to rest, me slate flat, thinking about that shape of a figure patted down in the grass, but not enough to stop any sleep.

*

Father shook us awake. *C'mon boys, we have to leave…*

It's barely light out.

Paul was not for moving. A limpet on to the pillow. I'd been having dreams about a soft comfortable bed – the very soft, comfortable bed I was on. *Why would we leave here?*

C'mon boys. We're not seeing those ladies this morning. We need to be out of here.

And Paul, Paul was lifted from the bed to father's arms, where he clung on like a baby monkey. I sat on the end of the bed and began to object, whilst trying to raise some life. But within a minute father had opened the bedroom door and was out, suitcase in one hand, Paul in the other – I quickly jumped out after him.

Why are we running father?

We're not. We're not running. But we outstayed our welcome with those ladies, what, fourteen hours ago. We can't go ruining their holiday now, can we?

He was running though, almost. Quick dawdling, trying to look calm, but most definitely propelling himself along the road with speed, gently weaving under Paul's weight like a dribbling footballer.

*

We don't stand and hitch. We walk, and we keep on walking.

I'm hungry.

Paul breaks first.

I'm hungry, da'.

He's always hungry.

Da'…

Be quiet. You can get some food. I have some food, but not for now.

He has some food? I wonder what – some sandwiches? More of the ladies' sandwiches?

The occasional old car trundles by, rattling. No one stops to pick us up, though they sometimes slow to have a good look at the loons in the road, *perhaps they know them?* But no, nobody knows us and nobody stops.

It was easier on Sunday. People were feeling charitable. But now – early week. Everyone hates early week.

I'm curious what time it is, though only in relation to father breaking down the food. I look to make out where it could be – it's not in his pockets, for sure, it has to be in the suitcase…

Father…?

What is it, Joseph?

63

*I'm just wondering… just wondering what the food would be? I'm
sorry to ask.*

Don't you worry, Joseph. There's starter AND a pudding.

And he grins at me.

Ok. One more hour, then we'll eat.

He looks up to the sky, as though he can read the sun – as though
he can even see the sun. I cannot. But one more hour, I can do.

*

We make little progress, the three of us slowing, freezing in the
sticky, cold gloom. The midges are out, terrible little beasts they are,
buzzing around our heads, looking for their next bit of food. Paul
responds in his usual fearsome fashion, not wasting actual words
but – *Gnnrrrr!* Or *Haeeerrrr!* as he swipes his hands around. Paul
looks at me with anger, then turns his face flat toward the road,
stomping forwards.

And we're lucky. We're lucky as father decides enough is enough
and we spy a grey iron gate and that'll do. Father peeks into the
field – to see who we'd be sharing our meal with – decides it is safe
and hauls us over. *Ok boys, but don't go far. If we hear a car – we're
out, back on the lane, to catch it.*

But, right now, I'm not interested in cars. Paul is not interested
in cars. Where is this food? This main course and pudding?

Father smiles – *ok boys* – and plays his hand. A brown paper bag
emerges from his case and from within he pulls a whole soda bread,
shallow, but as wide as his head.

Wow… Paul's eyes are stunned open – *I told you boys, right? Well
here it is…* and where he got it I do not know and I do not ask, but
it had to have been the hotel and maybe it was the reason we left
the hotel, but well, it is here now, in a field with us and there's no
taking it back, it just has to be eaten…

*We're saving most of it boys, ok? We may need it later, if we don't get
to Cork City.*

A third of a half though is enough for me, for soda bread is a thick cake of a bread and I get my piece and it's gorgeous and fresh and near enough moist and difficult to chew, but amazing and ours. Paul has learned his lesson and is slowly nibbling away, pushing flies off it, hiding it within his coat, father eating quicker, mighty chunks in each mouthful. He's beaming. *Just think boys, when we get to Dublin. Every day we can eat like this.*

There's a noise, slowly approaching – *Father –*

Shh, I hear…

He holds his hand in mid-air, as if a music man, conducting the silence…

Louder, louder – *It's a horse. Horse and cart – quick boys, let's see…*

A horse and cart?

We climb over the fence, or Paul climbs through it, but we're all three careful to not lose even a single crumb of the soda bread. I watch carefully as father puts the remainder back within its bag then back within the suitcase.

Here, neat yourself down –

He flattens his coats, straightens his shirt, as if it were a job interview. He pushes Paul's hair into some sort of place and makes to do the same with my own, but cannot, as the horse and cart has almost arrived, and it is *going the right way.*

We stand, all three of us, one thumb each, pointing in the air.

We smile.

The man sees us. And now he cannot un-see us. We are three people, in front of him, almost in the way, smiling and begging for a lift.

It will take a good thirty seconds for the slow clatter of the horse to reach us.

Smile.

Father whispers through his grin.

Paul farts. Then laughs.

Paul – stop it. Smile.

But he's laughing, then I start laughing. We're excited from the food. But the smell of Paul's wind is awful –

Jesus, Paul, what is that?

Sorry, da', it was maybe the fish...

And father's smile turns from fake to real, and soon we're all grinning, gurning, arms in air, awaiting the mannie on the cart... He's a big fella, dirty, filthy grey jumper stretched upon a visible belly.

Good day to you.

My father says, too early.

The mannie on the cart stares back –

Good day.

Again, no reply – but the third time –

Good day, sir – my father bowing a little with his head now, nodding downwards.

Well, what's this? The three little piggies?

No, sir, just me and my two children here –

Well. You're not from these parts – Scotland is it?

That's right, Scotland. But my children are Irish. Or half and half...

Mongrels?

I wouldn't... I wouldn't say that... exactly.

Mongrels? Who, me and Paul?

The cart continues to move, it's making little sign of slowing, finally now it's beside us –

Would you be heading west, sir? We're making our way to Cork City

You're not gypsies, are you?

No, sir. I'm a poet and these two...

A poet! A poet! Well, I'll be damned. A poet. Woah, Jehovah, woah.

He brings the horse to a halt – *Stop here, Jehovah, for we have a poet now, with his two little piggies. They'll surely entertain us for a mile or so.*

My father's eyes tighten, his arms contract, but for me, a lift, surely, surely is a lift...

Father asks – *Where is it you're going...?*

West – west as you said. A little while anyway. Then north, but you don't have to concern yourself with that part of the journey.

Father considers for barely a second, then – *ok boys, jump on. Paul, let me help you.*

For it'll be distance between ourselves and the owner of that soda bread, I suppose.

*

There's a small set of ladders at the side of the trap and I climb on. Paul needs a lift, but he's soon up and beside me, beaming. Above, there's a grey cloud, slowly moving beyond a white. I think this will be another wet day. I look for a cover, but there is none.

Is this – is this your transport, then? Your only transport, I mean?

This? No, not at all. I just like to take it out. Makes work a pleasure, you know. Keeps my eye in. C'mon Jehovah, up, up…

We lurch into action and straightaway the rattle of the buggy picks up on the uneven road, the lack of windows to hush the sound, the wind past our ears – it's loud. Paul grabs my wrist and squeezes as tight as he could possibly do. I peel his finger off my wrist and put them into my own, a more familiar, hand-holding gesture. He looks at me as though in pain, not sitting back, resting, but anxious and tight. I smile at him and point at a random bird. He looks back at me as though I'm the king of the eejits. Father and the driver are having to shout now, almost –

So, a poet you say?

Yes, for my sins. Just off to Dublin. Meeting my publisher.

Your publisher? Well, I never, very grand indeed… Would you say it's a well-paid profession, the poetry?

Well… No. But – you know. I have to be…

True?

True. A-ha. True.

And to the horse now – *ok, c'mon, keep going, that's it –*

We shudder around a corner, hugging the side tight – *And I have to be careful now, what with all the motor vehicles about…*

Paul gets whipped by a few thin, light branches. *Aya!* He shuffles over, pushing closer still against me, me with plenty of space to the other edge.

And where's their mother? How does she feel about all… this?

Well. There's the thing. She's no longer, you know, with us.

Ah.

We rattle along. The soporific, calming clop of Jehovah's hooves striking the ground. Paul is blessedly beginning to loosen his grip, to relax.

Would you take a drink? A beer? I brew it myself, you know –

I hope not. I hope he will not –

It's not strong. Just a morning drink. Flavoursome. Full of iron.

Well… No. I won't. It's too early, for me. With them. You know.

Good man. A man's got to know his limits.

Well… it's not that… Father looks at us. Then – *So – do you farm?*

I do. I do. A little, anyways. But this – this here cart can be quite an earner. People like the old ways, you know? And I like the old ways, too. This thing here, well, it's mainly just used for weddings, you know. In the summer, I mean. There's a bit of a chill, today, surely. It's only an old milk cart, though. I converted it – I put in that extra seat at the back, see – and I plugged the holes in the floor – and now I can take the bride and groom. Sometimes their parents, though that puts a bit of strain on Jehovah. I tend to climb off and walk him if that occurs. Until they get the hint, you know? The hint that there's too much weight for one horse, even a fine fella like Jehovah here. Isn't that right, Jehovah?

Jehovah clops on in agreement. *And the weight of your belly,* I think, but I don't say it out loud.

Are we… are we ok, now?

Eh? Oh, that's fine. Just you and the little fellas. That's fine, so. Jeez though, some of the big fellows from America, mostly, they haven't a clue, they'll climb on and the whole world will creak from side to side and I'll look at the bolts and hope they hold, it's over one hundred years old now, this old thing…

Really?

Well, maybe eighty. Fifty, certainly. Old enough. Here – reach into that bag now will you? Pass me one of those bottles. I'll try the batch. Test it out, for later, you understand, know what I'll be letting myself in for heh heh.

Paul's asleep now, his head upon my shoulder, me holding his hand now, keeping him upright, helping him stay comfortable. I wonder what the pudding was? Will we find out?

*

The journey stretches on – always just one more corner, one further straight, just beyond, just beyond, my bum now aching from the pain of every single stone or hole in the road, of which there are many. Who'd get married in this? But, within time, we pull into a yard, within that there's a small cottage, grey, its gardens green and waving and rising and falling, overgrown in places, but not neglected. More – allowed to roam. When the trap finally comes to a halt, the expected, longed-for silence is instantly broken by the sharp yaps of enthusiastic dogs, who come tearing over towards us snarling before miraculously being hauled back, mid-air and flung backwards – tied as they are by ropes, one rope round each of their necks and those long ropes tied to a third that's running from the house to the gate.

Boishin, Colleen – be quiet – silence now. Quiet – c'mon.

They seem excited to see our driver, but my attention is closer to home, as Paul's grip has tightened once more, his legs curled up around me, his other hand now clawing against my chest as he whimpers *Ennghh! Dada! DADA!*

Shh! Now – they're tied up, they can't get to you – here, I'll help you down.

*

An hour, two hours later, father and our driver are sitting round a small fire, burning away in a brown rusted metal container, drinking a brown liquid, beer of course, out of old milk bottles, the shape the same as the milk bottles we have at home. Paul and me are sitting a half-dozen yards away, looking over, bellies rumbling once more, wondering if we'll move on, move on out away from here.

Our driver is singing, though I cannot understand his words. They're Irish, I recognise that, but mother was not long enough alive to pass that down, if she even spoke it, and I've only ever heard the nuns use it. My father is listening, no doubt unaware of what is actually being sung.

Paul springs down, back to the brook we found earlier, making more work on our dam of sticks, mud and leaves.

When is he going to stop? That song makes NO sense.
I think it's in Irish.
Is it a riddle? A riddle song?
But it doesn't stop. How can it be a riddle that doesn't stop?
Maybe that's the riddle. How to make him stop.
No.
What's da doing?
He's just… listening. And drinking.
Is he drinking beer?
I think so.
We'll never leave then.

Paul kicks the ground in frustration.

Father's singing now – …*John Anderson, ma jo, John, you are a dirty devil…*
I think you're right.
What's that?
We're not moving today.
No. I hope we'll be eating, though.

*

We do eat. The man hands us a handful of muddy carrots, that we wash in the dam we've built and gnaw away on.

Carrots.

Father then appears and gives us some of his hotel bread, but I notice he has to share it with our host, which annoys me, as I'd've preferred that fresh bread to these muddy carrots.

Paul asks – *Do you think the carrots was the pudding dada talked about?*

No, they came from the man. But we can't ask father what the pudding was, as the man will want some of our pudding then also… And see – He's quite… big.

Carrot and bread is tasty food. Our host muddles over once more, gives us a small porcelain bowl each and says – *Here, you can drink from the stream. It's good and fresh now.*

I look at him, then at the chipped blue bowls, questioning. He notices my discomfort – *Sure, I drink from them – the dogs too. You'll be fine, young fella, fine.* He ruffles my hair with his clay-coloured hand. I pull back and he chuckles, before heading back to the other side of the yard where father is waiting, holding a milk-then-beer bottle at arm's length, examining.

*

At some point in the afternoon, they fall asleep. We're in our own little dwam, torpedoing big sticks with small sticks, then small sticks with big sticks. Eventually though, we notice the silence.

He's out.

They're BOTH out.

Here – is it the evening?

No. Not at all. It can't be.

I don't want to be here. I'm cold.

Then put your coat on.

It's on the cart.

Then go to the cart and get it.

I don't like the dogs.

Don't be daft – they're tied up –

I don't like the horse.

Well – it's not going anywhere, it's just… I look over… *standing there.*

Will you come with me?

71

I look around, at the swirling mud pool below. To think we washed our carrots in *that*.

Sure, I'll go.

We walk over and as soon as the dogs see us, they begin to snarl, to bark. They run up to us – all of two yards closer they get – until the rope tightens and once more they're left hanging, as if pulled back by an invisible master.

The barking though, it eventually gets father to wake out of his mid-afternoon slur. Our host doesn't wake, he must be so used to their impressive noise, he just turns on his chair and buries his face into the head of it, hiding his eyes from the sunlight.

C'mon, dada, we want to go. We hate it here –

I don't hate it here, but…

C'mon, dada. C'mon.

…Eh?

We have to go. To get to Dublin, remember? To Dublin…

Father shakes his head, cringing from the awakening, the sunlight, the dogs, the beer…

No. No… You're right, son. C'mon. Let's make a move. Before… before I fall back asleep.

We up and away, father at first barely moving, stumbling, but finally, as quietly as we can, making every effort not to bother the dogs and waken our host.

*

Father's sneaked a beer. Into his side pocket. First the bread, now the beer. We're tramping along the overgrown cartway, and before long the beer is finished, and the bottle thrown on to the verge.

Dada?

Yes, Paul?

What was for pudding?

Father laughs – *Ah, you'll see, you'll see. Here – let's keep going a while longer, eh?*

How and where my path began,
up, up to this summer,
I cannot say,
but I am full with thanks.

I hear the birds,
I see the reflections on the water,
I skin the bark off a twig, with a knife,
it's sharp, short blade an old friend.
I rub my fingers together to clear the earth.

Laid down atop this forest floor,
we drink fresh water, direct from the stream.
I pull a tiny leaf from between my teeth
then pop it back in and chew.

13

W E'RE INSIDE NOW, in a pub, quiet and warm. We poke at the fire, just a huge pile of steaming and smoking grass, so not really a fire at all, but that's what we're calling it – that's what father and *her* are calling it, so that's what *we're* calling it.

But we're not really fire tending. We're more listening.

Father is smoking, very strange to see him doing that, *he used to*, he told her, *when he was younger*. He puffed his chest out, a little, then coughed, the grey of the cigarette smoke swimming and hiding quickly in amongst the grey of the steam and smoke of the fire.

And will you be coming back through?

At that, Paul and me, we eased our poking and examining, but there was no reply from father. We returned to the exercise, poking holes in the piled cuttings, watching the spiders run from what remained of their homes, stacked now one on another.

We'll see how rich this man makes me!

Rich, eh? I look to Paul, but he barely even acknowledges the word. Instead, from the fire he rescues a centipede – or a millipede or whatever – a long crawling worm, but not the size of a worm, the size of a finger nail, it now scampering, charging over his hand. Paul's not worried – *I can't even feel it* – before blowing the beastie away and smelling the trail it'd taken over his knuckle.

*

We'd ended up in there yesterday evening. Father used the excuse of the shop adjoining to walk us in, then found us some bread and some crisps for our supper, and we were happy for that. He'd began talking away to the lady behind the bar, and well I wouldn't know why, but she was as happy to be talking to him as him her, and then we heard about his *lovely accent,* although it didn't sound lovely to us, it just sounded like father, you know?

He'd opened that suitcase of his and whispered to her a few lines from a piece of paper, before she giggled and he shrugged away and looked embarrassed, as well he might.

And a pint had appeared out of nowhere and right then we knew we wouldn't be leaving *that* night. But we were ok, for it was warm and it was dry.

There hadn't been a great deal of the day left and before long, people had snuck in and were disturbing my father's conversation, and for a minute I thought, I hoped maybe, that he may find himself stuck alone at the end of the bar too much, too lonesome and come sit back amongst us two, but no, he stayed, supping away at his one pint.

Where did you get that?

Paul had a little wooden car, not fancy, no windows or doors, but a car, for sure.

Where did you get that? Gies a go…

He nodded over to an open door, a door to a cupboard, I ran over and found brooms, a bucket, that sort of thing, some flags… but no car.

C'mon, give me a go…

But the car only ran up and down my leg at the speed I pushed it and as soon as I had it, Paul ran over to father and that disturbed my train of thought and soon the car was just wood again, no life in it at all.

Go on – just… shoo!

And soon we could barely see father, so full was the place, people walking in with so many odd-shaped sacks and boxes, musical instruments tied on to backs with string, huge, burly husbands and smiling wives, reminding me of a warmer, happier church, everyone in full flow, nobody giving a hoot for Paul and me, and slowly, music beginning. I think a violin first, an *air* which only meant a *slow one*, I think, and me listening in, imagining the music as a line, a horizon, rising and falling, dramatic cliffs and fast, surging collapses, before other instruments joining in, a boozy accordion, never in time, a man saying *Sorry* repeatedly, as he seemed to be playing a different tune to everyone else, but soon even him being taken under the wing of the collective, and now the whole bar, it seemed, playing or singing or making some noise, one man – no, one man and one woman, both jangling spoons, banging them on their knees, one man even with a matchbox, one match sticking out and him drawing his fingers down it, creating a fine clicking sound that somehow wove its way into the music... He was in time, I knew that. I knew about time in music.

And Paul was asleep by now, of course he was, his head resting on my legs, and every now and then father would poke his head out of the crowd and grin down at me, at one time licking some white foam off his nose whilst smirking...

But then it was all ending, slowing and calls for *Mary! You sing for us – go on girl!* and one voice coming through a lone voice, solo singing, not being able to see who, but a lady and then – yes, it's her, of course, and she has a voice soft and clear and effortless, and there – is – not – a – word – spoken while she is there, on the stage, behind the bar...

And the applause when she finishes and the shouting – as if they were expecting a free drink from her – but then, now she's talking – *A visitor... Scotland... Something for us...* and my heart begins to beat and I think of waking Paul, but too late, father is saying *No – no – NO –* and meaning it, but then there's a look I catch from Our Lady of the Bar and father is delving into his suitcase and I wonder what is going on but it becomes clear he is going to *Read Them A Poem* and I sink. But then he begins.

A Bottle of Lies –
When I was born, I was told –
and he starts strong, but quietens and soon people are murmuring

and talking and – no – *laughing* – not at him, I'd hope and I want to sit right up and punch them laughers in the gob but there's nothing I can do, especially with Paul's head on my lap and soon the whole pub is chatting away and I have no idea where father's voice has got to, in amongst the joy that everyone else is spreading and I know now we'll have to get out and father will be destroyed and we'll be sleeping under a bush, but then – then – another voice comes out, but no, it is the same voice, but this time…

…this time father is singing, and the little bar world quietens in a moment.

Behold, I am a soldier bold, I'm only twenty-five years old
A finer warrior ne'er was seen from Inverness to Gretna Green
When I was young, my faither said he'd put me tae a decent trade
But I didnae like the work at a' – I went and I joined the Forty-Twa

And I know this song, I know this song, so, so well, as father has sung it to me and Paul a hundred, hundred times in the bath, in the garden, on the walk to church…

…and without even thinking, I join in –

The wind may blaw, the cock may craw
The rain may rain, and the snaw may snaw
But ye willnae frichten Jock McGraw
He's the stoutest man in the Forty Twa…

And my singing, it awakens Paul, who sits bolt upright and begins to play at marching along, his thin little arms swinging back and forth and soon he too is singing.

And there is a domino of faces turning towards us unnoticed, our voices very audible in the silence of the bar.

The sergeant who enlisted me slaps my back and then says he
A man like you so big and tall could ne'er be killed by a cannon ball

And the colonel then when he cam' roon', he looks me up,
he looks me doon
And then said he, I'll take a guess – you must be the monster
of Loch Ness!

And Paul and me joining in when we can – a triumphant *Cannon Ball!!* A shouted *Loch Ness!!*

And soon the whole bar is uproared and on board and I look over to see father who is shouting the lead now, his arms swinging around as though conducting, his hand holding a whole full pint of stout, being careful not to spill and when the song ends, when it finally ends, there is such a cheer that I know father will be with them all night, a celebrity for the evening. I smile at Paul and him back at me, before he leans in again for sleep.

*

I'm lying down now, Paul beside me on the thick leather sofa. I think I have slept and awoken, slept and awoken, over and over. The music has soothed and feared me, the cigarette smoke drying my throat, leaving me wishing for water. The lady behind the bar has brought crisps and orange juice, and I sip away at the remainder, the ice slow melting. And father, he is roaring on, his voice occasionally soloing out a familiar song, less applause this time, but appreciated and studied, then on to the next, the next, the lady at the bar…

But as the people begin to dwindle, seats becoming empty, quickly filled by standers, so less standers now, fewer people at the bar stools, but father there and eventually, finally it is his turn to sing once more and I hear the call he gets and lie there, awake… and he sings, he sings, he sings our mother's song:

If I had the love of home
If I had the heart of a good man
Surely, I would follow you anywhere

Like a swan, returning home to Russia
My love for you is my all…

And I sit up, I look up and there on his thin, reddened cheek there is a tear, slowly rolling and soon falling and now there are many more of my own.

*

So, we stayed. When the pub had finally emptied, he'd moved Paul, then me, to the closest seat by the fire. He lightly placed some logs and peat on to the embers, left and returned, this time with a blanket, which he slowly, delicately laid upon us. I pretended to be asleep, and he pretended to believe me. Then, there was a bristly kiss upon my cheek and that was it, silence at last, almost, just the light wheeze of Paul and the purr of the fire to keep me company.

This morning has not brought comfort
only a sharp reminder –
a slap in the face,
a paper cut,
and a thump upon the heart.

This evening has not brought comfort
there's no relief in the spark and jump of the fire
they're too deadly for the memories they bring
and the poker too red to touch.

14

COME THE MORNING, we'd woken up and ran around the bar at one thousand miles an hour. Weaving in and out of the stools at a mighty pace, Paul's arms outstretched like an aeroplane, mine shaping a shark fin on my head, chasing after him – *I'll get ya! I'll get ya!* Until *Mary* had appeared and given us some more bread, but this one with some milk that tasted funny. She was using it in her tea though, I checked, I waited and checked, so it wasn't poison. It just tasted funny. And it had the floating white teeth that you sometimes see. The chewy bits.

But, Paul dipped his bread in, and I did the same.

Thanks, he'd said, quietly.

And I said,

Thank you.

And Mary, she smiled down at us.

*

When father appeared, he had that creased, cross-eyed look to him, but he was also carrying something else in there – like he was embarrassed. Shamed by his singing, maybe? I don't know. He sang well. He sat down beside us and I jumped on him, hugging, holding. He smelled different. He smelled fresh, somehow, yet he seemed distracted. He had Paul at the other side of him and was squeezing him to death.

Here – You can have your pudding now…

I looked up at him, examined his face – *Was he joking?* – but he reached into his top pocket and brought out two slender rods, flat, twigs almost, but coloured, then rolled them a little and they puffed out, then held Paul's hand out – *Here* – Father bit the top off one of the packets and out slid some thick golden rocks... *It's sugar. Go on, taste it* – But sugar is white? Paul stuck his tongue on to it and pulled it back in, before declaring *YUM!* And licking his hand, furiously, repeatedly, all over his fingers, where the sugar had never even been...

I took a different tack, I opened my mouth and gubbed it all in. It was sugar, but a sour sugar somehow. It made me grimace. It's not much of a pudding. But, within minutes, Paul and me were outside, exploring the yard and twirling like falling sycamore seeds.

*

She died. Drowned.
　　Oh!
　　The children... they don't remember. They wouldn't.
　　No.
　　...
　　We were – we were just horsing around on Lough Hyne –
　　Horsing around?
　　You know – just being eejits. We had an inflatable. A dinghy, but not some child's toy, it was... ach... It was SUPPOSED to be suitable for four adults...
　　And it was just the four of you?
　　Well... No. Three grown-ups and the boys. But they were only... tiny. Tiny then, Joseph was two or three and Paul just a few months... six months, maybe.
　　Listen... You don't have to tell me...
　　No – it's good. Good for me, to talk, you know? I can't... I can't talk with the children about it. Not yet at least. I mean, I know there'll be a time when they ask, you know?
　　Of course.
　　Of course.
　　So...
　　So – Well, it was myself and Sinéad and my brother, Joseph.

Joseph?

Yep. He was the reason our Joseph... my Joseph... He was named after him, you know. Joseph – my brother – was amazing... He was good at everything, he could run, he could paint, he could sing, do these ridiculous sums in his head, knew everything about all sorts... We were SO excited to have him visit...

Were you living down there, then?

We were. Sinéad was from West Cork, and I loved it down there. I was very happy with the pace of life, the lack of things to spend money on, you know? I felt we could live down there on a pound a week, and we quite often did...

...So, when Joseph arrived, we were thrilled to see him. Sinéad just loved him. Loved him. He was so... Just a great fellow to be around, you know?

...and Sinéad, well, she brightened up considerably, with him being there. She'd been a bit – blue, I suppose, you'd call it – I think it was from the children being born so close, and her stuck now in that little house... She was a traveller, you know? I don't mean a gypsy, I mean... an explorer... a free spirit. We'd met in Dublin, of all places... So, she was struggling to find herself back in the quiet of West Cork, for the foreseeable... Joseph brought some light in, you know? He brought in the outside, the outside world...

We'd been given that damned inflatable as a wedding gift. A wedding gift from an uncle and aunt of Sinéad's, who hadn't even turned up to the wedding! They didn't approve of the wedding not being in the church... I was considering selling it – we both were, but Sinéad decided we should keep it, for when the boys were older. It just seemed the perfect time to try it out, when Joseph was there. High spirits, you know? And Lough Hyne is always so calm, a perfect place...

But we went out. And young Joseph, well, he somehow got away from his mother and fell – just fell overboard. Slipped – just like that, and he was in and underneath and of course Sinéad... well, she screamed and fell to the side, then jumped in herself, as you would –

And you –

Well, I had Paul! And of course he was crying, then, at the commotion, and the boat was tipping and it seemed like forever, but my brother had taken his shoes off and those old thick woollen flared trousers he'd wear, and then jumped in himself – and boy, he could swim, he always could, and then – then it was just me, me and Paul, stuck on the boat… Paul bawling, me looking, trying to calm him, but nothing doing, of course, until – young Joseph came floating back up, then I saw two big hands around his waist and it was brother Joseph, of course, and he fair threw the baby into the boat – just threw him – and I grabbed, I grabbed him and tried to wrap him, but I could see he was not breathing, so I bent down, holding a screaming Paul and trying to work out what the Jesus I could do with Joseph, eventually just pushing his belly, pushing into him, squeezing the poor soul until, until all this water came out… water and slime… and then I did the kissing, you know, the breathing into him, just over and over, for ever, there was no response and I had him all the wrong position, but Paul screaming and me terrified for Paul, too, so holding him down, flat, hard, stopping him moving, breathing into Joseph and then finally, finally, young Joseph began to cough, to splutter and then to cry, and cry he did, he opened his lungs and shrieked and the elation, the joy, I was over the fucking moon, and almost breathing myself into a frenzy and I turned, sure to see Sinéad and my brother at my side, in the water maybe, but there was no one, nothing and all of a sudden I'm holding the two screaming boys but shouting myself over the calm of the water — calling Joseph! Sinéad! But seeing no one and then scanning the shore – I mean, we weren't far out, only thirty yards…

And then, all I heard was my father weeping. Quietly at first, but then full on, almost screaming himself, like a demon was inside him, hauling its way out into the world. I reverse back, crawling out underneath the snug seats, the same way I crawled in.

*

We were there for days and days, after that. Maybe two whole weeks. I was looking at Paul with different eyes, but at myself, also.

Searching for a memory, a memory of *that*. It was a vivid picture I had now.

*

And we were comfortable. We were fed. We were clean and we were stationary.

*

I grew up here, Fraser. And when my mother died… Well, it was known I'd take over. So, I did.
    She's cleaning. They're cleaning. I'm not. I'm hiding.
    Imagine. Can you do that, Fraser? Spending your life here, watching as that life passes you by? The same way it passed my mother by…
    …She died from the smoking, you know that? From the cancer… But, here's the thing… she never smoked, not one cigarette. But this place… Well, it can become a bit of a fog, as you've seen…
    There's a bath here. It only takes, what a minute to fill up? Can you imagine? Our bath, our bath at Creagh, well, it's not even worth attempting… there's never the water. The only time we have a soak at ours, is in those rare weeks that father calls *The Height of Summer* and even then, it's to cool us down from the heat generated using that pump at the top of the hill to bring enough water down to fill the little boiler… But, they have a bath here. We get in together, Paul and me. And we shout and we scream and blow bubbles with the soap. We hide in there for hours, lost in play.

*

In bed, I cannot sleep. I lie and I listen to the sounds from the bar, father behind it now, working, drawing thick black beer from the taps. I hear him, handing over the drink, taking in the money, his clear voice a regular amongst the murmur. And just as the noise eventually lulls me to sleep, the silence of the empty bar awakens me and I hear father once more, but this time Mary too, talking, singing lightly, laughing.

15

W E'RE OUTSIDE, IN the yard.
What a place this yard is. What kind of den can you build
on a long grey stone floor?

I'll bet you there are rats here in the summer, maybe the winter
too, with all these old tins of beer and the smell of it all... I wonder
if rats drink beer. I wonder if they LIKE beer.

We're kicking a hurling ball about, a *slotter*, or whatever it's
called. We don't have the sticks, so we're making do with our feet.
Paul whacks it away then runs behind it shouting *The planet has
been struck! The planet is in trouble! The planet is heading for the edge
of the universe!* Before it slows and rolls into the long stone wall that
separates us from the field next door.

In that field now, right up against the wall, there are three little
faces, and they are peeking over, seeing who we are, what we're up
to. I've spied them a few times, but we've never spoken and sure
why would we, with us only being here for a visit... As Paul walks
up to the ball, he lets out a *Hey! Who did that!* Rubbing his head...

Those GHOST children threw a brick at me.

Give over! It wasn't a brick –

It was – look –

And looks around himself to see what debris it was that hit
him... but there's nothing but a small clod of earth and moss.

It was THIS. This lump of dirty, filthy mud.

He looks at me, nose creased, expectant – then picks the thing and
tosses it back at the wall, where it hits nothing and falls, unspectacularly.

Take that!

Ye missed!

The boys behind the wall. And then they giggle. And then they throw another, and another, then more, until the sky is full of flighting wee clumps of wall moss, raining down and around on Paul. He retaliates, he spins his arms around as if blades from a helicopter, occasionally knocking one roughly back to where it came, but mostly just a noisy waste of energy.

IIIeerrgrghghgwghwaaaehghrghgrhrrrwhhehehehwwwww! You missed! You missed me!

He's down on the floor now, picking these things up, pushing them, squeezing as many as he can into one fist, then up against the wall and throwing them over, high in the air and inaccurate, but returning to the attackers with similar affect as they were received, them no doubt crouching behind the wall, but who'd be afraid of a bit of old moss anyhow?

I gotcha I gotcha! Hoi, hoi, hoi, hoi.

He's singing now, prancing around the yard…

Die, die, from the curse! Die, die, I made things worse!

And the three faces back up, wary of another attack perhaps, but seeing only Paul as some crazy ceilidh dancer and me still at the door, laughing.

One by one, they begin to emerge over the wall, heads then hands, forearms then shoulders, then the whole darn lot, white shirts, grey tank-tops, hauling themselves over and standing, in line, in a uniform or some sort – school, I'd guess, a dark maroon with white stripes tie, once-white shirts and just-above–the-knee shorts, the girl wearing some kind of sack-looking dress… One of them, about six, maybe, is carrying a stick. But it's not an impressive stick, more a bendy twig.

They stand and stare, before one breaks ranks –

We're the O'Driscolls. We live next door.

I walk closer – I think I'm the eldest here, they all look below ten, surely – *You live in the field?*

Don't be a dick. No. We live on the farm.

In the HOUSE.

He throws an arm around, vaguely pointing behind us, to a just visible house, surrounded by barns. Maybe three fields away.

The fellow in the middle seems the oldest.

Do you wanna get some rats?

How do you mean?

In the barns, ye eejit. Do you wanna squash some rats?

And who wouldn't.

I look over to Paul, but I needn't have bothered for he is wide-eyed and open mouthed. I nod. *Sure.*

*

A minute later we're running over the fields.

I'm Kevin – The oldest says – *This is Siobhan, and there is Kevin, also…*

I look to the younger Kevin, then to the elder – they look like brothers, but can't be – *Is he a cousin?*

No! He's my brother. We're both called Kevin. Jeez, it's a funny story, I was ran over when I was just little, two, maybe, and I was in hospital all broken up and in bits and lying on the operating table and they thought I'd live a week maybe, if that. And my mumma – well, she was in the other side of the hospital, giving birth to young Kevin there and she was so upset by the whole thing that she named HIM Kevin too and then, well, I only went on and lived, didn't I, so now they had two Kevins, and sure we've thought about changing names and the like but it's never worked out, so now here we are – I'm Kevin and so is he.

Younger Kevin turns and grins at me. He's lost his two front teeth.

That was a horse that did that. But only his baby teeth, so there's no concerns.

Young Kevin makes a rabbit face at me, but without the two front teeth, he just looks as though he has a black hole where his mouth should be.

And what about you, Siobhan, would you want to be a Kevin?

Nooo! And why would I? That'd be stupid completely, it's a BOY'S name. And with that, her and Paul run ahead, shaking their heads like wild men, Siobhan whipping at the soil and the crop, the dreaded Brussels sprouts.

Are ye living there now?

No, I don't think so… We're just visiting…

Ha. Mary is a necker. You know?

A what?

A necker? Do you even know what that is?

Of course I do!

Do yez?

But I don't, so I shout – *Look!*

And point to where Paul and Siobhan are, pulling sprouts off the stems and eating them down.

Ah Jezuz, they'll be causing an uproar later with those in their bellies! Siobhan come off those…

Little Kevin is lagging behind a bit, but there's no waiting.

He'll be fine, he knows where we're going – shouting then – *Don't ye, Siobhan?*

Eh?

You know where we're going?

There's no reply, but she's carrying on, hopping over the rows of sprouts, just like the rest of us.

My mumma's in heaven.

She's what?

She's in heaven. She was taken by the angels.

Was she?

She was.

He puffs his chest up and looks forward, far into the distance, owning the situation, boasting.

And mine too, maybe. Mine drowned. In a lough.

No. Really?

I nod.

Was it a big lough?

I suppose… I suppose it was, yes…

Well… and is she in heaven? Or in purgatory? Purgatory is where the people go who don't go to hell and don't go to heaven…

I know that!

Sure, how could you not know that…

She's in heaven. Father says she is.

But he never has.

Sure, MY mumma was in purgatory, just for a bit. It was awful, so.

Ah really? How did that happen?

Well… And don't tell a soul… you promise?

I nod, of course.

They thought my mumma… they thought she'd… DONE HERSELF IN. You know?

And then he's doing that long-distance stare thing again.

And they were saying because of that, she wasn't allowed into heaven, which was a nonsense, because everyone knew she was a good lady and kind and sure why wouldn't she be allowed in, you know?

Sure.

And it was distressing us. It was distressing me dad, he said. And me aunties. And me, me, also. The other children were teasing young Kevin a little about it… We were all distressed, dadda said so.

…so eventually, after the funeral – a big funeral, the biggest they'd had round here for years, I'd say – after they had the funeral, people were whispering 'poor soul, in purgatory' and I was wondering Jesus, how long will she need to be in there for, because winter was coming and we were told it was like being in a bare room with just a chair and no heat or company so my dad he went to the Bishop himself and he sat him down and explained that my mumma would no way of done herself in and that she must have just gotten tangled and the Bishop said he'd have a think and I know then that he must have talked to the Pope and the Pope told him that mumma was in heaven now and she'd not been in purgatory at all except for a short little while on the way up but she's ok now, she's in heaven all safe. And eventually, they held a little Mass and Father Brennan announced

that mumma wasn't in purgatory after all and now everyone knows.

*

Bigger Kevin asks me –

And was your mother Catholic, even?

She was.

He exhales. *Well, that's the main thing. She'll be safe somewhere, don't you worry…*

I know exactly where she is. Buried in the corner of a graveyard on a hill. Beside her a little hut where the keepers leave their tools and things, with the old flowers and the plastic flowers hidden behind the hut, but overflowing on to mama's grave, so it's always looking a mess anyhow and because Paul won't go and father doesn't want to go, well, we hardly ever go. But I think of it, almost every night.

…even if she's in purgatory. It's all right there, I know it is.

*

We reach the farm, Siobhan and Paul first, turning then and waiting for us, Siobhan whipping at the wall with the remnants of her stick, Paul more examining, watching. Little Kevin is a good way off, still.

Here – there's the barn. Have you got a barn?

We don't.

Well… here's ours. Grab a stick, if you can. Or a stone. And don't stand still.

Stand still?

They'll run up your leg and bite off yer knackers!

*

There's no door, just a great big hole in the corrugated iron sides. It seems held up by wooden beams, scaling up the inside of the walls… holes throughout and although it's not a particularly windy day, the sheets of metal are seemingly breathing in and out, causing a rattle, a rattle that makes me jump, the first time, the second, the third...

Inside, there's nothing much but a huge pile of haystacks... There's rat poison, of course, and a few hand-tools, although I wouldn't recognise what they were. Kevin the Elder picks himself a long, copper-rusted wrench of some kind, then hands me something else – it's like a short broom, but instead of a brush it has three thick metal hooks, all fishing out at different angles – *That's a good one, a wide top, plenty to catch them with...* and I imagine catching *anything* on the head with this and how the head would surely come off worse.

The bales are those small rectangular ones, but a load of them, one on top of another, then another, until they almost touch the ceiling at one end, a ceiling as high as a church roof, higher maybe, the bales at the top looking like the terraces at the side of a football stadium from a magazine.

Is it... is it safe?

He looks at me, as though a coward –

Of course it's safe! I'm here, am I not? I've been up those a meeellion times.

I blush, a little – *For Paul, I mean. I wouldn't want... can we climb on these...*

But before I can even finish, old Kevin is charging on to the lower bales, skimming his body along their surface, skidding two or three feet along before coming to a halt against the next. *Come on! Get up! We'll see them better from a height!*

Behind me, I hear Paul, him arriving with Siobhan, the two of them chatting wildly to each other, but also Siobhan holding on to the hand of the younger Kevin, who they'd been waiting for. I can't seem to be scared in front of Paul, so I jump up, and straightaway I feel the spike of the hay on my hands, followed immediately by the burn as I drag across *Aya!*

Jeez! Don't be soft.

I look up and see his rear and shorts, hind legs, as he begins the climb up to the next level. I straighten myself up and continue behind him.

Younger Kevin is loose now and is billowing from one side of the barn to the other, he's got some kind of thick stick in his hand – it looks like a hurley stick for a child, maybe – and he's whacking it repeatedly against the foot of the bales, and then the side of the barn itself, making an almighty *clang*.

Jeesus, Kevin, will you not do that?

The voice from above, from old Kevin, old Kevin who I'd guess was younger than me, still.

Keep that NOISE down. Ye'll scare the rats.

Sure there's plenty of them to go around…

And just like that, I spy one, running from behind a blue plastic pot and straight into the hay bales, right where I'd been climbing a minute earlier…

Oh! It's that fella! The OLD fella! He EATS the poison, you know! He must be some kind of…

SUPER RAT –

Super rat, yes!

I don't like that one – Siobhan there – *I'm going to kill it –* and she grabs another tool, this one with two long rusted handles, running to some kind of beak, and begins to poke it into the bales, roughly where the rat escaped. Paul's excited – *He'll come out! He'll come out!*

Then I'll chop his head off with me wire cutters.

And Paul rushes beside and begins to kick the bale repeatedly – *Come out! Come out, you scoundrel!*

I turn and ascend, old Kevin now almost ten feet higher than me it seems, and able to touch the roof soon, surely. *When you make it up here* – he shouts down – *you can see where the pigeons roost* – and he points to the beams overhead – *but even these fellows aren't safe from the rats – look! They'll balance on the beams and eat the young ones alive, before they can even fly!* And that sounds too good to miss, so I speed myself up, one leap at a time for this bale ladder now, before I'm head to head with Kevin and grinning, him pulling me up the last little step before pointing – *Look how small they are now!* – and I'm glad I am not scared of heights, for if I was, I would have been *then* as Paul and the whole gang look tiny, all that way down on the floor level and it is particularly weird having to watch my head against the cold metal roof of a building SO tall.

There's one!

And he jumps off, clearing two, then three bales before landing just where I'd seen the shadow of a rat, recently left at quick pace.

Missed him! He got away! He got away!

I stare down, trying to spy another, perhaps to look at, perhaps to jump at, but the choice is taken away from me as a moment later I hear a *Stcka* and no more than a foot from my cheek is another rat, running no doubt from the screaming below, but in turn making screaming up here as I inadvertently recoil and scream myself, causing me to roll down, one, then two, then three bales, finally managing to cling on to some binding string, right beside old Kevin –

Did you fall off! Did you run away! Did you ROLL away?

NO! I lie – *He came down this way… Sure… Sure you missed him, he was THIS far from your face* and I put my finger and my thumb SO close that there's only a slither of air getting through, a fraction of light…

One's on the run! One's on the run!

And Kevin's leaping about, from bale to bale, thudding his wrench against the top of the bales, making, a deep, satisfying, safe *THUD.*

And then –

I gotch one! I gotch one!

It's Siobhan, still on the floor, a brown rat dangling from her hand, held aloft by a rope it seems, but no, as I climb down, I see it's no rope, it's the tail of the beast, with MASSIVE front teeth bared, bared and scored, red-eyed, manky-skinned…

It's been poisoned! Put it down! Put it down Shiv…

But Siobhan is waving it, over her head now, like some kind of animal lasso, and bits and pieces and whatever else are coming off it – dirt from the floor, fragments of hay, I'd hope, but maybe muck and piss being forced out of its belly…

It's alive! It's alive! Paul now, shrieking with all the excitement, but it's surely not alive… *Look! Look! It's paws are grabbing out…*

And they do appear to be, they seem to be moving towards us, as though swimming in the air, trying to escape…

WHAT DO YOU THINK YOU'RE DOING?!

And all stop.

Siobhan drops the rat in fright and it flies down to the floor, those paws making no effort to break the fall, the body tumbling like a stuffed sock and then the head crunching, taking the brunt of impact before lying still as a stone.

I'VE TELT YE A THOUSAND TIMES – KEEP OUT OF HERE AND KEEP AWAY FROM THE POISON AND THE RATS. IT'LL KILL YE! IS THAT WHAT YE WANT? IS IT? IS IT NOW?

I'm guessing this is the farmer, the dadda, but whoever, our new friends have stopped dead still in fright at his arrival, all weapons dropped, all mouths closed…

AND WHO ARE YOU TWO? IS THAT YOU I SEEN AT MARY'S PLACE? WELL, WHEREVER – YE SHOULD GET YERSELVES BACK NOW, BEFORE I KICK YOU WHERE IT HURTS! GO ON! GET GOING!

I run by Paul and grab his arm – careful not to grab his hand in front of our new pals – and drag him outside, running toward the field. As we gallop away, we can still hear, just –

AND WHAT WOULD YOUR MOTHER SAY? IF SHE WERE HERE? TELL ME THAT!

Before we hit the soil and leaves of the field, our run slowing gradually, down to a walk.

Did you get a rat?

I didn't, Paul, no. Did you?

No. I never even seen one, until that dangly one… Do you think they have them in the pub?

I think of the rubbish stacked up outside… *Probably not.*
Good. It was a big fellow, was it not?
It was.
Well, I hope they stay in their barn.
I laugh. *What use would they have crossing these fields?*
No use.
No use at all.
Can we get back now? I have a sore tummy…
Sure. Let's get back.

*

As we approach the yard, the house, the pub, we hear laughter, father's laughter, Mary's too, but it's father's we quieten for. They're too far away to make out any words, but, entering the yard itself, Paul and me decide we're not going to go in, not now, not whilst father is happy like this. We find a clean space, a couple of dry wooden pallets and sit down. Paul gathers up a small stick, and the stick grows wings and becomes a plane, or perhaps a space rocket, and weaves in front of him, left to right, up and down, right to left. But it is a silent rocket, for too much noise would stop us from hearing the curious sound from inside – Mary's voice – my father's voice – *throwing* the joy out of their lungs in a way I've never heard before, a father I've never heard before. And this happiness becomes the soundtrack to Paul's game, as I watch and listen in wonder.

In the heart of the matter, during the event,
I didn't even notice the silence.
Between onlookers, heads spinning,
And the waves, screaming.

Then –

That bare realisation.
Clawed at, hit, unstoppable.
'There is now nothing more I can do'.

Pulled ashore by strangers, their fee
a silent, staring.

The Garda arrive and
'Was this your wife and is this your brother and what were they
doing out there together?'
Our lives. Split and taken and noted, grey pencil upon white paper.

16

THE NIGHT AFTER, there is no laughter, and I fear I hear far worse – snarling, charged whispers barely audible, but rising up like waves, waves full of anger and defence, and when we charge down for some breakfast, there is nothing left out for us and we are not alone, as father is already in the kitchen and looking as though he's barely slept at all, as though he'd even slept on a thin leather seat in the snug of a bar. He smiles at us, of course, but this is his old smile. A barrier to whatever is behind the smile, you know? And now we'd seen how he could smile, well… we wanted that back.

And when Mary came downstairs, well, I don't know what father was planning on saying, but what he said was just –

We have to leave. We have to get to Dublin. I promised. I promised. I can't be here… A kept man!

Jesus, Fraser. No one is after keeping you, did you not get that? Don't you flatter yourself.

And then a cruel, piercing silence, a silence that made every drop of my food lose its taste and my stomach want to throw it all right back up there and then.

*

I'd been pleased to be here, with Mary and her milk and her bread and her crisps. We even had a room, though a room we had to share with boxes of those crisps. Those O'Driscolls hadn't been back, though I'd seen the shouty man in the bar both nights since… But, we saw less of father when we were here, and I wanted to see father… And, there's only so much one can do in the dusty backyard of a bar. Throwing rocks. Balancing bottles. Throwing rocks at balancing bottles then being told off…

Paul, he liked it all – the bar, and the food, and the fire, and the no nuns and not walking.

Father said to Paul *It's not that… we've been here too long. We have to get to see the man. To Dublin. To see the publisher man. I can't stop now. We're so close… We have to think about that and not anything else. Do you understand?*

And how could Paul understand, him being younger than me, and me not a clue about any of it, about any of it at all.

Can we not stay, da? Joseph and me? And you'll be back tomorra?

It wouldn't be tomorrow, Paul. But… we can maybe come back. I hope. Or maybe… maybe Mary would come back home with us.

He whispered that bit though, anxious *she* didn't hear. Perhaps not believing the words himself.

*

Do you have to go, Fraser? I mean, could you not just… send the… send the poems?

No. I need – I need to see the man. And see what he says.

I'm not liking this… I'm feeling… I'm not some staging post, Fraser… You could send him anything you needed to, you do know that?

I know, I know… but this ONE time, this one, first time, I need to meet him, the man who wrote back, you know?

Jesus, Fraser… If you're making a run for it…

I want to stay. I want to stay here in my hidey-hole, stealing Tayto Crisps and munching them until my tummy bursts.

I'm not making a run for it! Sure, where would I run? I just – I just made a promise – the writing, the poetry… it hauled me through all that – that time, you know? I've got to try it – I have to at least try – does that make sense? I can't risk it… I can't risk it to an… an envelope!

But only a fool would move from this luxury dwelling now, surely? With its Cheese 'n' Onion with its Salt 'n' Vinegar with its warmth and water…

Oh, Fraser, Fraser, do you not think I've heard that before? Running, rather than being… trapped here. What a fool I've been…

You have not!

Then what am I if I am not a fool? Tell me – who am I to you? Are you scared, Fraser? Because, if so, do you think that I am not? Do you think I provide a bed for every man of little means that passes through? Because believe me, I see a hell of a lot of them, and believe me, I do not. You're chasing a dream, Fraser, and dreams do not come true. I know that. And YOU should know that.

You have to trust me…

Jesus, for a man with words, you have little to say.

Then –

Fraser, there's nothing here, I know that. And Dublin… with the bright lights and… who knows what else, who else…

And father –

You're here, Mary. You're here.

A scattering of sand on glass
and I am awake.

The room then silent, ice, still.

I feel you, around me,
and I am lucky.

Until the rain.

More sand, thrown harder,
wet and heavy now, shut outside.

How you'd pull yourself upon me on nights like this,
we would share our warmth, our bodies
whilst the curtains slowly danced.

Wait for me, my love.
Wait for me beyond these fearful nights, beyond these overran years.
I will raise ours, and I will raise them well, for us.

17

THE BUS TO Cork arrived, as she said it would. We climbed on and were barely waved off by Mary, Mary who'd been silent the whole little walk from hers. She'd ruffled my hair though, Paul's too…

She'd tried, I'd seen, she'd tried to talk to father, at least catch his eye, but father distracted, counting and recounting, telling the driver Paul *was only six*, which he hadn't been for two whole years, and finally him being allowed on for free and finally us away, though the stories, mother's story and Mary's story… the thought of them all came with me. And when he had finally turned to wave, she'd already begun her journey back inside and can you blame her?

*

We shared the bus with many different people. Ladies, mostly, dressed in their finery, sat at the front, chatting away. We climbed on and sat closest to them, in amongst that peculiar rose smell that posh ladies use to scent their cludgies.

Behind us, though, the smell was altogether different. For a start, it was almost all male, a few foreign-looking girls aside, and there was a thin grey cigarette fog that floated toward us, choking.

I don't like this bus, da'.

And neither did I. The seat itself seemed to be a worn-out fuzzy orange blanket over a bare piece of wood and Paul and me were practically on top of one another. Father was holding his precious suitcase tight to him and the weight of him was slowly but repeatedly pushing me off the seat and on to the floor.

Move over!

Paul was trying to snuggle his head into father and I don't blame his attempt to anchor himself around father's arm.

It's not long now, boys, this part of the journey.

And I wonder, was Mary and her house just part of the journey?

I'm hungry da'.

We'll eat at the bus depot. When it's more comfortable. Mary... Mary gave me some food for you. For us.

Mary.

Mary. Mare...eee.

What are you saying, Joseph?

The road bumps and my bum jumps a foot into the air, the bus moving aside before it could land and me flailing all the way down to the grime of the floor, the raised bit of the footwell landing between my bum cheeks and almost splitting me in two.

Ah Jesus! Heck! Fuck!

I'd never said Fuck! before, but I'd heard my father say it plenty now, but me saying it, or worse – shouting it, it brought me all sorts of attention. And of course, that attention then on to father –

Oh Lord have mercy!

What language from such a youngster!

You should be ashamed!

And from the back, just laughter –

Jesus, will you look at him!

Ah he's taken a tumble!

A Ha HA HA HA ha.

Then the great arm of my father appearing and lifting me straight back on to the seat, poor Paul being squashed aside in the movement

Get back up, ya clown.

Then, brushing me off, invisible dust from my shoulder, straightening me up, visible creases not budging.

And where did you learn THAT language?

Loudly, though, for the audience, because he knew fine where I'd learned it.

And I'm sat back, quiet now, looking forwards to the seat ahead, my hand clasped on the edge, keeping me grounded. Worried for more of a telling off, but peeping round to father and seeing him glinting, grinning out toward the window, something working awoken in his eyes that I'd not seen for a long time, if ever at all.

18

WE SLOW WHEEL through the city streets and finally arrive with the *sheesh* of the breaks, climbing off slowly, stretching our legs, waking ourselves up.

The bus station is filthy. And I don't mean filthy like the house we've left at Creagh, or filthy like the school floor, it's strange, black, unruly filth, a filth that I cannot rub off my fingers.

It's the oil. Don't touch it.

And I know not to, now, though the rainbow of it all is appealing.

PAUL, I SAID DON'T TOUCH IT.

And Paul jumping back –

And keep close. The pair of you. Keep close to me.

My head cannot stop moving, back and forth, waltzing between the views. There are people here who look as though they roll in that oil every day and people here who are obviously drunk. They are mostly the same people.

An elderly lady approaches me, mewing, or squeaking, but not really talking…

Get away you. We've nuhin for you –

Father batting her away – there are creases under her eyes like a ploughed field and her skin is almost as brown. She has a tooth, I notice, but only one…

Eeeeuuuggg Have youuuu…

Go! Go now! You two – come on. Stay close.

And he wrenches us away from her …

Jesus…

He looks nervous, father. He's dragging us from one place to another, standing still momentarily, then off we go again. He's looking up at boards, at times, at platform numbers, one arm clasping his suitcase close, one hand firmly wrapped around Paul's. And Paul's other hand is with me.

What are we doing?

Shh! The next bus… Mary had a timetable from the newspaper… I know what to do… There – there's our bus – now – wait…

He stands – we stand, but not close, no – we stand a stone's throw away. Father patting us behind his back, trying to avoid being seen by the driver – but the driver isn't paying us any attention whatsoever.

What are we doing, father?

SHH!… Any minute now…

I turn and gaze up the hills surrounding us, hills covered in multi-coloured houses, tiny places it seems, like match boxes, piled up one against the other. I can see the people buzzing in and out the doorways, up and down the street – we could live here, maybe? This looks good, to me, once you get away from the filth of the station.

Look! There we are… They're getting on now…

And sure enough, a queue has formed at a bus, a bus with a sign on the front, proudly declaring *DUBLIN.*

Shall we go over then?

NO! Stay here… wait… wait…

And the slow procession continues. I wait, watch, then – *Father, will we not get a seat? We'll need a seat…*

Wait… ok – wait… now – hang on –

I look back at the houses, but suddenly, Paul's arm is pulled and then my own. *Come now. Quickly. And keep quiet, you hear? Dead quiet.*

I look to our bus, but the driver is walking away, hopping slightly, back into the bus building –

Now's our time. Come on – keep up –

And we're at the door, which has been left open. *Follow me boys –* We climb up the stairs, Paul struggling with their height, a bit, but soon lifted on – *Lucky we've got tickets already eh, boys?* Past the faces of the passengers, bored looking mostly, heads in books, resigned. *Just made it eh, boys? Lucky we got tickets earlier, eh?* Why's he rabbiting on about tickets? I don't remember getting any tickets… He leads us as far down the back as we can go, right into the stinking cigarette zone, with the mad laughing men and the cursers – but this time, the company seems a little different, younger, ladies wearing floral baggy trousers, men with long tied hair, and an altogether different smell, a sour, fruity…

We'll sit here boys, in you come –

And he brings Paul right up on to his lap and grabs my arm, pulling me close beside him. *Keep quiet now, boys, and still. Keep quiet and still. And don't look at the driver. DON'T LOOK, Joseph…* Father's shouting, but whispering. Whispering, but shouting. *Shh…* Then he's smiling, conspiratorially, at the people around us… *Heads down, boys…*

But there's no worry, for we hear the door *Slam!* And almost instantly afterwards the bus's engine grumbles into life, we lurch forward and are off, off to Dublin.

Sleep, boys, sleep.

And with Paul on his lap and me on his shoulder, we sleep.

*

Every now and then, the bus will slow, then stop, but the engine remains on. Some new people will emerge, looking for a space to dump themselves, their bags… *Keep your eyes shut boys… It's not for us to move… Keep yourselves still…*

*

Can we eat? Can we eat now, father?

All around us, people have food. Sandwiches, fruit, steaming hot drinks… There's smoke, too, but less than the first bus.

Sure. Paul – move over with Joseph – here – Joseph – this is yours…

I grab at it, a brown paper bag with a J written on it and within… well, within there's a roll, almost not too old and within that… cheese. Perfect. I snarl into it, right away. Before long, Paul is doing

THE BOOK OF THE GAELS

the same, but father – well, he's reading something, a small piece of paper that he found on his way into his own bag… He's smiling and reading, then reading again. He catches me looking and shoves it into his top pocket, before pulling out his own supplies – another roll, this time accompanied by a small bottle of beer. He puts that back into his old leather case.

*

The bus stops. I look out of the window – *Is this it? Is this Dublin?* But it can't be. There's nothing here but one shop, connected to a pub and nothing else. A field, I guess. But there's not even a road, other than the one we're on.

TOILET STOP!

Quick and to the point. I spy the driver jumping down the stairs and hopping over to the building, quickly followed by the first row, then the second, then everyone, all standing together. Father holds us down. *Not us, boys, not us…*

But I need, da', I need…

So do I!

NO! He'll see us and… maybe he won't let us back on…

I thought we had tickets, da'?

Shh! Now…

But everyone is leaving. There won't be a soul left on. It's one thing hiding in a crowd, but if the crowd has gone, you're just standing there alone, like a tree in a field.

Ah Jesus… Jesus now…

And the last people around us stand and leave – *We'll have to go, we'll have to go boys* – So we stand, to go, but father is not sure what to do with his suitcase, eventually shoving it tight down below, underneath our seat. He then removes his scarf and places it upon the seat, to mark that this is ours, this is where we are. *If I have to climb back on and get it, you boys stay outside, ok? Just let me run on alone…* Then we're quickly up against the back of the last few to leave and down we go, quickly on to the tarmac.

The driver is there, smoking a cigarette. He nods at my father, but there's no smile, no humour.

C'mon, boys.

The queue to the cludgie snakes all the way through the shop, up to and past the counter. People are picking up goods – biscuits, apples, crisps, drinks… Father is not picking up goods, and neither is Paul.

Father is muttering under his breath *Jesus, Jesus…* and he's looking, out of the window, over to the bus. The driver has disappeared. *He better not be getting my suitcase…* When it's our turn at the counter, we have nothing to buy, so Paul and me smile at the lady, who looks tired but happy. A busy time for her. She must live on these bus visits.

Nothing today lads, eh?

We shake our heads. Paul looks at the chocolate, the different colours, the golden wrappers…

Nothing today, eh, boys? Come on – our turn in the lavvy.

But on the way out, she gives me and Paul a chocolate mouse. Each. No bigger than my thumb, and as thin as a penny, but a chocolate mouse, all the same. *Thank you, missus.*

Yes, thank you missus.

And they're gone, straight into our mouths before another step is taken.

*

We're not the last, as we approach the bus. Some people are still out, stretching their legs, choosing this moment to have a cigarette, thankfully, rather than puff it away on the bus.

But the driver is watching us, as he finishes his cigarette.

My father has his hand on my shoulder, as we approach, it tightens. He's pushing me back and forth, as if with affection, but it's too strong…

A word with you, sir?

And we stop.

He takes a final drag from his cigarette and throws it on to the floor.

You've no tickets, do you?

My father looks down, speechless.

Where is it you're going?

Dublin. He mutters. I look up to catch father's eyes, then the driver's, but they're squared against each other.

Dublin. Again. As if the driver didn't hear.

Why did you not get a ticket – when all these good people did?

My father coughs. But there's no answer – until, Paul squeaks out – *Dada's got a job. In Dublin. We're going to his job. We've been riding carts and walking and eating nuhin. The bus is better.*

And father doesn't chastise, doesn't *shh*. He just looks at the driver, who offers little sympathy.

So… have you the money? I'm guessing not?

I'll… I'll need to get my suitcase off.

You will. Look – I'm sorry, but… if the inspector gets on between now and Dublin, well, that's me in the serious brown stuff. You know?

I understand. I'm sorry…

No look – I'm sorry. I really am. I have two children of my own. But I can't…

He reaches over and fluffs Paul's hair.

Best get your bag, so I can keep the bus moving.

And we stood there, Paul and me, we stood by the door of the bus, as father crawled on, head down and made his way to the back, gathering his suitcase and scarf, then making his way back. Lord alone knows what he said along the way, though I'd guess at nothing at all.

19

THERE'S NOTHING. THERE'S nowhere near here.

Father's looking up and down the road. Occasional traffic, that's all. No road signs, houses, no one to ask... If it wasn't for the shop, this'd just be a roadside verge. At least we know which side of the road to stick our thumb out.

He's rubbing his face, looking down at us, then to the ground, then over to the shop...

Here – Let's at least try –

So, we stand at the road and he sticks his thumb out. A family of three, with one shoddy suitcase. We look ok, I think, to me.

And I think to myself – *When I get a car, when I grow up, I will pick up people from the side of the road...* nobody stops. The cars just fly by, we feel the wind in their wake and close our eyes from their dust.

I need a wee, da'.

What, again? So soon?

I do though, I do...

Ok, hang on a moment, there's a van just on the horizon... hang on, hang on...

It just whizzes past us, blaring its horn.

Forget it. Let's take you inside.

I make to stay, to hitch, by myself – *I'll call you if anyone stops...*

What? Don't be ridiculous. C'mon, boy. Maybe... Maybe the lady in the shop will have some ideas.

*

I was watching yez.

Heh.

No one stopping for yez, eh? That's the story of my life…

Can we – can he use…

The jacks? Sure – go ahead.

Father shuffles Paul through the door, leaving me and the lady. The lady and me. I look at her and wonder what to say. But she beats me to it.

And how old are ye then?

I'm ten.

Ten years old, is it? That's a fine age.

I'd say she's forty, maybe. Or fifty. Old, you know? I feel proud of my age, that I am still here, that I have defeated the ageing process, at least thus far.

And where are you lot off to?

Dublin…

Dublin! Well, you've a long way to go still I'd say.

I look at her, for an answer, an answer to the obvious question – how are we going to get to Dublin?

Will ye be buying anything?

I look around – I'd love to be buying. There's plenty of things here I'd be happy to eat, but I strongly doubt it. I don't think father has a single penny left in those pockets of his. Maybe, if we're lucky, he'll have a roll to share.

He emerges, Paul under his hand. *Hello again.*

Hello yourself.

Ok, Joseph – on you go now –

But… I don't need…

Go on, you'd be as well to, now –

I look to the lady, who shakes her head and nods me through. *Go on, son. Everyone else uses it, so you may as well.*

*

It stinks, through this door. I don't need to pee, so I just stand here, waiting until enough time has passed that I can pretend I have peed. On the wall there are posters, slowly peeling off. A barn

112

dance. A hurly match. A fundraiser. I wonder where these things take place? When there's nothing within eye-distance.

I can hear my father talking, through the door –

Is there anything you'd like done?

Eh?

Is there anything you'd, you know, like done, whilst we're here? You know...

What? I can do everything I need myself now –

I meant, maybe, in exchange, you know, for some... food?

What? I'm not a charity –

Oh father, father – I burst through the door – *He could clean the lavvy! It stinks!*

My father looks at me with incredulous eyes –

Heh! Would you do that? Would you clean the jacks?

His head turns, slowly, towards the lady, hand still on Paul's shoulder – *Would you feed us?*

She snorts, softly – *Not for life, but, sure, you could take a roll...*

Each?

Ah, I can clean it myself, for nothing. Takes a moment, no more – I have to make a living here, you know. I rely on these bloody buses... I can't GIVE you food that others would pay for now, can I? I'd be a fool...

There's a shaft of light coming through the window behind her head, and it's pulling out the dust, floating in the air, reflecting and visible now. My father doesn't speak.

Can I have another mouse, then?

A what? What did the young one say?

Nothing. He said nothing... Come on boys, we'll get going... Joseph – get back from there, come on, we'll walk along the road a bit and keep on trying our luck. Say thank you to the lady.

I make to move, to move out of this cavern of delights, these treats and comforts... Surely she'd not miss one? She'd not miss one small bag of crisps...

But I'm under father's guidance now, his spare arm around my shoulder this time, his suitcase held above, shuffling me out – *I'm sorry to have bothered you, lady.*

Well.

Paul's face too, is taking in the surrounds as we leave, the parcels of treasure, but they're not for us, not for us…

*

And then we're outside. Back to where we began.

Father looks to the road, then back to the shop. He shakes his head. *Wait here, boys* and he's back in.

We know not to follow him, so we stand. Paul gives me his hand. Cars pass, a light wind, the sun lowering still.

Father comes back out – *Here – give me that suitcase, Joseph…*

…then he's back inside.

We cannot hear voices. Paul tightens his grip and I squeeze a reply. He kicks a stone, or the gravel as a whole. Digging his toecap in.

Watch your shoes! Father will go mad on you!

He stops and looks at me. He's accepting of this, I think. He doesn't know. And he is trusting father. And so am I. What else can we do?

We move closer, for it is getting cold, slowly.

I need a pee.

What? You can't already…

But I do… I need to go inside…

No! Father said not to…

He's dada, why do you call him father, he's not a priest, you know.

I know!

He's dada, and he won't leave us here.

Why would he do that? Of course he won't.

He's gone back to be with the food, to see the food…

He may be getting us something…

An apple?

Or crisps…

Or some Pepsi-Cola?
You've never TASTED Pepsi-Cola…
What, I have so!
Have not.
Have –
Not –
Have –
Not –
Here I'm going in –

And before I can stop him, he's released his grip and is running in – I follow him, of course I do, as quickly as I can –

And we burst through the doors, together.

Father turns, the lady turns. They are at the counter, together, and they both have their hands on something, something short and small. A bracelet? A watch? In an instant, father pulls his hand away and puts the whatever-it-is into his side pocket – *You two! Outside now – I won't be a minute… Go on…*

And the shopkeeper, she says – *here – let them take a bag of crisps each…*

And father, he shrinks – *Are you… sure?*
Sure. And we'll sort the rest.

We grab a bag. A bag each. Paul has Cheese 'n' Onion and I have Ready Salted. We run outside and pull them open, but Paul's bag bursts – it bursts open and goes everywhere, all over the floor and miles away and ten feet away and immediately, we're down with the escapees, picking them up, piling them back into Paul's burst bag *This one's got black bits… It doesn't matter, it'll be potato, not from the floor* – and it probably WAS from the floor, but he's eating now, and crying a bit, but eating and soon I'm doing the same, more careful, giving Paul a HUGE crisp, to make up for his loss.

He sniffles – *Here, this is the KING of the crisps.*
It is!

He gives me a baby one, like the wafer we had in the church, that sort of size – it tastes… it tastes of an old cheese, it's a peculiar taste, very dry, but better than the wafer, no doubt about that, and the flavour runs into my next crisp of my own that tastes of… salt.

And Paul has finished then and is rubbing his fingers in the bag, then licking his fingers, then just licking the whole bag, inside out, all around. I don't do the same, not with mine, just the salt in there – he sees me watching and – *Want a lick?* But I don't, no. I don't want a lick…

*

Father emerges.

He doesn't look happy, he doesn't look sad. He just grabs a shoulder, rubs our hair. *You ok boys, now? Here – we're sorted. Look. Next bus is not until tomorrow, but we can get it…*

How can we get it, daddy?

…well, the lady – she has lent me some money…

Lent? What does that mean?

It means… I can pay her back and then we'll all be back to normal… But anyway – don't you worry about that – look – she's told me where we can stay, this evening. There's a campsite, apparently.

A what?

A campsite. Come on. You know what that is, don't you? Don't be an idiot. We'll have a tent. Together. It'll be fun. Your mother – she loved camping. She'd love us doing this.

Did she?

She did. She did…

And we are paralysed by the thought of our *mother*, loving to camp… *Did she ever camp with us?*

Well, no… But yes – inside the house she did, yes…

But surely that's not camping? Or maybe it is… Our house wasn't the warmest, I know that.

Well. Come on now. We have a bit of walking. Not much, but a bit. C'mon, boys. It won't take long. Let's get there before dark.

20

B UT WE CANNOT find the place. We walk, and walk, and walk, but still we cannot find the place.

Did we go the right way, dada?

Of course... It'll just be... over there...

But it wasn't.

Until, finally, as the sun was setting, we began to hear peals of laughter, far away at first, but something to aim toward.

And then, and then, just as the sun went into its final descent, there were... flickers of light?

Here – we're almost there – Last stretch, eh, boys!

Paul's feet dragged. Eventually, he was picked up and carried. I offered to take the suitcase, but it was more of a weight to me than him and we both knew it, so I just continued beside father. The best I could do to help was not drag my feet.

And father, he sang, to keep us distracted –

And in that bog there was a tree,
a rare tree a rattling tree,
and the tree in the bog
and the bog in the tree
and the bog down in the valley-o...

The voices got louder, then softer, as though they had heard us – for they HAD heard us, they had heard father, surely, and maybe Paul, as he lightly whimpered, or maybe me, the effort of trying to keep up and not be a burden, surely that was audible...

...and I do not know what a campsite was supposed to look like, but it surely wasn't this – for within half a dozen steps we stepped up a verge and were immediately in amongst a circle of high, tall stones, a large fire burning in the middle and all sorts of grown-up men with long hair and grown-up women dressed like girls, with long scarves and wild, messy hair, all lit up by the flame of the fire. *Hello! Hello! Join us!* they said. And father considered *not to* for a moment but then agreed that maybe we should and I was relieved he did, for it meant we could sit down, close to the fire and release the effort on my collapsing legs.

Paul whispered to me – *That man's wearing a SACK!*

And it seemed Paul was right. Father was the best dressed amongst them, heck, almost the only who'd made any bother, in his tweeds and his once-white shirt… The others looked as though they were in a pantomime – some of the women had painted their lipsticks on their cheeks – all of the men had seaweed beards, like old tramps, but thin, flat bodies like younger men…

They were dancing, some of them. I think. At least, they were waving around, as though pretending to be the wind. They offered father cigarettes, but he said no, and took out his beer from earlier – *This'll do me…*

We were offered some cake and who's going to say no to *that*. We thrust our hands out and delivered them the open palm greeting, to catch any precious crumbs, to estimate the size of the *cake*, to show our acceptance. One voice said – *Sure, don't give them any of that cake I made, it's…* and that made us more eager still, shuffling off our backsides and standing now, not queuing, but not pushing ahead, either. We both knew the other would share, if there was only one piece of cake –

It emerged from a bag, probably brown paper, though hard to see in the flame light. Father seemed happy with the thought of us having cake, and why wouldn't he be? And for one brief, beautiful moment, we had one dollop – for I cannot call it a slice, more a sling of mud – of cake each, before the naysayer hopped over – *It's too much, too much* – and removed Paul's slab. He began to whimper, but I shook my head – *I'll share, you know I will* – and his whimper ended as quickly as it began. He sucked and licked his own hands, finding any remainder of his once-full handful, before prodding in the gloom at my lot and eventually pulling the main piece in half *Hey! Watch it...* But there was plenty enough for two.

But, the first mouthful made clear that this wasn't a chocolate of my dreams, this was most certainly made for grown-ups, for there was a dry, clumpy bitterness to it that made it as much of a chore as a joy. I just knew that Paul's face was going to be screwed up in horror and disappointment. How could you offer someone chocolate cake then give them this? It's not cake at all. It's like eating... earth.

Euuurgggh.

Paul threw his away, his sudden sharp movement visible, even in this low light, and all around there was laughter.

Just as well!

I grinded away at my mouthful, took one further nibble, just in case I'd had a bad bit, but no, the further nibble was even worse, if that was possible. I discreetly dropped the remainder on the floor. Who'd make a cake that tastes like a shoe?

The attention very quickly left us and we sat back down, just off the inner circle, but within the reach of the warmth of the fire. I was SO tired, and after a minute or two just I began to feel dizzy, from the walking, I'd guess. Paul's head began to shudder on to my shoulder, and soon it'd fall toward the floor, only for him to rescue it and return to my shoulder. After that happened three or four times, I lay down beside him, but I found I could not, for upon my head resting on the grass, I felt I was falling into the ground itself, then somehow turning split somersaults, over and over, as if I were rolling down the hill. I sat back up and tried to focus on the fire, but began seeing faces within the flames – demons and ghosts, open armed and grabbing, long tongued, evil eyed. Paul was asleep to my left and without warning I turned and vomited, but thankfully, to my right...

Nobody noticed. I was discreet, and there was little in my stomach anyway, except the cake.

That cake. Ugh.

My arms were dizzy now. I've never had dizzy arms. I could barely hold myself up so I shrank down beside Paul, turning away from the sick and into him, his familiar smells and sounds. I was ok still, eyes open, but the moment they were closed I felt I was lying on a dinghy, floating in a mildly choppy sea.

The singing, the commotion – it all continued, it just would not stop. Some of the pirates had musical instruments, handheld drums, guitars, I think, maybe something else. They were singing, but the music had no tunes I could hear or understand… This was like thirty people all singing different songs. Paul, lying beside me, would shuffle and crunch then wake and say *Make them stop!* So, I put my hands over his ears, but then it was louder for me, so I'd have to remove my hands from Paul's ears and put them back over my own. He'd begin to growl, and I'd feel his body tensing up further. He'd be pushing me toward the sick. Eventually, I'd take father's scarf and tie that long woollen beast around *both* our heads, our ears. But it didn't lessen any volume. *Make them stop!* Paul said, *Make them stop!*

*

Eventually, through exhaustion, Paul got to sleep, and I could concentrate on his light snoring, which lulled me into a sort of sleep. It was colder, but we were close enough to the fire, and we had ourselves…

*

Later, father's voice woke me. He sounded happy, so I did my best to stay awake, to keep this moment, which of course, sent me to sleep…

…until the next shudder of laughter, which would wake me again, for a second, waves of sound, waves of sleep…

…and once, it was the silence that woke me. My ears panicked, it'd been SO loud, so busy, with the howls of the girls and the yells of the boys, and then, the silence broke through and within the silence, was my father's soft voice, floating –

I pray, come and tell me your name – and tell me when your dwelling be
My name it is dear Sully, I earn a living out on the sea
For I am a man upon the land and a selkie in the sea
And when I'm far, far from the strand, my dwelling is in Sule Skerrie

A song I half knew, half remembered, the melody, the story…
And all around, I heard the voices were whispering – *Listen to this! LISTEN to this… It's the real thing… HE'S the real thing, man…*
Father, my father, the real thing.

*

The cold snuck around my neck, up the base of my back. I heard a sound, it was a tiny wave, breaking on a shale beach. It said *Shhh…* and again, *Shhh…* and, you know, I think it was some essence of my mother, calming me, stroking me to sleep, which I finally did.

They'd sing songs for this, you know?
In the old days.
To spread the news.
Well —

Come gather around me and I'll tell you a tale
Of when I was younger, before it all turned to hell
Of when I had a lover that I loved so well
Oh, come gather, gather around me...

21

WE WOKE AND were soaked. Sleeping on grass, waking on dew. Paul says –

I need a pee.

But of course, of course you do. I jump up after him and run behind, but to where? There is nowhere around, just an open field...

Paul is not shy. He begins, right there, and I turn, a half-angle, and begin myself.

The grown-ups are all asleep. They are splayed around this tall circle of stones as if a giant has dropped them from above in groups of ones and twos and threes, arms and legs flopping out from the bundles like errant branches. Father is lying by himself, curled around his suitcase, cuddling it like a cushion.

I'm hungry. Shall we wake da?

No! Don't do that, he'll be mad...

But I'm hungry!

Leave him...

BUT I'M HUNGRY.

SHHH!

I wrestle him down, and soon the two of us are rolling slowly away from the stones, slowly towards the edge of the field –

Blackberries!

Where?

Look – Over there! In the hedge...

We stop wrestling and examine from afar, then within one second we're up and over, and a second after that we are picking and eating...

These are delicious...

Our fingers become purple from the fruit, our lips the same. Paul examines each berry, throwing some away, peeling off leaves and *a beastie!* The fruit is sweet, it's sour, it's delicious it's everything that stupid chocolate cake was not and soon enough we've worked our way down and we're sat squat down in amongst the bush, not hiding away, but out of sight, certainly…

Look – A spider web…

Beyond – look the other side – more berries…

Raspberries! *No…*

And reaching through the gap, pushing past the web, neck against the twigs…

Ow!

You pushed me!

Did not!

Did!

Did not…

All right, out you come… and Paul suddenly floating out of the bush, his legs still tight against his body his hair getting scrapped through by the branches – *Hey!*

And some great giant has grabbed him, but –

I turn and see father's shoe, with his trouser sodden now, from the long grass he'd've walked through to get to us…

So THAT'S where you two got to, eh?

I reverse shuffle out, no desire to be lifted as Paul was. But as I'm exiting, there's a *Whack!* on my behind – *Aya!* – and I'm worried there'll be more to come, but father, well, he's playful, not angry, almost buoyant – *Come on, squeaks, we need to get that bus. It's a good long walk back to where we came, you know…*

Not *that* walk again… *No! That's SO far…*

It's not far and it'll be easier in daylight – sure, we'll just follow the sun – I can see where we were, from up here – And what a glorious day it is, eh?

And he grins and points over in the general direction of nowhere in particular – *We have a good three hours to get there, now, I'd say* – and I look, I do, I try and see – but no. For there was never anything to see there, no landmarks or pointers, just that shack of a shop. Father begins to walk and I rush to follow and as soon as we get beyond the long grass, just as he said, it gets easier.

Father's eating some of that foul chocolate cake. We don't ask for any. As he walks, he sings. He hums, he smiles, and he softly, softly sings.

*

The bus journey is incredible. Father is hungry and whatever food he managed to get from the bus shop yesterday he is happy to share. *Get it down you. Soon we'll be rich as kings…*

It's a peaceful ride. Paul and father and me, we all sleep a lot, seemingly taking it in turns to be the one awake, watching the other two doze, then head back down as somebody else surfaces for air.

The towns shake me awake, mostly, and we crawl through the tiny, close streets, a rainbow of colours on the houses and every second house a pub. Young mothers, old, cigarette-smoke-coloured men in worse suits than father's own, peering up to us on the bus, we who are going places, seeing the sights… No change between towns, just the size of each one, on occasion people jumping on or off, holidaymakers in their blue raincoats and shorts, young boys looking at Paul and me with suspicion, them with T-shirts with ladybirds on and tight red shorts, fancy pumps and plastic toys, us in our grass-stained once-school uniforms and clumping leather shoes. Father spits on his scarf and wipes our faces. I stick out my tongue and they retreat, clutching their mother's arms closer, tighter.

Leave them be, John, leave them be. Turn around now.

I have the last laugh. I think *It must be really bad where they live to come on holiday here* and *We're going to Dublin* and *Your dad looks like an idiot* and *My dad has a magic suitcase…*

*

One of the towns though, doesn't seem to stop. It just goes on and on and on… Paul is staring out of the window, father too.

This place is massive!

Father's quiet, occasionally peeling his head round, as if spotting a familiar landmark. Then, whispered – *This is Dublin.* And then – *I lived here for a while. With your mother.*

Really? We both lean closer to the window, as if we'd be able to spot her, or her ghost or a friend of hers carrying a picture of her aloft or maybe with her smile, that we'd somehow recognise or, well who knows what. But there's no sign of her. Of course not. After a minute, I sit back and gaze.

The streets are full of cars. Not like where we were, there'll be one each street, maybe. Well, maybe two, or three. But here, every space seems to have a rusty bluebottle car piling up and down. It's a grey old place, a dark grit covering scattered on top of it, the colours of the towering houses scarred and cowering, as if fighting off an illness, but still there, peeping out, showing everyone they are still alive. Plenty of dogs, horses too, who'd've thought that? I wonder if mother had a horse?

Father smiles at Paul, still glued to the window, ruffles his hair, kisses his hair.

And as we get further in, words begin arriving on buildings, but not like earlier in the journey, where it was most likely the name of the lady or gentleman inside behind the counter, these are HUGE letters, a lot I recognise – GUINNESS, HARP – And now… *Look, Joseph! Look, dada! This building must have a thousand windows!* I peer out, and behind yet another peach-orange bus, there's a building that seems to stretch on forever…

Is it, is it, is it… Buckingham Palace, dada?

Ha! No, Paul. It is not.

The people look busy, leaping about as if they've somewhere to go – and the colours they're wearing, vivid pinks, lime greens – and not every man is in a suit, no way, some wide, floppy trousers, bright jumpers under huge overcoats – Plenty of dogs… And *look!* – a factory – *Look at the size of THAT! And the houses – there are houses on top of houses – this must be the tallest building on the planet!*

We drive over a bridge and there's at least five lanes of traffic.

How does the driver know where to go, dada?

Heh. He'll know, Paul. When you grow up here, it's different. You get to know things, gradual, like.

Look at that lady's hat! It looks melted…

But the bus is away past her before I can spot anything.

Honestly, it looked melted – LOOK! A horse and cart – Ohhhh the bus will hit it!!! Watch out!!

It doesn't. We turn off the bridge and drive alongside a river. Soon enough the people thin out, the buildings just as tall, but mostly the signs say HOTEL now, or B&B. This town is huge, never ending. I have no idea how father is going to find his way around.

We swing under some bridges, Paul, myself and father pushed against each other, against the window, then the bus slows, and finally, the engine cuts.

All off!

I didn't realise quite what a noise that engine made until it was over. My ears feel a relief and scramble to take in the new quiet, though it's not *too* quiet as all around there are plenty of other buses and straggling groups of people, all ages, couples, schoolchildren, plus our own bus emptying now. *Wait, just wait* says father, so we do, allowing for the commotion to subside, before we stand and take our place at the back of the queue to exit the bus.

We would hide ourselves within
the city's bars
where we could dance

Your flowing red skirt

And the strength of you!
to peel me once more
from the side of the wall

Too strong a temptation.

Off we go again
in amongst the smoke
and the stares
the golden, the black

We quicken, we rush and we share
over and over
until your legs grow tired
but long, long after my own.

Oh! What a life we had,
us two young Gaels.
There were diamonds in the rough of the roads, those nights.

22

*H*ELLO? HELLO? *Is Mr King there? King — K I N G? Who? What, aye, haud on —*

He shuffles the paper with his one free hand —

Padraig? Padraig King? Trí Dé Dána Press? — Ah ok — Yes, I can wait…

(*to us*) — *He's just coming.*

Who's that, dada?

The man — now — stay close. Stay close — Joseph, don't wander…

There's an altogether different feel to this bus station, compared to the gleaming streets we drove through. There's a smell, the loos, or *the jacks*, the diesel, the dirty grey men walking back and forth, the cigarettes and pipes… Young people here, probably my age, but looking more like grown-ups, marked, ripped coats, forced, deepened voices, cigarettes again and threat. I try not to catch an eye. I *don't* catch an eye. Instead, I look back up at father, for his eye. In his raggedy suit, filthy shirt and now very old-fashioned looking flat cap, we do not look rich pickings for any passing criminal. Father has his suitcase wedged between his feet and is beckoning me over. I walk back, trying out a cowboy swagger.

Have you wee'd?

Eh?

Have you wee'd? In your pants?

No, Paul, I have not.

It's just you're walking…

Shh!

Well. You are —

Shh!

129

QUIET the both of you – the man's back – Hello? Hello now – Padraig? Is that you? Hello! It's Fraser McLeod here... Fraser... McLeod... From Skibbereen? Skibbereen? In Cork, yes... I, um... You – you sent me a letter, you'll remember... My poems... that's right! That's right! Great, great, well, I'm here... Yes, in Dublin... Dublin, yes. The bus station. Could I come... Well, to see you, as you suggested? Well... Yes, we were kind of passing... today maybe?... oh... oh... busy, I see...I see... How about tomorrow? Hold on... hold on...

He shovels into his pocket, bringing out some more change and thrusting it into the slot. I look around and over, seeing if anyone is watching, but no, we're just another minor event...

Ok! Tomorrow! Good – Great – what time – nine am?... No. Midday. Lunch. Lunchtime? Ok – great. Grand. Thanks very much. Ok – we'll see you tomorrow at lunchtime. Grand. Ok. Bye now – bye now – bye, bye, bye...

He puts the phone down and he's grinning ear to ear. *Sorted. Now, c'mon boys, let's find us a place to sleep for the night.*

Father picks up the case and we leave the station, a few tough-looking boys watching, me grabbing Paul's one free hand and not glancing back.

*

We pass one place, then another. A third. Father looks up to them all, inspecting.

What does that BeeBee sign mean?

It means Bed and Breakfast.

Oh.

Does that mean we'll get tea?

No, it does not. It means we'll get bed and breakfast... Here – we'll try this place –

Red writing on white board – *The Rose Hotel, B&B, Rooms Available.*

We climb a small set of stairs and father puts the case down, then pushing the *Reception* button which sets off a distant ringing

sound. There's no immediate answer, but a voice – *Wait, wait…*
and finally, the mottled glass door is opened –

Now. Who are you? She looks us up and down *How may I help
you? I don't have any charity, if that's what you're after…*

She looks amazing, like from the telly, a bright red jumper, hair
touching the moon, as though she's had an almighty fright, an
immaculate white apron with a picture of an old man wearing a
cap –

No – It's just a room we're after, please – the price of a room –

*A family room is it? And have you the money? It's up front here, you
know. Before you get the key.*

Ok…

*And no disrespect, but we have our standards, you know. We can't
just let any old soul in here – this is a tourist hotel, you know, plenty
of tourists come here. Regularly, you know. Americans. Australasians.
Brits.*

*I'm Scottish, missus. But my children – they're half-Irish. Their
mother has left us alone on this earth now, but we are doing well, thank
you very much and a room for the night would be most welcome, if
you'll have us.*

*Well, if you've the money, and it'll be ten pound for the three of you.
Good clean sheets and a warm room. Toast for the children. Sausages for
you only. Sausages are wasted on children, I find, wouldn't you agree?*

But father's still stuck on the ten pound.

Ten pound?

*That's the price, like it or not, I couldn't give a family room out for
less you understand.*

How about… with no sausage?

How do you mean, no sausage?

How about – what would the price be, if I don't have the sausage?

Paul pipes in – *Keep the sausage, dada, I can eat it easily, I could
have it now…*

Shh now – Then – *Ten pound is too much.*

Well. I'm sorry, son, but you'll need to find somewhere else.

131

Would you take five?

Five pound for the three of you? Who do you think I am? I tell you this – You will not find cheaper than ten on this WHOLE street, you understand. I'm not over-priced. I'm the same price.

Father looks deflated, he looks to me, as if for advice, but what can I say? Then to himself – *Ten pounds is... it's too much. No. We can't do it. I'm sorry lady, that's too much. Thanks for your time.*

Well, good luck to you. And good luck to your children. I hope you find somewhere. Now, excuse me, I have rooms to clean.

And quickly, she closes the door.

*

The next place was twelve pounds, but it included sausages for all.

*

I don't know what to do, Joseph.

We're sat on a cold concrete step, outside yet another of these hotel B &B places. I'm not sure what to say. Paul is, though – *Go to sausage place, go to the sausage place...*

Father is looking in his purse – *We can't, Paul. We're down to the last of it. There's no more...*

He looks up to the sky. We're lucky there's no rain, though it's not warm and it'll only be getting colder. He shakes his head.

No. We'll have to keep on looking. Come on, boys.

23

DELIBERATELY, IT SEEMS, we're walking away, out from the colour and the noise of the city centre. The streets stay wide for a bit, a good bit in fact, but then, in an instant, they pull in close and tight and different sounds appear, of family life, arguments, dogs barking, children playing... Father is fitting in here though, in his clothing. We all are. There's no one more or less well dressed than us. *Do we know someone here, dada?*

Shh now, Paul, I'll find us somewhere.

And the eyes follow us, curious, then move on to whatever's next. We pass a young girl, stroking a cat. She sticks her tongue out at me and I reply by thumbing my nose up, then quickly catching up with father and Paul.

Are we nearly there, dada?

We will be, we will be...

But he's not slowing, and we pass through another street, another street still then –

Here. This may do. You two – wait here. I'll just be one moment.

And before we know it, he's opened a glossy black door and walked inside. Paul and me just look at each other in surprise at the pace of it all, and then up to the building – *O'Hallaran's.*

It's a pub.

I know that!

Will he be long?

How would I know that?

Pub with rooms, it says.

Shall we go in?

No! He said to wait...

Colour TV, it says.

We should go in. I'm hungry.

No, Paul. Wait here. Look – He's only been gone a minute.

Is he having a drink?

No, he won't be.

I hope not.

Sunday Roast, it says. Paul spies that – *Is it Sunday today?*

No! It's not.

I don't think so, anyway.

Will they have any roast left?

Well how would I know?

I'm hungry!

I KNOW!

And then we're wrestling, in the street, with all the noise that makes – *Aya!* – *PAUL* – *Get off!* – but father is out in an instant – *Stop it, you two. C'mon. Stop. STOP.*

We stop. Paul is looking at father and I'm sure he is just about to ask about food, but before he can father dangles a key, bearing the number 7 –

We have a room here. And listen to this: Two pound a night! One bed, but she doesn't mind us sharing.

Is there…

Paul was wondering…

Was there…

The roast…

Anything left?

Heh. You two. Don't you worry. Look – And he delves further into his jacket pocket – *The lady sold me a roll each. We'll be fine here. Don't worry boys, we've landed, we've landed. Ten pound indeed! What were they thinking!*

We climb the narrow stairs, thin, sky blue carpet, worn through to the yellow. The noise of the bar follows us, as does the smell, the ever-present nicotine, the sticky alcohol, the unwashed attendees…

Here we go – Room one – Room two – must be further down –

Me dragging the case along now, father with key in hand, ready to explore and display, Paul peering into key holes, but mostly keeping an eye on the rolls, trying to work out what they contain, which one will be his...

Ah, here we are – number seven...

The end of the corridor. Different door type, this one a paler wood, newer looking.

In we go...

And we enter a corridor, with a bed at the end and behind that, another door, with a sign reading EXIT. I look back where we came, through the door... same colour walls, carpet...

This is just the corridor, dada...

Where's our room?

Are we sleeping in the corridor...no...

This is it, boys...

But there's nowhere to sleep – the bed is so narrow, like a ladder turned horizontal, almost – then there's no window, no anything...

But... where will we sleep?

Be quiet. This is – fine for us. Sure, a bed's a bed...

But there's only one of them!

If that.

Father tenses – *I said – be quiet. Do as you're told.*

And we did.

Now – you two boys can take the bed – sleep top to tail, maybe – and I'll be fine on the floor. Sure it's warm and dry. Ok? That's enough. That's enough for us. For now. Ok?

We nodded. I look at the filthy, soiled floor and am glad I am not the grown-up, the one sleeping on *that*.

Good. Now. Who's for some food, eh, boys? Who's for some food?

Paul leaps on the bed and turns to father grinning, expectant.

*

It's late, now. Paul and me are sitting on the bed, in the pitch black. Except it is not pitch black, there are streams of light coming from every which end of the door, it not fitting properly in the corridor at all. And how we're supposed to sleep with the noise of everyone coming up and down the stairs and the sounds of the bar easy enough to hear anyway.

*

And the sheets stink. And the mattress has thick black hairs sticking out into us. And the air is stale. No real air reaches the end of this corridor for there is no window. I want to open the exit, but who knows about alarms and anyway father said to stay here and to stay put. He wouldn't be happy with us opening the door.

The suitcase is under the bed, but even that is peeping out a little, the bed not large enough to hide it.

I can't sleep, Joseph.

I know Paul.

Where's dada?

He'll just be downstairs. He'll be back.

The noise and the stench and lack of air and Paul and me left alone to share the uncomfortable nature of it all and now I think father may have been right to bagsy the floor.

We sit like that for hours. Paul whimpers, lies down. I move the horrendous, stiff, old blanket over him and eventually, he sleeps. I stay upright, on alert, though for what I do not know.

The swamp of noise from downstairs was rising, ever rising. On occasion, there'd be a slight drop in volume, but it'd charge back up. Eventually I too lay down, too tired to keep awake.

But I awoke with a start. For now there was a very different noise going on. The crowd, the furore – that had moved on – and now there were only two, or perhaps three voices, but they were shouting, no laughter within, and one of them was most definitely father. I stood up and walked to the door, I even put a grip on the handle, but I could not turn…

You fucking Brit bastard…

GET OFF HIM, JOE! GET OFF HIM!

Get yer fucking hands off me, ya tool…

GET THE FUCK BACK TO ENGLAND, YE CUNT.

I'M FUCKING SCOTTISH, YA TIT.

YAR A FUCKING BRIT BASTARD that's what ye are… I'LL GET YOU…

And the collapsing of furniture, the smashing of glass, the squeal of a barmaid, maybe, more swearing, shouting…

I look to Paul, just visible and stirring, but hopefully still asleep… I'm hardly breathing, barely moving…

A slamming of a door, the voices still shouting, but outside now…

AYE YOU JUST FUCKING TRY IT!

Them falling further afield… Some distance between us… Hoping father is inside, safe… I have a sudden rush of nerves, I buckle over, slip to the floor and am sick with fear.

*

I stir and awake once more, but this time it's in father's arms. He's lifting me up and placing me on the bed. Straightening my legs, stroking my hair, manoeuvring the blanket, covering me up. I don't want to question, or know, so I allow him the luxury of believing I am sleeping, but the relief I feel when I hear his soft voice *C'mon you* and feel his strong arms underneath and then around me… And I listen and I listen and he doesn't leave the room, and as soon as his head is laid down, I finally fall into a proper, deep sleep.

The road over can be fun
with company,
sure.

The laughter,
the collapse,
the sharing.

But solo?
No.

It's a killer of a walk, this,
when you're sipping regret
awaking with your brain outside in
and your teeth inside out.

And anyways —
the next morning
everything is still there
it's just been framed
by
A sharp kick to the side of the head.

24

I WAKE UP TO Paul's sniffling and shaking of my leg – *Joseph, Joseph… is he dead, Joseph?* I heave the life into my eyes, focus, look at Paul, remember this terrible room we are in, then follow Paul's gaze down to father and then the shock wakes me fully, for his face is a terrible red colour, there's blood caked into the carpet around him and his once–white/grey shirt has now a large rose of pink upon it. I lean down, straightaway – *Father, father* – I push his shoulder, I shake and call – *Father, father* – and the relief, the delight when he lurches up and blinks his eyes open is immediate, though very short, for his eyes, or one of them at least, is blood red, with a huge pus of fat around the cheek below. Jesus, the purple bump on his face…

Father, are you…

Arrrghhhhh… His eyes, though glazed, are dizzy. And his breath… He'd had too much to drink, I recognise that.

What… What time is it? He looks at his wrist – *Where's my… Ah.*

Then he collapses back down. *Joseph – be a good lad – go and find out the time, will you? We need… We need to get to the man's place. The publisher…*

Where, father?

There's… there's a clock, in the bar… ooph.

I stand up, grapple the handle and run out, straight along the corridor, and down the stairs, greeted immediately with the glazed door, intact, thankfully, then into the bar. The clock reads… I think – just after half past the eight. Turn around and run back up the stairs, this time spotting a bloodied half-hand print on the wall. Straight along the corridor, then in.

It's almost nine, father.

Is it? Is it? Well. We'd better be getting up then…
And father…
Aye?
Your shirt… it's got some, um stains…

Don't mention the face, don't confront, don't bring up the impossible…

Has it? Ok. Right. Ok then. I'll just… He points down the corridor, to the loo – *I'll just have a look.*

He steadies himself, one arm first, then the second, and pushes himself upward. He sways over me and for one awful moment I fear him sicking up all over me, but he doesn't, he makes to wipe his face, spotting the blood on his cuff, his hand *Holy Jesus*, wiping it ineffectively upon his trouser and making his way out.

Jesus.
Don't swear!
He said it. Dada said it.
Doesn't mean we can.
Is he dying…?
What? No!
How would you know, then?
Well… he's walking, for a start…
His face…
I know, I saw…
Is his face dying?
What? No – it doesn't work like that…
Did he… did he fall down the stairs?
I wish he had, I wish he had.

*

The door opens and he's back. The man is back, the big, bloodied dad man.

Well, how's about that then, eh, boys? See what sleeping on that floor has done to my face!

He points at the bruise, the boil, the bang, the whatever it is.

And this shirt… Well, I'll be needing to change this now… About time, eh!?

Paul's hiding, knees pulled up, back of the bed.

Now, let's get the ol' suitcase open, eh? See what I can put on, for the occasion, the occasion…

Father's swaying. Paul's weeping, a little, but father doesn't notice. He pulls out a whole stash of papers, a thick handful, *These, these, these we need to keep… but here – here we go –* and out comes a shirt, as white as paper, clean, straight… *Well boys, I was married in this, and it brought me luck with your mother. Now, let's see if it can do it again.*

And I wonder what kind of luck it brought the marriage, brought mother. We don't need *that* kind of luck here.

*

We leave, quickly, without ceremony, or breakfast. Father says – *We'll go this way, boys, I think –* and he pushes, pushes again and finally manages to open the fire exit door at the end of the bed, a door that takes us on to a wrought-iron staircase that leads down to the back alleyways below, a quick scan and father chooses the left turn, encouraging us to stay close behind. A corner, another corner, a street of houses now, much quieter than when we arrived, curtains closed, the people inside no doubt enjoying their sleep.

We struggle to keep up, Paul and me, but father extends a hand, so Paul gets his speed boost and then it's just me struggling to keep up, so making to run a little ahead, as though leading the way –

Right here, Joseph –

And now there are buses, heaving themselves past us, coughing out thick black smoke. We're overtaken immediately by countless walkers, this street very much alive, people dressed neat, off on their way somewhere tidy. Paul and me now with our eyes in every shop window we pass, especially at the catapults, space dolls, footballs, board games.

I'm hungry, dada…

And so am I. I wonder how much money is left in that purse of his, after all that time he spent in the bar…

We'll eat soon enough. We need to find the man's office though. He'll… he'll sort us out.

People walking toward us, getting close enough, then taking a wide berth, when they see father's bruised, cut-up face. His clean white shirt isn't helping, it seems.

Do you know where we're going, father?

I do, I do. I asked. I asked last night… It's a… it's a bit of a walk.

Do we need to get the bus again, dada?

No… No. Not today. Maybe afterwards, we'll get the bus somewhere else. Or maybe we'll stay somewhere… closer. That we can walk to. We'll see. We'll see.

I catch another glimpse of his swollen, sunken eye and I flinch.

*

We're sat down, on a bench that is most likely meant for tourists, but it fits us, also. People are walking by with food, pubs and cafes are open offering yet more evidence of food, the smells, the availability.

Father has had his little purse open, but there seems to be nothing left within. But still he looks, over and over.

And he checks his pockets, once, twice, thrice.

He rubs his neck, though the shirt is too big for him, if anything. What's going through his mind – the last time he wore it? Or, is he like me and Paul, most likely, and just wondering where the next meal is coming from?

Not long now, boys. We can go up and see him shortly. Then, we'll get some food. I promise you.

I wonder who this god of a man is going to be, who is to supply us with food and lodgings. I wonder if he's going to supply us with soft pillows and a room without an exit door. I wonder if we'll be allowed to take the pillows home to Creagh with us. Will there be a fresh face for father, even?

There's a dog, a stray, I'd guess, sniffing around the bins, pawing open a discarded chip wrapper and licking up the bright red sauce. Paul is watching, enviously.

I'm hungry, dada.

I know, son. And so am I.

He wipes his face, looks up and down the street, again and again. I can see his hands are shaking, he's twitching and tutting, rubbing his nose. People are swerving around us still, staring a bit, but not communicating.

Father bends forwards, then sits back and says –

Ok.

We look to him, Paul and me both, waiting for more, but all we get is –

Ok.

But then he stands, straightens his coat and begins the walk away. We jump up after him immediately and fall into his wake.

*

We've circled around the grand stone square twice now, father getting more and more agitated. When we arrived at the square, his face was unbelieving, *Look at this, boys*, but now, after maybe three times around, repeatedly looking for the missing doorway…

It says number sixty-two C, but where is it? It just doesn't…

He's flustered, a red face now hosting the spreading purple bruise.

Excuse me, excuse me…

A lady, walking towards us, smartly dressed, blonde hair. We've seen plenty of them as we've careered around in circles, but this is the first soul we've asked and she can't have heard father, for she gives no reply, just speeds on past.

Fuck sake.

Paul glances at me, and me him.

Fuck sake.

I barely dare breathe.

Hold on. Hold on boys – wait here – I'm going to… I'm going to ask –

And he walks up to the nearest door, as far as I can tell. There's nothing to distinguish it from anywhere else near here, just a huge wooden door with a polished brass handle. He knocks, frantically, loudly, then spies a bell and pushes that, too. Paul hustles up beside him and clings to his leg. The door slowly peels open and I hear... *We have nuhin. We have nuhin for you* and begins to close, but father sticks his foot in the gap and says – *No, no – we don't want anything – I just need to know where 62C is?*

I have no idea, sorry, now...

They're still trying to close the door, but father's foot is still stuffed inside.

It's a publisher – I'm a writer. A poet...

I have no idea, now go – get your foot – c'mon – go.

And father releases his foot, the door slamming behind him instantly. He's shaking his head, looking all around him, then – *There boys – he'll know* – a man in uniform. Father hops down the steps and run–walks over – *Excuse me, excuse me...* The man instantly moves his arms to the defensive, palms out – *Now, now...*

Hey – do you know where 62C is? I've been looking... I've been looking around this square, but I can't... I can't find it. I've got an appointment... they're my publishers, you see, but I've never been and...

What number is it?

62. 62C – but the square only goes to 48... I just... I've been... we've been walking in circles...

It's around the back, sure...

And he gestures, a circular hand movement.

Round the back?

Of course – look – behind there –

And he points to the other side of the square. *That little road – that will have the other numbers on it.*

But... that's not part of the square?

No, I suppose it's the not the square official like, but the address is the same. You see?

I don't think father does, but he says his thanks, then looks down at us two – *C'mon* – *over we go.* And he's jogging off now, us two youngsters at a full pelt to even keep sight of him.

*

He finds it.

62C.

It has not the glamour of the large stone square, no way. It strikes me as being back to our level. It's the doorway to an outbuilding, and that building only maybe the size of a large shed, the door still wooden, but narrow with unpeeling varnish, the grass around overgrown and full of litter. An old garage, perhaps? A stable?

This can't be it…

And now he doesn't *want* to have found it, but he has, for to the side of the door there's a small paper label that has a list of a dozen or so names, and near the bottom are the words *Trí Dé Dána Press.*

Well.

He looks down to us, and wipes his face, then looks up to the sky, then around about the door, in case there is *another* door. A bigger door that leads to a brighter future.

Well.

Then, slowly, he lifts his hand to the door, knocks three loud, slow knocks and steps back, placing the suitcase on the step behind him and one arm around Paul, one arm around me.

25

THE DOOR IS opened by a man in a filthy brown cardigan, with unkempt, curly hair and thick black glasses. In fact, it's barely a man at all. He can't be more than twenty years old, if that. He looks out, sees father, or the current state of father and recoils, before – *Mr... Mr McLeod?*

Yes, that's me says father, slightly bowing, *and these are my two boys, Joseph – say hello, Joseph – and Paul. Say hello, boys.*

Hello.

Hello.

Heh.

And you must be... Padraig? Is that right? Or is he in?

Father is hoping that this young lad is not Padraig, I can sense that, but – *No, that's me, Padraig Brennan. In you come, you lot. Step inside, it's not huge, but you're welcome, welcome...*

The corridor is unlit and barely fit for the name, for inside there is nothing but seven doorways, all almost touching one another, all bearing the name of at least one or two other businesses. Our own door – *Trí Dé Dána Press* – is shared with *Temple Laundry Services.*

Here, here – we're not too big, there's not much space, but in you come, in you come...

And the room, if possible, is smaller than the corridor. There's only one desk, even. He must share this desk with the laundry people. I look around for sheets, but there's none. There's a small bookshelf though, not built into the wall, no, but a standalone, leaning slightly away from the wall, but full of paper, a few book spines.

Well... well...

He's shuffling his chair back and forth, opening and closing drawers... *And how... how was your journey, now?*

...fine...

Sit down – go on – sit –

The one largest object in the room, a huge leather easy chair, brown worn through to yellow, thick black horse hair poking through – it remains on our side of the desk and father inches it towards him, before realising it will not inch easily and sits himself further back in.

So. So... Mr McLeod...

Fraser, please...

So – Fraser, now. I loved, loved, loved your work now, you understand.

My father inadvertently exhales, a loud, long release *Good... Good.*

And, and, and as I said...

He shuffles more paper, paper he appears from nowhere, paper he takes from the bookshelf, just in order to shuffle, then return...

This work of yours...

You see, the thing is, Padraig...

I would be willing, perhaps...

It's cost us a little to get here...

We could think of...

And I was wondering if we could...

Get the best of the poems and maybe...

Have an advance?

Print a small pamphlet?

And then silence, the pair of them staring at the other.

A pamphlet? A... pamphlet? You mean...

Well, well, you know, as a start, I think a pamphlet, look – look here at this –

And he reaches over to the bookcase, before removing a thin red jotter – *Look here, see, this is one, this is one of our biggest sellers now, this is Seamus O' Riordan – You'll have heard of him – this one, now, this has sold almost one hundred copies, now. It's quite a, it's been, quite a...*

Is, is… is there an advance? For the pamphlet? Before the book? The book of poems? Is that – is that for…

No, no, no, no, no, no – it's, it's, this is, what we do here, you know. It's only a small run, sure you wouldn't have been expecting more, would ye? No, no. No. You're a man of the world, clearly…

Father is white. All that blood he'd worked up inside his head has rushed to his feet. Or is in his heart somewhere, struggling to keep it going. *You boys. You two. Go out into the corridor now, while I talk to Padraig here, you hear?*

And straightaway we're out, feeling and fleeing the tension, opening and closing the door as quietly as we can.

Oh no…

Shh!

But we can hear every single word still, of course we can –

Padraig. Your letter…

Now, now, as I said yesterday on the phone…

And your letter said you were interested in publishing my work!

Yes, yes, and I am, but you, you have to understand, there's little money, little money in poetry now. At least, at least at this stage. We have to start small. But – Seamus, Seamus there – he's earned well out of his pamphlet –

How well?

I'm sorry?

How well has he earned?

Well, that's, that's, that's confidential, but, I can tell you, I, I've given him at least ten pounds, even last week I had a man asking if there was a second volume – it's progress, progress, long rocky road, you know, the poetry road, there's seldom riches, sure I write myself…

Ten pounds? Listen, Padraig – I've come all this way…

Well, I know, but we have to keep things realistic, you know? Heh – I never said, I'm SURE I never said there were riches awaiting ye', Mr McLeod…

My children, outside…

I look to Paul, who again is shaking, quietly, visible in the gloom. I put my arm around him.

I need an advance on this – this pamphlet. I need – my children. They're hungry. You know?

An advance! No! But I can't, I have none, I can't...

And look... And there's shuffling – *I've brought...* then the opening of the spring of a clasp, and then the second... *I've brought some more... more, see? I've edited... they're ready, there's twenty-three poems here, all good – we could do a book with these, I think? I think so? Or two, maybe three pamphlets – I could, I could leave these with you – take an advance, and leave these with you...*

I've seen them. They're together, tied together by a thin bit of string, barely a string, but thicker than a thread. Written on the front, in father's lonely scrawl –

The Book of the Gaels

Twenty-three? Twenty-three poems? Well... they'd have to be very long – almost laughing now – *Or at least one of them! I can't do a book, even if you had a hundred poems... We... I...*

But father is insistent – *What will you give me? What will you give me? As an advance?*

Well – I don't know, I have never done an advance...

Well, let's work it out – the poems you had that you liked – that you WROTE me about, how much for those?

I, I, I don't know, maybe... a pound?

What!? A pound? One fucking pound? Jesus, Padraig... I put my HEART into those poems...they're my life!

There's silence now, until slowly, the man's voice begins creeping back in –

Well... yes. I know that. I know that. It's just... Fraser, I'd have to sell ten copies to make that pound back, then I could, I could send you any profit after that point?

I can hear father's deep breathing through the door. He's trying to calm himself, I recognise the sound of it.

... And what about... what about all these?

Well... well... I haven't read them...

They're good. I wouldn't bring you them otherwise...

Oh, I don't doubt it, you know I like what I've read so far but…

So, what will you give me?

I, I, I don't know… I don't think…

Would you give me ten pounds?

What! No, I…

Because then I could get home, Padraig. I could leave the work with you and I could get my children some food and then get them home…

No! No, I don't have ten pounds, sure I only make that myself a week with my work…

So you have it?

No! No, I don't have it, it all goes on rent and food and staying alive – look – I am just me, it is just me here – I only do it for the love…

What have you got then?

I, I, how do you mean?

Well, if you don't have ten pounds, what have you got? Five?

What? No! I told you, I can give you – a pound. Just a pound. I'm sorry.

*

We're heaved out of the doorway and into the street by father, him fuming, raging angry. Suitcase in hand still, Paul and me clever enough to keep quiet, not to mention our stomachs, keep out of his eyesight – *the bastard, the BASTARD* – and if we could have shrunk any littler, we would – *One pound! What a joke. What an absolute joke.* He turns – *Aaaarrggggh* – takes the suitcase and kicks it, over and over – *fucking, fucking thing* – he throws it to the floor, placing his hands around his head and how he's shaking and he's breathing deeply, slowing, trying to calm, bring himself down. *I'm sorry. I'm sorry, boys* – Still shaking his head – *We shouldn't have come… I… I knew it* – I can't talk, cannot look, but Paul does, and he says *It's ok, dada. Let's just get some food* – And father, well, he laughs at that, he laughs, and shakes his head more, and when I meet his eyes I see clearly that he's crying through the laughing and he looks broken and he looks exhausted and he looks completely lost *And where is this food coming from, eh, Paul? Tell me that?*

After all this,
this declaration
of love business,
we built a campfire
in the ruins
of a castle.

The stars peered down
applauding,
despite their distance

'So!
we fit in somewhere,
after all!'

I see us, old, and sat upon
a rough-hewn wooden porch.
I see us drinking a toast
to life
and to one another.

26

FATHER – *I need... We need to be able to get home. Or, to that... back to Mary, at least... and we need to eat.*

We're sat back in the centre of town, tourists bustling by. We're walking back towards where the pub was, but the thing is, I'm not sure we're even going back to the pub.

We need to eat...

Mary would be my vote. She had food, old food ok, but food. And it wasn't cold. It wasn't clean, but it wasn't cold, or wet. If we left now...

But we have money for neither.

Father has the purse open again and is looking, counting through, but the money remains the same. He's looking all around, trying to catch some inspiration. *I don't know... I don't know what to do.*

It's well past lunchtime and we haven't had breakfast, even.

Oh, Sinéad. What to do, eh? He's muttering now, quietly to himself, but I pick it up and look around for this mysterious mother of mine, should she suddenly have appeared.

I'm hungry, dada...

Shh! I tell him. *Dada – Father's thinking...*

No. He's right. We have no choice. We have to eat – C'mon now, boys, we're not dead yet.

And he stands, pulling us both behind him, one by one, then strides off, in the direction we came. *C'mon, boys, we'll soon be eating...*

He's making a fine pace, us walking against the stream, it seems, people parting as he approaches, partly down to his broken-down face, I'd guess, but also the commitment. Paul catches my eye, over

153

and over, partly to make sure I'm keeping up as father drags him forwards, but partly I know to share his excitement *We're going for food!*

There's music coming out of almost every shop, every bar, but we take a sharp left and suddenly we are on a small, almost empty street. *I spied this earlier, look* – And hanging from a building, maybe thirty yards away still, are three golden balls –

Is it a restaurant, father?

Eh? No. No, it's not. It's something else altogether, c'mon and he hurries us along, until we get to the steps – we wait, then, as an old lady is emerging from the doorway, clutching a few paper notes. She looks at father, and then at Paul and myself and then back to father. *Good luck* she says, then scurries off back to the main throng.

In we go, boys, c'mon.

There's a single bulb illuminating the room, which contains only a blood-maroon leather upholstered bench. My father gestures to it – *Sit* – so we do.

This place doesn't look as though it sells food. And by the smell, I'd hope it doesn't…

It smells DEAD in here.

Dead and damp and cold and unwelcoming.

A small brown hatch opens –

What's your business?

Umm… We have, umm, a ring…

Is it yours?

It is, yes.

The half-face looks down at us, then to father – *Room number two. Quickly now.*

And the hatch closes.

Father opens the door to enter room number two, then considers and returns – *You boys – you should come in, too. Ok?*

We walk in and now we are in an even smaller room, no windows to the outside, just a scarred plastic serving hatch, covered by a rusted metal grill. There's one seat, which father takes, gesturing to us to sit on the floor, but the room smells of a dog kennel – if the dog had been smoking cigars – so I stay upright.

Latch the door. Latch the door at the back, will ye?

The man appears at the other side of the hatch. Just as well, really, as there is no space for him this side. He has a spectacularly bald head with busy black hair around his ears, emphasising the dome. He's wearing thick spectacles and his shirt is similar to father's – once polite, once a dress shirt perhaps, but now an everyday item, worn and tired.

My father turns and leans past me, then pushes at a thick iron bolt, locking us in this peculiar place.

Good. Now then. Fine day, eh?

Fine enough.

And where are you pilgrims from, then?

West Cork.

Oh. You don't sound West Cork, you sound more… Scottish, I was thinking. No crime there, we get a lot of the Scottish fellas in for the rugby matches, you know.

The children are Irish, though. Their mother…

Ah, I see, I see, I love Scotland, I've been to Edinburgh, you know, to see my cousin who has a place and – ah – now let's see, is it a ring, you say? Here, here, bring it out… Put it in that tray, will you?

My father hesitates, then opens the suitcase and feels along the lining, before finally removing a bright gold ring, with shining rocks of some sort.

Diamonds! says Paul, but how he'd have a clue I do not know.

Father breathes in, looks at the ring, examining… then places it in the tray, the tray then instantly sweeping through to the other side, the man chuckling, then picking it up.

Hey!

What? Ah don't you worry, you'll get it back if we can't come to terms… I've been in business for almost fifty years, you know. I have no call to cause trouble… Now. Wait one moment – and he places the ring on his table, out of reach of us, but still in view, before disappearing and returning with a tiny magnifying glass.

Now, is this your ring, is it? Are you sure? You'll be asked to sign for it now.

It is.

Hmm... ok... ok...

What's going on? Paul whispers

He's looking at father's ring, I think.

Shh! Says father.

And I whisper, even more quietly *Mother's ring, I think.*

And Paul's eyes widen... *Mother's?* As though he'd never thought about her at all.

Well, well – I can certainly make you an offer for this, but it may, it may not be what you wanted...

How do you mean?

And my father is no doubt worrying about the single pound in his pocket and how *this* better be more than *that.*

Well, it's gold, but only nine carats, and the diamonds, well, they're very, very poor quality, and the one on the right – did you have that replaced, somewhere?

My father nods. *My wife, she lost one of the diamonds when she was cleaning nappies. Using the old water pump at the top of the lane...*

Well, it's not a diamond at all anymore, I'm afraid to say. It's glass paste, that one. Did you know that? Very close match, it's been done well, but most definitely what we in the business call costume jewellery. So... all together...

Glass?

Paste, yes, sir, sorry to tell you that, but just that one, and it's been done well as I say, and the others are real enough... And you know, it's not – the whole thing – it's not worth a whole lot – I mean, it's a pretty thing, it'd sell, but I don't think... I don't think I could offer you more than seven pounds for it.

What!? Seven pounds... but it was her engagement ring! It cost me almost twenty pounds!

That may be, that may be, sir, but they lose value the moment they leave the shop and without the second diamond being an actual diamond and what with the gold being… Just nine carat…

But it's worth more than seven, surely!?

Well… If you sold it privately, I suppose you may get eight, or nine? But I have overheads, and I need to make a small profit myself, so… No, it has to be seven. Sure, I have a million of these things.

*

Father slams the door behind us, suitcase in hand, ring in suitcase.

What a thief! This city – everyone grasping at their money… Grasping at my money… Well, I'll not be giving in to them. C'mon, boys, we'll figure something out…

*

But we don't figure ANYTHING out. We just sit. We sit on another step, surrounded by more noise, more music and more tourists, scurrying past us. *I'm hungry, dada.*

I know you're hungry! You're always bloody hungry!

And with that, we are quiet. I watch the trouser legs, the bare legs, the tights, the shoes, the boots, the sniffing dogs. My stomach is curling in on itself with hunger. It's not fair, this, sitting in amongst all these people with money, them just streaming past. What on earth have I done to be here?

I turn and father is crying, softly, silently. He's kept it under control, but now there are tears, and they soon bring on Paul's and then it's the pair of them weeping away to each other, father's arm around Paul now. I rub my face in my hands, wondering where my tears are… Father should have taken those seven pounds. I don't know why he didn't. Because that would be food for now, wouldn't it? And a room in the two pounds place? And then tomorrow we could begin the journey to Mary's place.

There's a *chink* noise, just ahead of us. I look down and – someone has thrown some money on the floor – I leap to it – *Hey!*

You dropped your money! – but the person, whoever it was, just scuttles on, so I keep it in my palm and sit back down – *Father look, I just got this – five pence. I can maybe buy a roll with it?*

He looks at me, then above at the people passing by.

He thought we were…

He puts his head in his hands.

And then, a minute later, another, another coin – but this one – *Ten pence!*

Paul grabs it *Dada – dada – we can get some food now! We can definitely buy some crisps at least!*

Wait a moment… His eyes focusing.

And we wait and we sit and we stare up at the passing folk and every once in a while, one of them will root inside their purse and throw something our way – ones and twos mostly, but the occasional five in amongst them.

I'm not doing this, I'm not begging… No way…

Father is arguing with himself, shaking his head, but there's no escaping the delight in Paul *We can eat! We can eat, dada!* And father angry, but realising there's little he can do, little we can do now, but accept where we are.

Two pence. I grab it.

Ok, boys, give me – give me it all. But I don't. For what if he wants to hand it back? I keep it and Paul, he does the same – *It's money for food, dada, it's my money, I'm hungry…*

GIVE IT TO ME. NOW. Then, quieter – *Now, boys. Let me… Let me count it up.*

We hand it over, sadly, bit by bit, and watch, as father counts.

There's almost a pound! And he laughs.

We've made a pound, just by sitting here for an hour… That's the same as…heh. Jesus, I can't believe it…

There's a shop a few doors down, with a sign that reads *Soup and a roll – 20p.* We could afford those. We could share – two of those would be enough, it'd be a huge feast, in fact, for three of us with two of us just children – soup and a roll would be perfect.

Can we eat, father? Look – and I point to the shop.

He's smiling, but scowling also and still shaking his head, back and forth. Then, finally, he hands me the money – not all of it – *Sure. It's your money. You've earned it. Go on – knock yourselves out* – and I'm up and at Paul – *C'MON!*

We run over to the shop, through between the tourists as though they are not even there and we're in the shop in seconds, Paul ahead of me, face against the glass counter, looking at the food on offer…

White rolls with orange cheese.

You two boys – can I help you? I'm going to ask you to buy something or you'll have to leave right away – I can't have anybody window shopping my food…

We're not window shopping – we've got money – look!

I hold open my palms and show him the mountain of money – *We'd like soup and a roll. Each. A soup and a roll each, like it says on the board.*

Please says Paul.

Yes. Please. I agree. *Soup and a roll. Please.*

And how much money is there in that mighty little pile?

There's forty pence. We've counted. Two soups and two rolls. Please.

Ok, ok, that's fine – now what sort of roll do you want?

What sort?

Umm…

Do you want ham and cheese or…

HAM!

HAM!

HAM AND CHEESE!

HAM AND CHEESE! YES. SAME FOR ME. HAM AND CHEESE.

PLEASE.

YES, PLEASE!

Ham and cheese!

Heh. Ham and cheese it is, fellas.

Two!

Yep, I've gotcha – there's two of you… Hold on now… You pass that money over first – go on –

And he nods, eyes wide, encouraging – *Come on boys, there's other people to serve now…*

I look to Paul and him to me and we decide right then to trust the man. We scatter his counter with pennies, which he pulls together and counts.

Forty-two pence. Two pence back, boys –

I take it.

And then a roll appears – it is massive, almost the size of Paul's head… *Remember to keep some for father.*

And Paul halfway through it – *I said – keep some for father, or it's not fair…*

He mumbles something back to me, a mouth full of food and then my roll arrives –

And there's number two now, fellas.

Immediately, I sink a long, deep bite and Paul says, between his own chews – *Save some for dada! Save some for dada!* And I see he has barely got a mouthful left of his.

And here's your soup, boys – it's pea soup. Good and wholesome. Put some heat in you. Ok?

Pea soup? Well, I've never had that before… I carry on munching away, reach up and take one of the cups of soup, motioning to Paul to do the same. He grabs at it and we're ready to go, both chewing, both almost burning our hands on the soup, laden down now and – *Thanks!* – then leaving the shop into the busy street.

Bye now, boys.

27

A ND I KNOW father will be pleased with this, for Paul's left him a mouthful of roll and he can have all of my soup, for it is green and who wants green soup, but as I look over to where father was, well he's talking to some new people now but they don't look too friendly and before long one of them, a filthy bearded man, has grabbed father and pushed him over and father has responded by getting upright and punching the guy straight in the face and in a second father is overrun by two other men, both ragged and worn. Paul and me run over, the best we can while balancing the soup *STOP IT! STOP IT!* But they're not stopping, not one bit, in fact they're going in harder, father with one hand being held, then both behind his back and the third man, the original one, well he is SHOUTING at father – *YOU COME ON TO MY PATCH AGAIN AND I WILL BREAK YOUR BOLLOCKS YOU UNDERSTAND* – and then another *thwack* to the stomach and father's broken down on the floor, knees buckled, coughing, held up now by the two apes – and Paul, well he's ran at them, spilling his soup. *GET OFF HIM GET OFF HIM GET OFF HIM* and Paul is whacking one of them on the leg, but being held back by the palm of the man's hand, the man himself laughing, and then pushing Paul over, over on to his back. Father screams, then body charges into the villain, knocking him over, him landing near a couple of tourists too, and then when those tourists realise something is up, the whole atmosphere changes as now there's a whole area of people screaming and staring. I get down to Paul's side and sit him up, he's fine, just a bit of gravel on his face and tears coming out – someone kicks over *my* soup, but never mind that, father is throwing his hands at the

161

original bearded guy, slapping and clawing and pushing him away, before the three of them notice the crowd that has gathered, *Peadar – Peadar – we have to go – now – leave.* And the bearded guy taking one more swipe at father but missing and then they're off, leaving just father, Paul and me and a handful of surrounding tourists.

*

Are you ok, fella?

Ignore them. It's just tramps, fighting.

Tramps?

But father is not listening, not responding – *Paul! Paul, son – are you all right? Come here, come here* – and scooping Paul up, holding him, cuddling him – *Did he hurt you? Did he get your face? Here, let me look* – and Paul playing it up, I'd say, for the sake of father's attention, but no, Paul's shaking, also, and crying, *here, here, c'mon, son, we'll sit back down, sit back down* and father reversing, and now I see his face has a fresh wound, a cut or a hit or something, but new red blood has appeared and I think – *The city doesn't suit us* – and when they sit, I sit as close to them as I possibly can and father puts his arm around *me*, even though I did nearly nothing apart from sit with Paul, but the arm feels very good indeed and before long the three of us are crying our eyes out, just sitting there, shaking and crying our eyes out and my tears are flooding now and I know not why and Paul is covered in snot and maybe some blood on his cheek too, though it could be from father and the concerned tourists have all gone, leave us three unfortunates and I feel hypnotised into this damn cry so I try to shake myself out of it and remember the roll, the half-roll, then see it three feet away, being kicked along by the parade of tourists and feeling I've lost my head entirely, only for father to say –

Where's the suitcase? Boys! Where's the suitcase?

And that, in an instant, snaps us out of it.

Did you see it go!?

I shake my head – *Of course not.*

Paul, you? Paul sniffles, shaking his head, *No, dada.*

Fuck!

I look to Paul, but there's no reply. I try it out myself, quietly, mimicking the same anger as father... *fuck!* and father looks at me, his face sharp and raises his hand an inch from my face, pointing his long, gnarled finger – *Don't you start, boy* which pushes me right back to tears, tears that I fight back, twisting my neck all around, as though looking for the suitcase, but really just fighting the shock and the fear of father's raised voice.

C'mon, boys. We have to find it. Now.

Is it mama's suitcase? With all her things in...

Mama.

It has her ring in it, that's for definite. I didn't not sell it to that bloody loan-shark just for it to be stolen by some filth...

And our clothes... and your poems!

Father's clothes anyway.

Well, my poems were with the other man. The publisher. At least they're safe...

And I wonder if he's being serious, I think I may have preferred they were stolen long ago, before we left our house at Creagh, or maybe just before we left Mary's, stopping us coming on this ridiculous journey, stopping us from being sat here in the street, half-hungry, full filthy with father shouting at me, when all I'm doing is my best...

Ok, we'll look down this way – c'mon now –

And he puts his arm around me, pulls me close and kisses my hair and I'm so worried about all that blood and whatever else getting lodged there that I almost pull away from him.

*

We head down the first alley we see, but there's nothing to be seen except the river at the end of it. We follow that down, then go back up the next alleyway, this one busier, a few bars, people milling around – my father approaching one couple, dark skinned, bright clothes, more tourists – *Excuse me, have you seen...*

And they back off, showing father the palms of their hands and shaking their heads, then the second father loses eye contact, they turn and quickly walk away.

C'mon… and he's off again, leaving us behind, so me taking Paul's hand now and keeping up, just, but father stopping every twenty yards or so to look for the thieves, giving us a chance to get back to his side.

There!

And it's me who spots them, giving me a rush of pride – *There, father!*

It is them, for sure, up a side street, maybe twenty yards away, the same filthy three people that father got caught up with.

Come on! Shouts father and he sprints off towards them, but I don't know who he thinks *we* are, but we're not some army, ready to back him up in a fight, we're a child and a smaller child, but we follow after him, weaving in and around the tourist bodies, my hand squeezing tight on to Paul's, blindly following father, watching father, a good bit ahead of us, running full pelt at the baddies, and shouting – *Oi!*

Which of course causes them to look up and see my father charging onwards.

They're sat at the front of a small shop, the suitcase is open, I can see that, but as soon as they spot father, one of them slams it shut, stands and runs off, leaving father's second-best shirt remaining in the street. But unfortunately, the other two do not run off, they slowly stand and wait for father to arrive and when they do, well, it isn't pretty.

Father is out of breath, but there is no polite recovery time. As he arrives, he is greeted immediately with a fist to the face. We hear the cracking sound from where we are – half the alley away – and it stops us dead. Not just me stopping, no way, Paul too, the pair of us, terrified of what is about to happen, what is actually happening.

And father's entire body sways all the way back at his knees, but somehow he does not fall over, he recovers and throws his own fist, and it must have landed well, for the fatter of the two filthy men falls straight to the ground, landing on the cobbles with an audible thump. As he struggles back up, the second man grabs father by the neck and pushes him against the window of the shop, where he rattles against the metal grid that is protecting the glass. My father pulls his head back as far as it will go then thrusts it into his attacker's own face, causing an almighty scream and the man to reverse, holding his face, crouched down double. Father moves away from the window, but the fat man is up and runs into him, the weight of the fellow heaving father backwards, tripping then and coming down all the way on to the ground.

The blooded, broken-nosed man steps over, hand still over his face and angrily begins kicking my father repeatedly around the head.

No! Paul and me run up, but keep our distance, we cannot fight, but we can scream – *GET OFF HIM – GO AWAY – GET OFF DADA – STOP IT! STOP IT!* and finally, I run up and hit the bleeding nose guy square on the back. He turns and swats his arm at me, knocking me straight down to the ground. Father is struggling up again, leaning toward me, and I wonder what's to happen next, but the fat guy has had enough and is heading off away from us, soon the bleeding nose is following him, laughing away – *Ye fucking idiot! Now stay down!*

I watch them disappear and half-crawl towards father, Paul meeting us in the middle and the three of us once more a sorry bundle, sat in the gutter, crying our eyes out.

*

Are you ok, son?

I can barely nod. Father little resembles the father of just yesterday, now. He has blood all over him, his face having been kicked a few times, that one eye completely closed now, his nose looking all squashed... My head hurts, it feels wet and on fire, but every time I check for blood, my hand comes back clean and dry. But the ache, the ache is something terrible.

What are we going to do, father?

I don't know. I don't know, son.

Paul is a baby once more, clinging to his father, his fingers white with the grip on father's soiled, old coat. And so much for his best shirt, for his second shirt that has been abandoned in the scramble, is lying on the floor, covered with foot prints and grime, and this second shirt looks in better condition than what father is wearing now.

Are you hungry, boys? That food you had looked pretty good – here, did you save some for me?

He's smiling, trying to make us laugh, or trying to make Paul laugh, but he doesn't get it – He looks like a blood-covered Halloween man.

It spilt, dada, it spilt on the floor, I'm sorry…

No, no, no, no, no, don't be daft, it's not your fault at all. This whole adventure has been my folly. I can see that, I can see that now. Sure, we were better off at home…

Do you remember that moment
deep in song
a crowded, airless, silent bar,
you singing, me listening?

When your words were done, you opened your eyes,
slowly, but
straight into mine.

Later, you told me
'Sure, I thought you were rude to stare like that.
I almost told you to shut your gob,
hanging open as it was!'

But, another singer began their song, and you kept my gaze,
throughout

And do you remember that moment, deep in song?

28

ON OCCASION, WE'LL be passed by. This little street a dead end to nowhere, the shop father was fighting with locked up, a book shop, *Closed on Wednesdays*, I see. But we're left on our own to work out our own situation.

We've walked, as ever. The tourists miraculously parting for us. Father has been looking, but for what, I do not know. Paul is silent now, grabbing my hand, staring straight ahead, just following, following… there's no danger he'll run off anywhere.

I feel sick, then ok, then sick, then dizzy, the bump on my head from just the fall enough to keep the fight fresh on my mind, if I needed any reminder… I'm proud I helped, or tried to help. I'm pleased I ran in, but I feel sick. And father, with the disgrace of injuries on his face, putting me right back in amongst the fight. No wonder Paul is staring straight ahead. Where else can he look?

This will do.

We're not quite back in the main drag, but not far off. Still plenty of company around us, avoiding us, not seeing us yet somehow steering around us.

Ok, this will do.

It's a doorway, just another doorway, smelling a little of pee, but not too bad.

This will do. Sit down, you two.

Where father?

Just where you are…

In amongst the pee smell, the stained concrete step. Never a comfort, would rather be walking still than sitting here. I look up and father is rubbing his hands together, as though warming them. His head is twitching around, perhaps looking out for our attackers. He shuffles his feet and I catch a good look at the tweed of his trousers, ripped now in a couple of places and stained in a great deal other. He has taken his scarf off and is wrapping it around itself, slowly, making a sort of pot shape. Paul glances at me, finally, and I pull him closer, to share the warmth, the fear, the worries. Father crouches down amongst us both and places the scarf pot on the floor, just in front of us, muttering – *Keep an eye on that, boys, you hear?*

I nod, *Yes, father.*

And he stands, shuffling his shoulders, rubbing his neck, settling his feet…

… and then, and then, and then… father begins to sing.

'It's narrow, narrow, to make your bed and learn to lie your lane…'

And despite it all there's peace in his voice, peace and comfort. Weariness, fatigue…

'For I'm going over the sea, fair Annie, a braw bride to bring hame'

And I think of him, him and mother, a mother I cannot remember, other than from a photograph and a fresh horror story.

'With her, I'll get gold and gear… and with you, I'll get none'

Mother's gold, her cheap, yellow gold. Was it worth it, the ache in my head, the mess of father's face?

And a coin lands at father's feet. One penny. A start, at least. Father, he barely registers, just carries on –

'But who will bake my bridal bread or brew my bridal ale?'

Paul's head is leant against my shoulder, sniffing, wiping his nose, his eyes, and surely keeping an eye on the money, him twitching now, watching as folk pass by, watching their pockets, their hand movements…

And another coin falls, this one a two-penny piece.

Keep your eye out for the thieves, I tell Paul. *If they come near, grab that money off the floor.*

I look up at father, the beautiful, rough sounds coming from that ploughed face, bringing in money like occasional rain, small amounts, but it adding up, and I can count already we're between five and ten pence and I'm hoping it'll continue, to what I don't know, but I suppose, if I were to ask, I'd ask for a meal and a bed and a bus all the way home for all of us, for I have had enough of this city.

*

Paul is asleep, and father is still singing away, but this is many, many songs later. He's swaying, with the sound of his own voice, the rhythm of the tales he is telling, but with fatigue and hunger also, surely. We've got almost another pound now, father on occasion bending down and placing it all jingling into his jacket pocket.

It's been raining a while, not a heavy rain, but it has been spitting and it still is.

I'm cold, dead still this last while, neck moving only, keeping an eye out for any trouble, my head still aching, but mercifully easing off... Doing the arithmetic – father got one pound for his poems and we spent forty pence on the food and there's almost been a pound here in his scarf – we can get a room, I know we can... Maybe not in that faraway place that we deserted this morning and maybe not so easy with father's face looking so awful, but there's hope... I wish him to stop, I wish him and wish him once more, but he continues, on and on.

The crowd is getting rowdier, more beer filled, younger, more male. On occasion, a fellow will peel off from a group and watch – *Will you look at this sight?* – but on the whole, we're getting less attention, less interest and less money.

It's harder to see what's what now, who's who, but at the end of the alley there's a man with a cigarette, still, watching perhaps, but certainly listening. I can't make him out and look the other way, then back – and he's still there.

Finally, father gives in and slumps down beside us, him looking exhausted and drained. He ruffles Paul's hair, wakening him up – *I think I've got enough for some food and maybe – possibly – a place for later. If we can find somewhere cheap enough...*

And tomorrow?

Well, Joseph – tomorrow is another day…

My concentration is with father, who has a handful of change in his hands that he is counting, before placing it in his other pocket. Counting each handful, adding it up, over and over.

I don't notice when the little light we have is blocked, until it's too late. We look up, father and me, at the same moment and standing right above us…

You've done well, I'll give ye that.

And father's up in an instant – it's the same guy, the same tramp guy, Jesus, and he's smiling at father like a friend, arms up, defensive. *Hey! Fine voice on you –*

Get the fuck away from me – father has stuffed the change back into his pockets, it jangling away still as he moves, struggles to stand –

And a fine little earner you made – what was that? Quite a few pennies landing there I saw – That should rightly be MY money.

How do you work that? This isn't your street…

Oh, but it very much IS my street. This whole area is mine. Why do you think you were warned off earlier?

Is that what you call it? A warning off? Well, I'm warning YOU to get away from MY family right now –

Why, what are you going to do? Do you think I'd be down here, in front of a man like you, who's proven he'll fight, if I didn't have my friends close by?

I look, up and down the alley, but there's no one, just groups of normal men, men who don't look smelly and ground in the dirt, like this man, men who could not be friends with *this* man.

…No. I came to talk to you. You see – I don't like people on my street, taking my money. But I figured – you weren't to know that… Sure, you're not from these parts are ye? And after all, how would a – Scotsman? – know about local business affairs like this? No. I'm going to guess that you're just passing through. I'm going to HOPE that you're just passing through. Is that right?

My father nods. *It is.*

Good. Well. In that case, I think we can help each other out.

I'm not giving you this money – this money is mine.

Ah, no – you misunderstand me. You can keep your pennies… You earned them. But you see. All these disagreements – they're bad for business. Put off the tourists, which annoys the shoppies who call the guard… and on and on. No. I have… other work. That you may be interested in. Short term, you understand? And… and I could help you move on. Wherever you're going. Which is?

Home.

And where's that?

That's no concern of yours.

Fair enough. So long as it's far from here, I wouldn't care. Now look – this rain is coming down heavier and your fine singing is emptying pockets before the customers even reach my people – So let's get inside and discuss this.

Do you think I'd be going anywhere with you?

Ah, don't you worry, we're not far – just around the corner there's a fine, respectable public bar where we'll be guaranteed a slot. You can bring the children in, get them some food – some PROPER food. You must be hungry, eh, fellas?

We nod, too soon, for father says *Don't you even talk to my boys.*

Fair enough, fair enough. You talk to them, then. You ask them to follow us. I'll get you some stout and them some food and then you can listen to my proposal. All in full view and with no danger and with warm bodies and full bellies. Sensible heads. And drier than out here. Agreed?

He doesn't even wait for an answer, he walks off, turning his head just the once to make sure we're following, which we are.

*

I'm sucking on a chip, wide-eyed, Paul licking his chip for the salt and the tomato ketchup. It is very welcome, this food, and what's more, we have a fizzy Coca-Cola each. It is heavenly, this place of warmth and laughter. Father has a stout, which he is but sipping.

172

He has long since finished his own chips but I'm hoping he's paying attention to keeping a clear head as our provider is still with us. He's on his own though, or so it seems, the fellow who knocked me to the ground is nowhere to be seen, and I have looked…

Paul is rolling back, overjoyed, his stomach must be bursting.

Father is talking. And of course, I am listening.

So – what do you want? For all this? See – I don't owe you for this – he gestures to the food, the drink – *the way I see it, you owe me. This is an apology – and a cheap one, at that.*

You're a strong man, Mr…

McLeod.

McLeod. And my name is Fallon, McLeod.

My father nods, as if this was a first meeting.

Well, McLeod, you're a spirited man, I'll give you that. And a good one – providing for your family so…

Don't you patronise me… Fallon.

Oh, I'm not! I mean it. Most men would have crumbled after being asked to leave, so – they do, I've seen it – and who knows why you're even here in Dublin, but a lot of men would have ran off with their tails between their legs long before they found themselves messing with the likes of me.

Well, we're not staying.

He nods. *I'm glad to hear it. It's not for everyone… this city.* He takes a sup, then returns his drink to the table. *But, I'm thinking – well, why not make your short stay here a little more comfortable, eh?*

In what sense?

Well. Where are you staying? In a doorway? What are you eating? Food bought for you by a beggar – a beggar like me! You can do better than that. And I saw how you could stand up for yourself, back there. Most men wouldn't. But you had fight. You had fight in you. He gestures to us, to Paul and me – *You had fight in you, for them. And that fight, that may be of interest, to me…*

In what way?

Well, I'll put you in a little hotel I know – a nice place. Warm. A few nights' rest. And some money for food. So you can prepare. Get these little ones off the street – and then, after it all, I'd give you a little bit more money – to get you wherever you're going next. You'll be refreshed, though. The little fellas can get a wash. Somewhere clean to sleep. Somewhere safe… Is it agreed?

Is what agreed? I have no idea…

I need men who can fight, McLeod. Other men enjoy watching men like you. Cowardly men, the audience, I'll agree there, but they're men with money, McLeod, money they gladly pay me and gamble with on top of that… A new face like yours… Well, they always like a fresh face in the mix, though you don't look too fresh right now…

To what…? To fight?

No, no – that's too strong a word, it's more… to wrestle. It's like wrestling, McLeod. In a ring. And… You'd have – I could give you five whole pounds now, plus, a room until Friday arrives and for the night itself… for, you know… afterwards… Then, for the job itself a further five pounds just for turning up.

There's no way I'm doing that…

A-ha. But it's twenty pounds if you win, McLeod. Twenty pounds. And that room, remember, would be good, would it not? For where are you sleeping this very evening, McLeod? There's that rain, coming down outside and what have you got – a pocket full of coppers? That'll not pay for anywhere comfortable, McLeod, though I'm guessing by the look of you, you'll know that…

Twenty pounds?

Twenty if you win. Twenty pounds could get you wherever you're going, McLeod.

And how long is the fight?

The… event – it takes as long as it takes. But – you'll not be paid a penny if you turn up and throw in the towel, so don't even consider that. No. The crowd would want their entertainment. That's what the twenty promise is for. It's your motivation. As if you'd need any more, what with those two, and all three of you needing to eat and rest your head somewhere safe, McLeod.

And if I don't?

You do not need me to answer that, McLeod. This place here – this meal – this will be the end of your luxury.

29

*T*HIS IS YOUR *room – look –*

She opens the door, a thin, light thing, but opening to an actual room this time, no corridor for us. We curl in, Paul and me, and straightaway Paul shouts out – *Dada, there's a loo, see!? Dada, there's a loo! And… what's that!?*

That's a shower, Paul, EVERYONE knows that…

For it is. A shower, *all to ourselves*, I think.

And you're here for how long?

Three nights, Mrs Marra.

Three nights. Well. Until the Saturday morning then. And we all know what he gets up to on a Friday evening, don't we. And with your looks, I'd say you'll be joining him…

My father doesn't answer, except to say *Is there a beer for me? He mentioned an evening drink?*

She tuts – *Did he now? Well, he never told me, but I'm not one to argue and surely I can bring you something up… Will a stout do ye?*

Father nods.

He'd done his best, father, to strike some kind of deal, but he had few cards to play and his main desire was the return of the suitcase, but Fallon denied, denied, denied he had it, that any of his associates knew of it… And why they'd hide an old suitcase, I don't know.

Father had pressed on *For sentimental reasons – It belonged to their mother – Will you at least keep a look out?* And Fallon had finally nodded – *If I find it. And you do well. You can have it.*

The door closes, and we examine further – red carpet, still some colour to it, a large, fat grown-up's bed, small sink in the corner, windows covered by a flimsy curtain, bigger, heavier curtains ready to be drawn for later, wallpaper, bubbling a bit off the wall, but generally clean enough, and warm, it's certainly warm.

Father is counting the money, again and again. Finally, I ask him –

Are you doing it, father?

What's that, son?

The wrestling? Are you doing the wrestling? Because I was thinking… We could just take that money – we could take that money and go, father?

What, and just leave?

I'm surprised he hadn't thought of it – *Yeah. In the dead of night. Like… like a cat burglar…*

A what? A what burglar? Paul now, joining in, but father shakes his head… *No, we can't just – can't just leave.*

But why not?

Well… They'll be… they'll be keeping an eye on us…

But we could run, father?

But then they'd want their money back, Joseph, don't you see? And you'll remember – they weren't shy to ask last time they thought we'd taken their money…

He pauses –

Listen – Why do you think he put us here? He obviously knows the place. Old Mrs Marra downstairs knows him too. Don't worry, son. It won't be too bad. Easy money. I can take a wrestle, sure. Who couldn't?

Paul is bouncing on the bed, jumping up and down, causing the floor to bend, shaking me and father out of the conversation. And I wish I could be jumping on the bed, that oblivious…

*

Whatever he has on you, give him it and get away. As soon as you can…

It's not that easy, you see…

He's hooked you – he's hooked you, Mr McLeod. I've seen it many times. He hooked my son and then got me and I'm still here. For the sake of those little ones, you need to get out of it. It may not be easy now, but it'll be harder come Saturday morning, believe you me. If you do well, there's not a hope in hell he'll let you go, he'll hold back, hold back, offer you more for another – and if you do badly… Well. Whatever he's promised you will not get. Do you understand?

The door opens and I spring back, pretending I wasn't listening through. Mrs Marra pushes her head inside – *Here, you boys – do you like the comics? I brought you some. They belong to my grandson. Sure, there's crayon on some of the pages, but they'll keep you occupied so.*

Comics!

Don't leap on the bed, now, good lad…

Thanks, Mrs Marra.

Oh – that's not a problem. Just you listen to what I said, you hear?

Father nods and the door closes.

*

Paul's asleep and the room's dark to keep him that way. Father and me are looking out into the night, over the river, occasional passing barges, to the other bank, most lights off in the buildings opposite, but the odd sign of life, a curtain being drawn, a fellow scurrying into a building, a dog being walked… Further down the path, there's a hulk of an old vessel, with a large glass tower.

That's a lightship, my father says.

A what?

A lightship. It's like a lighthouse, except… it floats. On a ship. It warns the other shipping to avoid a shallow piece of water, or an old wreck…

And what's it doing here?

Well, I don't know. Sometimes they're used to lure people in, show the captain of a ship what way they should be navigating, avoiding rocks, you know…? Or maybe it's just… being fixed for something. Having a rest.

It's like a giant Christmas light, and I'd love to see it working, for it'd surely be SO bright…

*

There's the occasional bird flying past, breaking the light a little, but it's mostly quiet. Peaceful.

You know, your mother loved this city.

I turn to him – *Did she? In what... in what way?*

She loved the people. Just SO many. And a cosmopolitan place.

A what?

Do you not know what that means, son? It means there's people from everywhere down here. Look at old Mrs Marra here...She's from the north... but there's English, Scots... Corksters like yourself! You're a Corkster now...

A Corkster. I think of mam, how if she'd been a Corkster, she'd've floated and would be here now. And there's no chance she'd be thinking of letting father wrestle, I'd bet on that.

I don't think she'd let you fight.

What's that?

I don't think mother would let you fight. That's all.

Ha. And how would you know that, Joseph? Listen – You're not worried about the fight, are you? It'll be fine. I'm not expecting to win, but I won't get hurt... there'll be a referee, you know? All I have to do is put on a good show...

And then?

And then we're out of here! No need to hang around – We'll go all the way home to Creagh... Or maybe stop with Mary... For a short while at least... See if I can help her there... Did you like her? Did you like it there?

I liked the food! And... And I liked hearing you sing...

Heh. The singing... Your mother sang, you know?

This talk of mother – I think about waking Paul, to help remember what father may say, to help build the frame, paint the picture, keep the picture...

She did?

Yes. That's how we met. With her singing, and then me, and then together... I was here – in Dublin – teaching... But mostly, I was, well, you know... socialising.

Soshawhatting?

Heh. Meeting people. Making friends.

Drinking?

Yep, I suppose that was in there too… But sure, it's a young man's world, Joseph. You've got it all to come…

And… was mother… drinking?

No! No – not at all. Not at any level anyway. No. She was there for the singing. The music… It was always me leading her to the bar, you know? Not the other way around. I tell you. She had the most beautiful voice…

I think of her screaming, as she drowned.

It wasn't fair.

What's that, Joseph?

It wasn't fair, mother… going.

No.

He nods his head.

You're right there, young man. It wasn't fair at all. But, we're doing ok, ain't we? Me, you and the little man over there? Sure, we'll be fine…

There's a gull, a night gull, flying back and forth, back and forth, hovering above a nest, perhaps, then off again, over and over. Their wings look huge and black, though that's just the light, no doubt, playing tricks on my eyes. A chill's coming in from the window, a window that has shrunk and grown through so many seasons that it's not sure where it fits in the frame anymore… the slight wind it's allowing is just a wisp, but it's tickling up my neck, up to just behind my ears. I look up to father and there's a glint in his eye, a reflection. He blinks, blinks again, then turns to me – *C'mon, anyway, let's get some sleep. I need a proper rest, get my strength up for the big day, eh? Sure – he won't know what hit 'em, whichever poor soul I'll be boxing.*

I… I thought it was wrestling?

Well. You know. One's the same as the other…

It is not.

I don't want you to fight.

A father has to provide. You'll learn that one day. I have. Poetry is a nonsense… I mean, who wants to buy it? That fat boy – the publisher boy – he only gave me a pound. One pound! He laughs. *That's no living.*

He shakes his head, then, quietly – *I tell you what that was, Joseph. That was a crushing. No fight can hurt as much as that…*

But all I can remember is that big fist hitting my father and my father falling straight down. And who'd want to see that again? I'd rather be asleep on the street.

*

There's a dream I often have, where we're all together, in the middle of a HUGE field, overlooking the sea… We're eating a picnic, on a large white sheet, gloriously white, thick linen, comfortable, with warmth beneath it somehow, and I can barely see the distance, for the glare of the sun is too much, but I'm happy and Paul is happy and he's cuddling mother and father has his arm around me and he's eating a sandwich the size of an iron and I try to see mother's face as who would not, but every time she turns I wake up and that is it, me done up until the morning.

Is that a scream of delight,
as we fall down these hills, as though chased?

As we raise to a canter,
should we beware of the danger?

No. It is not our job to question
such a blissful, lunatic fall.

So, I take your hand in mine
but it's not to slow us, not to slow us...

30

W'E'LL GET SOME *breakfast – C'mon now.*
          Where is it, father?
   There'll be a room… we'll be down these stairs – c'mon now, Paul, I could do with a coffee…

It smells musty, this guest house or hotel or whatever it is. And I didn't sleep, well, not very well. I was too warm until father got up and opened the window in the middle of the midnight gloom. The witching hour, that's what Paul calls it, though I don't know where he read that, as there are no witches in the city, everyone knows that.

He's kicking me to get past, to grab father's hand – *I'm hungry, dada.*

   Well, let's get moving then!

In the stairwell, the sun is shining through a hole in the roof, catching us as we walk out, momentarily slowing as we feel for the banister, then descend. There's an amazing food smell now…

   Is that bacon, dada?

   Smells like it, Joseph! A breakfast for kings, eh? And that's us three – three kings! And once we've eaten – we'll go out – out for a long walk, eh? Walk alongside this river they've got, maybe spend some of this money that's burning a hole in my pocket…

   A word, if I may, Mr McLeod.

We stop. Foot of the stairs, there's a thin-looking fellow. He's wearing a suit, a few sizes too big for him, but clean, new maybe.

   And who will you be?

   I'm an acquaintance of Mr Fallon. I just have a – I just have a little message for you.

183

Mrs Marra appears from the snicket at the side of the stairs, sees this new man and recoils slightly. She looks up at us, still a half-dozen steps from the ground level, then back down to the man.

Here – you boys – come on through with me and I'll get your breakfast started. Let your father talk to this… this… charming young man here.

She lets her words out, but they're cold. Father lightly pats us forwards – *Go on boys. I'll join you in a moment.*

*

And we're in a grand square room. Huge. White decoration on the ceiling, a pronged light hanging down with maybe six or seven bulbs. A handful of people are sat and are eating, that's the bacon smell we got – and there's eggs, too – Plus there's piles of cereal and bottles of milk on the side, and that peculiar coffee smell… But I just feel a bit sick, now, seeing that man. I'm grasping Paul's hand, too tight, I know that, and he's wriggling it free, so I relax, but when I let go, he doesn't move anywhere. He's looking up to me, for support, reassurance, then back to the door.

Is dada not coming in?

He is.

Come now, boys – sit yourselves down and I'll bring you some food –

She pulls out a chair, then another, two chairs out on a table for four – *Here – sit.*

But we don't move, either of us. I'm not leading Paul, I want to stay right here, close to the door, waiting for father.

She looks at us then – *Well, suit yourselves.* And turns to the table over by the window, two young men, dark-skinned, foreign, maybe – *Now then, lads, can I get you anything else?*

We're left, to stand. Ignored. I twitch to the side, hearing father's voice, a little raised, but nothing to lure me back into the corridor.

Paul has leaned over to a close-by table and grabbed an old bit of toast, discarded by the previous occupant. He's munching away on it, tearing at the crust as though he were a lion and it a bit of meat.

It looks good, this toast. Maybe we should have sat...

And the door opens, father appearing, looking annoyed and sour. He gets us to a table, straightaway – *C'mon, lads – no dillydallying – let's sit ourselves down.*

He's muttering under his breath, his cheeks red, his chair torn back and slammed upright on the floor before he sits down and pulls it back beneath him, all the time shaking his head and looking left to right, left to right.

I know better than to talk, but I must – *Is everything ok, father?*

Ttt! It is and it isn't. Now. Where's that Mrs Marra. Let's order our food, shall we? Heh – I see you've started, Paul! Ah well, never mind, never mind... He's rearranging the salt and pepper, the knives and forks... *Now. Now. Oh – here she is... Ah, Mrs Marra –*

*

While we await our food, father tells us that he won't be allowed to leave the hotel. For his own safety, he's been told. *The fella – the fella there – he told me that sometimes the other boxer – the other wrestler – sometimes their team try to injure the opponent, see –*

How do you mean, dada, injure?

Oh – you know – they may try to trip me up. Or, perhaps tire me out. Ask me to carry something heavy...

I doubt even Paul believes this explanation.

Father shakes his head.

No... so, you see, I have to stay inside. We all do.

All of us!?

Well – You can imagine, I don't want you out on your own, now, do I?

The food arrives. The plates themselves are HUGE and there's more food on my own than I swear I've eaten my entire life. A full white egg, plenty of beans, two hunks of bread, some black circles, sausages the size of father's fingers and there – three long, thin strips of bacon.

So.

185

Thank you, Mrs Marra, this looks incredible.

Well. It's the least I can do. If you're going to be guests of mine, you may as well be comfortable. And here – the boys can come and watch a little television later on, if it'd help. Days can be long, stuck in one little room, I know that.

Television! I shout out – *Thanks, Mrs Marra!* – and even Paul stops eating, but his mouth is too stuffed with beans to say anything other than *Hmmmememe.* – But – Television!

She smiles. *No problem, boys. Anything I can do to give your father some peace and some rest, I will. Now. Eat up. Eat up and enjoy. You're growing men and you need your food.*

*

Father's upstairs. Mrs Marra brought up a newspaper and a radio and he's sat by himself, reading, perhaps, drinking tea, resting.

We left as soon as we were offered the opportunity for *television*. But now we're here, the only thing on is a lot of horses running in a race, over and over. We daren't touch the dial much as Paul tried it once and the thing started screaming a rainstorm noise at us. So, we're just watching a horse race, in black and white, with a picture that has lightning flashing all over the place, leaving the horses with mighty Zs across their bodies, then shrunken, then huge, then normal...

Paul doesn't seem bothered. *Look! Look!*

As if it's the first time he's *seen* television.

His face is right up against the screen, one hand on either side – *It's making my eyes all funny! Look! Look!*

Then he leans back and waves his head around, as though exhausted, or a lunatic.

This room isn't as good as our bedroom. There's dirty laundry everywhere, hanging on the edges of the sofas, the backs of the wooden chairs, dumped on the floor in large, unruly piles, newspapers and magazines gathered and dumped, mugs full of sticky white whatever, stained and abandoned.

A floor lower from the bedroom, too, and looking outside the window, we're only just above the head height of the people passing by. It's a colourful place, this Dublin, all sorts of yellow suited ladies, men with flapping trousers, bicycles sharing pavement and road…

…And right down below, reading a paper, but facing our way, that man from breakfast, in his baggy suit. He looks up and I drag my head back inside, quick as I can, before slowly peering out again…

And he waves at me, nodding also.

I don't wave back.

Paul is still on the television, literally almost, hugging the thing as though it's a great gift. No horses now, just men talking about horses.

Paul!

Paul!

Shh! I'm watching…

PAUL!

WHAT IS IT?

That man is there…

Which man – the horse man?

No – not a horse man – the man from the bottom of the stairs…

…

PAUL! The man from the bottom of the stairs is there!

SO WHAT! I'm watching television now…

But what can I do anyway? About the man in the baggy suit OR the horses? Nothing. I can do nothing. I don't look out again. I move away from the window and join Paul beside the snowing television screen.

*

Shouldn't you be practising?

Practising what, Joseph?

I don't know… Your fighting?

187

And who would I practise against? You? No. I'm resting. I deserve a rest. And so do you. Enjoy it!

But it is boring as a Mass, stuck here in a no-fun room. I've either got father's snoring and farting or Paul getting excited about the flickering shadows of horses.

*

We end up running up and down the stairs, as if we were the ones who were having to fight. Paul racing beside me, pretending to be some racehorse he'd liked the name of. Over and over, up and down, down and up, up and down.

Keep it down out there.

Some Irish voice, a crackly sounding lady, perhaps old, but never seen...

Shhh! Paul.

MMMMweeeeeeooooo – Overtaken at the final hurdle by The Mighty Joseph!

Shh!

KEEP THAT RACKET DOWN!

But by then we're on the next floor, along the straight and to the final set of stairs...

UP! LAST FURLOING!

And me scrambling to keep up with him, burning my hands on the carpet, scraping my knees, him winning and celebrating *YESSS!!!! THE GRAND NASHNOL WINNER MIGHTY JOSEPH! HURRAAA!!!*

And then straight back down again, aeroplane noises this time, as we zip round corners, jumping two steps, then three, then four, avoiding on every landing the tiny tables with solitary flowers, me quietening when passing the shouting lady room, but Paul screaming like a machine gun in full tilt – *DADALADA ISHE! DADALADA ISHE!* And finally, the woman now opening the door and screaming at *me* even though I was the silent partner – *AH'LL HAVE YUSE THRAWN OUT!* – and *that* shaking Paul out of his game and suddenly crying and running down the stairs even faster then crashing into our own room, where father is sitting on the bed, same newspaper in hand but this time a pen too, as though he's doing a puzzle. His face though, red and clenched, looks anything but relaxed.

Dada, dada, that woman shouted at me!

And I can't blame her! What a racket you've been making! Come in now. Come in and sit down. You have to behave boys — you hear me? BEHAVE.

And now HE'S shouting and well, it takes the pair of us by surprise, for we'd hoped for a friendly welcome in our own port. Paul, well he starts crying *even more* and these tears seeming more real and unstoppable and are accompanied by a long whine and Paul no longer running but now turning around and around in circles, as if looking for somewhere else to run to, but there being no place at all he could think of.

Father, he shouts, but not to us, to the bed, it seems.

SHITE!

Then climbs down and breathing loudly, tries to calm himself, then invite Paul over, saying *I'm sorry, Paul, I'm sorry, I'm just so tired of being stuck in here and what with everything going on my nerves are a little edgy, here, I didn't mean to shout, look we can read those comics for a bit and here — we've not long before tea. I wonder what Mrs Marra will cook up for us this time, eh? Now THERE's something to look forward to...*

*

So, we were weary after that. Father didn't sleep and the whole night-time was spent keeping as quiet as we could, dare we wake him from those few moments where he may have actually been asleep...

...and that fed into the days. He'd lie there, in a fury, fuming away. We'd go, for as long as we could, we'd sit in the linen room and watch the fizzing television screen, but even Paul finding that boring now.

The breakfasts were good, but after that first day, father said he *couldn't eat much* and we dare not stay down below in the breakfast room by ourselves should that man appear, so we'd stuff our mouths as quickly and as best we could, smuggling all we could roll into our jumpers back up the stairs.

And Mrs Marra would bring father up a roll at lunchtime, full of whatever he'd left over at breakfast, which would be plenty and he'd eat that. She seemed good, Mrs Marra. If I'd had a granny, I'd want her to be like that.

*

But the week was only half a week and that half a week was too short and before we knew it, the day itself had arrived. And in a way it was almost welcome, because it meant we could leave the hotel, the pressure cooker... Father had batted away any talk of the fight – of course he had – but Paul and me had been discussing it, quietly, him asking me *How long will it take? Will it be on television? Will dada be famous? Will we get fed? Will he get hurt?*

As if I'd have the answers to any of those.

*

Father slept though. I know that, because I did not, and I heard him snore. Paul and me just lay on the mattress on the floor, eyes open, staring at one another, each willing the other to close their eyes. But I didn't close mine and I do not remember him closing his.

*

No, Mr McLeod, you're not running off half-eaten today. Sit. Stay and eat. You'll need all the strength you can get.

I was not hungry, not one bit. Every bit of food being forced back out of my throat as it went down.

*

190

So, the plan is tomorrow we make our way back to Mary's place. I may… I may need somewhere to rest.

Does she know? Does she know we're coming?

No. No, she doesn't. But it'll be fine. It'll be fine.

*

Here – just pack what you need.

As if I have anything at all to pack. I'd be struggling to leave something behind.

I'll leave… I'll leave these Beanos…

Joseph?

Yes father?

You take my wallet, ok? Put it tight in your jacket and do not take it out to look at or show or feel or anything. And – And keep the jacket on, ok? However hot it may get. You got it?

I nod – *ok. I know. I know.*

And keep a hold of Paul. That is the most important thing. Understand?

I nod.

And Paul – I don't want you watching anything that's happening. You just… You take those Beanos and read them…

But I've read them sixteen times, dada, maybe a hundred…

Well, read them again. Read them again.

*

We'll be back, Mrs Marra.

I hope not.

We will. Keep our room fresh.

They'll send someone for ye'. They'll take care of it.

And if you could wash the sheets, I think Paul may have…

Sure, sure. I'll wash the sheets. Of course.

We may be late…

Well… Here – you can leave these two here, you know that. There's plenty of that static on the television they can be watching…

He nods. *Thank you. But… we may just leave straight after. Depending how long…*

She nods. *I see. I see. Well… good luck.*

We'll maybe see you later.

I hope not, she says.

*

We're called downstairs. Father looks at himself in the mirror, then ruffles our hair – *C'mon, lads. This won't take long. This won't take long.*

The ill-fitting-suit man is awaiting us.

How are ye? My father asks.

We've a car for you, the reply. Then, a look at us, at Paul and myself, and a break of character – *Jeez, are they coming? This is no place for them…*

They're coming.

Are you sure now?

Absolutely.

He shakes his head. *Well. They're your children. They'll be grown soon enough.*

We're out the door, down the stone steps and straight into the car, which smells of fresh leather, polish and clean. There's not a spec of dirt on the floor and we slide across the seats with ease. We're so low down here. I think I prefer the height of the bus. It's hard to even see out of these windows, but as soon as we pull away from the kerb, father right beside us and the fellow too, we can hardly hear the road and it's as though the car is gliding…

Paul has a spoon in his hand – a small spoon, for the sugar maybe – and he's rubbing it, over and over. There's no sign of the *Beanos*. I tap my heart and the wallet is still there. I put my hand down on to the leather and father takes it and squeezes, and I can feel the sweat in his hands but I squeeze back, not looking up, for I have wet in my eyes and if he were to see it, well that wouldn't be helping things one bit would it.

I have a strange, quick vision of mother, leaping out of the water, like a dolphin, but then gone, and I turn and look out, the car passing shop after shop, sometimes stopping – at traffic lights, I'll guess and – could we not just jump out here and run and run?

And Paul, well Paul now is humming a song. Or one part of a song, over and over. My father talks –

How long will this journey take?

Oh… I don't know. It'd take a short while, I'd say. No more than that.

Then back to the silence of the road, before Paul takes his humming up once more. Father leans forward, talking direct to the skinny man, whispering almost, but I can hear him, fine –

And the fight?

What about it?

How long will that take?

Eh? How do you mean?

Well – how many rounds are there? Is it the standard – I guess – twelve, I guess?

Rounds? Oh. No – there's just the one big round, I'd say. Sure, why break it up? It won't take too long, I'd say, but that's up to you now. I mean, if you go down, you won't be taking home much of a pay, will ye?

Well, there's the five pounds, Fallon said…

He did, did he? Well. You'd do well to remember that was before your warm bed and all those breakfasts and dinners you've been having. Sure, you've almost bankrupted Fallon, I don't doubt. You'll be NEEDING to win just to clear that debt… and here's the thing – so will the other fella – the fella you're fighting – as you can imagine. Different fella, different problems, but just as keen. So, you see – these fights – well, they can last a while, can't they? No one wants to be the one lying on the floor with nothing but loose teeth to show for it, do they?

And father slumps back into the seat beside me, me pretending I'd not heard a word.

I don't know why my father didn't interrupt or argue… Maybe he'd known it'd be something like this all along.

In the car there is silence. Even Paul has stopped his humming. So, what are we going to do now?

The car stops, suddenly.

Well. We've arrived.

Oh no.

*

And he's out quick, the man in the too big suit, and in that moment of him out and us in, father leans over and whispers – *Keep the wallet close. And keep Paul closer.* He squeezes my hand and ruffles Paul's hair, then, louder, *C'mon, boys, let's show these eejits what's what.*

We're still right by the river, but it's opened up and widened considerably. There's a huge old shed, some small one-storey brick-built efforts, but not much in the way of housing… A few winches dangling over into the water, rusted brown, nearby a giant old ship, maybe the size of six houses, but that too has splotches of brown rust on it, covering its once-red shell. There are chains on the ground with links the width of my arms – wider even, maybe even father's arms. And it's funny, nothing is growing here, between the bricks on the floor, the poured concrete, there's no shoots of grass or flowers… just grit. Grit, dirt and oil.

This way.

And we trip our way through the debris, Paul looking back, over the river, wide and open. Father catches my hand and Paul's too, one either side, as if we are wings, curled into his side.

*

We walk straight, straight toward the largest shed, waiting at a door, hearing too-big-suit man knock loudly on the outside, a knock echoing around, deep, metallic and cold. An opening appears – more a hatch than a door – and he beckons us in, himself standing on the outside, but waving us through. Father ducks and we follow, in, and the first thing we hit is the stench, of fish and the sea, and we're in to a HUGE building, the likes of which certainly I've never seen, bigger than any church or barn I know, just the walls and the ceiling and no stairs as they'd have no place to go, a few windows, well, not windows, but panels letting in light and in the middle of this space, there's a ship, a similar size to the one outside, but in slightly worse condition.

It's a fishing boat – look – and Paul points over to the back of the boat, where there's a pile of chains and maybe, just maybe a net, so he could be right.

Are we going to the sea? But surely even Paul can see that that particular boat won't be going anywhere soon.

My father is looking up, up and around, peering down towards the opposite end of the endless shed… *Where's the ring?*

The what? Oh – for later you mean? Oh, don't you worry about that – this way, now and we're led further down, past the boat, until we see a small white building, itself built within the shed – it's like half a bungalow but inside, not out – and gestured over, towards – *here we go, now. If you fellows just go inside there and have a little wait, that'd be grand.* He winks at me and I look away, as quick as I can, to his laugh – *Hehe, now – make yourselves at home, it'll be a while yet now. You'll be fine in there now, you have everything you'll need.* And again he waits outside as we walk in, slowly though, for it is dark, and father stops maybe a few feet inside, with us coming up against him, only for suit man to flick a switch and the whole place is lit up by one bare lightbulb. *Ok, lads? I'll leave you to it –* and the door closes, with a loud *click* of a lock.

It's just ourselves again. But in a smaller room this time, smaller even than our hotel, one tiny table, two small wooden chairs beside it. A door – or a doorway at least, and inside the rim of a loo, sticking out. I hope there's a door to that. On the wall, there's a radiator, with a little heat coming from it, warming the corpses of a dozen or so flies.

Newspaper on the floor. A bucket – I peak in – blue paint and a broken bit of yellow wood. The paint looks solid, it's gleaming but there's balls of dust, scraps of other paint, all sitting on its surface.

And now, we wait, wait.

Father's talking, but to no one in particular. He leans down and picks up one of the old bits of newspaper, reads it once, turns it over, then throws it back down.

*

He's sat in the corner, head in his hands. Paul and me are sat at the table, flicking that same bit of newspaper back and forth. It's in a ball now, of sorts, or at least a crumble. We're making as little noise as we can, so as not to disturb father.

Is dada going to be killed?

Paul's whispering, though father can surely hear.

What! No…

Like mama was?

No – this is – no –

And then he's humming away to himself once more, but still flicking the paper ball, still returning my own flicks.

JOSEPH – Keep quiet now – and keep your brother quiet. And – and turn that light off, will you? I need some rest…

I lean back and flick the switch and the bulb flicks off, leaving us in the grey-black room. I reach over to Paul and feel for his hand, before standing and making my way over to him, pulling him, first up, so he's standing, then over to my memory of where father and the wall is, then down and beside, so we're resting, cold enough, dark certainly, but together, father's breathing clearly audible and within a second his arm around us both, pulling us close.

*

I sleep and I dream. I dream of the sea. I dream of boats, I dream of mother throwing me a lifebelt, throwing us all a lifebelt and me myself grabbing it and climbing within and pulling myself forwards and up to the boat, up the side, as if being lifted, lifted and seeing my mother's hands and looking up to see her face and…

Father moves or Paul moves or somebody moves and I awake,

but slowly, slowly, I fall into a deeper dream still and in this one mother is taking me by the hand and leading me through a market place, surrounded by voices, people I cannot see for I only come up to their knees and I love this warmth around me, this gentle buffeting from warmth to warmth and there – up ahead – I spy a squirrel, in a clearing of legs and boots – a red squirrel looking directly at me and nodding, nibbling and nodding, twitching and winking until –

There's an explosion of noise and a flare of light and I awake to where I am, sat against the wall still, Paul leaning beside me, awoken himself now, and father the other side, but his eyes look well awake and aware, no surprise for him – and the noise, well, that'll be the door being open for as soon as bad-suit man closes it, the sound halves, but it is still there and I remember it briefly as the sound from my dream and how I wish THAT was the reality and this just a little nightmare…

I follow father's eyes and they're looking directly at the door. And within a moment it opens and closes once more and that Fallon man is there. Amongst all else he has disturbed my dreaming and for that alone I would not like him one bit.

*

McLeod. Good to see you.

My father is up, but he doesn't beckon us to follow and we don't. But I do crawl my hand along the floor, tapping it along into Paul's.

What's this I'm hearing, Fallon…

And father's walking towards the filthy man

…about us paying for the room, for the food – about us being in your debt, somehow, I don't like the sound of that…

But Fallon, he just laughs –

No? You don't like the sound of it? Heh! Well – you shouldn't have eaten all my food then, should you?

There's a grease on his clothing, giving it a peculiar, mirrored sort of look, it's down his front, his sleeves, his stinking trousers…

I told ye – I told ye – I'd find you a bed and gift you some money, which you've had – but you WELL overstayed your welcome there – three meals! Three meals, two, three times a day! How am I supposed to pay for that? Gosh, you must owe me, well, what is it I said I'd pay you? Five for the fight, minus what I gave you, minus all those meals – it has to, it has to be a debt now of, say twenty pounds! I can't chalk that off, McLeod. You know that…

My father, in this situation, looks like the sane, sober man, though his face is still battered and bruised and his clothing one step away from rags, be this a normal household…

Twenty pounds? Are you off your nut!?

But Fallon is not for stopping.

What!? What!? Me!? Did I sleep in that bed? Did I force you and your family to eat old Mrs Marra out of house and home? No. I did not. YOU ate the food, enjoyed the comforts, the warmth… You took the offer, McLeod, you can't back out now, for we are in a VERY different position from the last time we met. For now, you're not just a nuisance, you're a debtor. You know what a debtor is, McLeod?

There's no way I owe you that amount… You GAVE me the room, remember?

Did I heck. I SHOWED you the room. YOU took it. You sullied those sheets. You ate that food… Look – You owe me now. I know it and you know it. Win this fight and then we can talk, you can pay me off – understand? In fact – win this fight well and we may even be able to come to an agreement for the future – for if I like what I see in that ring, I can be a generous man, McLeod. Isn't that true, Tony?

And bad-suit man grins *T'is.* And shrugs his shoulders, lifting the suit, drawing attention…

You may even grow to LIKE me, McLeod. Isn't that right, Tony?
T'is. Still smirking.

No. If I win this fight, that's us even and it's over, Fallon, understand?
Well, that's what you say – but I'm not sure it's what I say, McLeod…

He's calm, father, he's not shouting, he's being as clear as he can –
Then what if I don't fight at all –

Well – heh – however much of a tough man you may think you are, I don't think you are a stupid man – just remember – there's not only you here to worry about, is there.

He stares down, down at Paul and me, and father rattles –

Don't you even dare…

Hey! Hey! None of this raised voice business – keep your energy, you're going to need it – and – we can still be friends, McLeod. We WILL be. Once this little business is over.

No chance. No more. I finish this and I – we – go.

Well, if that's what you want to tell yourself… and he walks closer, closer to father, raising a finger – *But let's hope you win, and let's hope you win well, McLeod. For if you end up swimming on the floor out there, well. Then we have a whole different situation again. Understand?*

My father looks away, and Fallon's out, taking Tony in the bad suit with him.

*

The outer shed sounds busy now. There are voices overlapping and shouting, slowly becoming one big uproar. Father looks over to me and nods. I nod back, but it cannot be the nod he was after, for I have no answers to this.

Paul is keeking out of the filthy, scored window – *There's people coming in! Lots of people!*

And father, pacing up and down this tiny room, occasionally kicking at an old cigarette packet or other bit of litter, stops and looks out – before shaking his head and carrying on. *This is not who I am, this is not who I am…*

Then, to me –

Look – You get out – if you can get out – do. Meet me at the lightship. Understand?

I nod, but I do not understand.

And just wait for me. Right? I'll be along…

…and keep yourself hidden. And keep Paul with you. Right?

I nod *right.*

Ok. Ok.

Then back to back and forth, here and there, up and down, pacing, pacing...

Do you mean... we just go? And leave you?

He stops – *I do. If you can. Do you understand?*

I nod, again.

I wonder what is going through his mind. Is he thinking of mother? Would she have advice? I can't think how... I look to Paul, still gazing, counting now – *38, 39, 40 – father! There's over 40 people here! 52, 53, 53...*

A knock at the door, and Tony is in – *Five minutes, son. Are you ready? – I'd take that coat off, if I were you.* And out, the audible lock on the door still there.

Fuck. FUCK. Sorry – Excuse me, boys –

Shock. We look down, or I look down, I cannot see Paul for I am looking down. He's probably still gazing out of the window.

Father's in the tiny loo space now, kneeling, his head almost in the bowl and I'm wondering if he's going to take a drink, but no – with a mighty hurl, he's throwing up in there, sick as Paul and me sometimes are, vomiting, then coughing, then spitting into the lavatory. It makes me want to do the same, the sound and the smell of him... I don't, but I do stand, and walk to him, and lightly place my hand on his shoulder, the way he does with me, has done with me on so many occasions.

It's ok...

He turns, and his face is violent red and full of tears, but he's not angry, not with me anyway, and he whispers – *I'll sort this, Joseph. I have a plan. Don't you worry, you hear? Just... if you're in that crowd... take Paul's hand, hold him tight and you fellows sneak out, you hear – and listen – but he's quieter still now – If I don't make it to the lightship by the morning – which I will – but if I don't – open that wallet and use the last of the money, get yourselves down to Mary's and I will join you there, understand?*

To… Mary's?

Yes – get the bus to Cork, then the bus to Ballyheada. Can you remember that?

I nod.

Then tell me it back, Joseph.

The bus to Cork, then the bus to Ballyheada.

Good lad. Good lad.

But this does not sound like a good plan and is not what I want to hear at all – *But – father – I don't want you to fight…*

Don't think about the fight! Your job is to get out, now. Joseph – you have to be strong. This isn't just you now, this is Paul and you and me and we have a responsibility to your mother… We have to keep this family together – be strong – right?

I'm blinking out the tears, but a big yellow thumb of his appears and wipes them further aside – *RIGHT? I'll get us out of this. I promise. I have a plan, Joseph. I do, but you need to be out of here. Do you understand?*

I nod once more and I attempt a smile. And I do promise back, but I am terrified.

You? You were lucky. You escaped.
I've yet to leave the scene.

And I now need three lungsful
for every single breath.

Perhaps here, they will know you, somehow.
Perhaps here, which was once our heaven.

There are sticks by the door that you gathered for kindling
that I cannot bear to burn.
There's a pot of dried herbs, brought over
from France,
their fragrance, almost gone.
There are books you've cherished
and written in.

I search through them all, looking for clues.

31

THE DOOR IS opened and father is taken. I look to Paul in shock, to see his wide-mouthed return.

The door closes with a click, and there's a ROAR from outside. That roar subsides, but only by a fraction, and it is punctuated by shouts, screams, *C'MONs!* and *LET'S SEE 'IM!* I jump to the door and turn the handle but – it's locked, of course. I look to Paul, and he's still on the table, kneeling over, looking out into the gloom. *They're going to kill 'im! – They're going to kill 'im!*

But I cannot think about *that*.

Come on, Paul, we need to get outside...

The door is still locked. Of course, it is.

Come on, Paul, come down and help! He's not coming down, so I look up to grab him and I see – The window that Paul is leaning against. *Does it open, Paul? PAUL! Does it open?*

He looks to me, shocked – *What?*

I climb up, via father's chair and look – there's a lock, of course there is – but it's on the inside, as it would be, as it should be, I turn it and – swift. It goes.

Paul! Paul – Can you see anyone?

Sure, there's HUNDREDS of people...

He's crying, panicking...

No... I mean – is anyone watching us?

No! And why would they be – look...

I look properly through the glass and into the main hangar. All that is visible is that big ol' boat and it's lit up – there are spotlights, kind of, but from above, shining down on to it – and on the deck of that boat, just arriving, is father. And beside father is that filthy

203

Fallon man with his Tony in the suit and opposite them – well, there's a HUGE fella. A long, wide man with a belly like a whale and six feet something tall with arms as white and as wide and as fat as a well-fed calf.

We have to get out.

It's a colossal wave, the sound of a few hundred excited men, the noise turning, birling around the huge shed, rising and rising more, directed and my father and this other fellow, a fellow who has his arms raised and is bringing his hands together, clapping the crowd, who respond in kind.

Father's going to be flattened.

We have to get out! Now! Open that window…

There's a push – and a slight movement –

Just kick it! Just kick it in! – Paul now, he's got the gist of the idea – but there's no need to kick anything, I burrow alongside and *heave* and it's creaked fully open in seconds. We're good to go. I look around – *Father's coat – will you get it Paul?*

Why should I get it? You're bigger and I'm all the way up here!

So am I! I'm right beside you…

YOU get it…

There's another eruption from the crowd and that solves the issue, I slide back down and pick it up – nothing else to be seen – I then put father's jacket on over my own, and it almost fits, what with the bulk of my own coat widening me out…

This time – now, let's go –

It's too high!

What is? It's right there…

No! Not this side – the drop – it's too high –

He's feared, terrified, shaking.

I get up beside him and look out. It's not too high at all, it can't be. It's just a ground floor window – *Come on, Paul, jump out!*

But I can't see the floor!

What?

I CAN'T SEE THE FLOOR.

Look – I'll go first, hold on –

With the noise of the people – it's like climbing into a roaring kettle... I land easily enough then hold my arms up – *I've got you, come on down now –* he hesitates, for a moment, then shifts his feet out, then his legs and I ease him down.

Ok, we have to find a way out!

WHAT?

WE HAVE TO FIND A WAY OUT – FATHER SAID...

I KNOW!

Then,

LOOK!

He's pointing, vaguely towards the door we came in – *LOOK!* – But we can't go that way – there must be a dozen people scattered about, stragglers at the back of the crowd

There's an almighty *AAAAAAHHHHH* – I turn and see the fight has begun, or at least father and the other man are circling each other... I cannot watch it, can't let Paul watch it...

THERE!

It's the door he's pointing at again – *THERE'S TOO MANY PEOPLE! WE NEED ANOTHER WAY!*

NO! LOOK – LOOK!

He's not moving, so I stare, I squint over, and there, by the door, underneath a flimsy looking wooden table, is father's suitcase.

COME ON!

He's off before I can say a word. At first, I worry – as though people are going to stop us, but then I realise – who even knows we're here? Has father been advertised as the fighting man with two hostage children? And the way we're dressed, now, after the scuffs of our journey – we look like street children, suited to a situation like this.

We get close to the table and there's not a soul looking our way. There's a couple of big fellas close enough, but they're not anchored to the table in any way, and their eyes are hooked on the boat, the boat with the fight and the fight with our father.

YOU GO AND STAND BY THE DOOR AND I'LL GRAB THE BAG OK?

His eyes are moon-wide and he nods to me, before running off, his arms swinging from side to side in the most ridiculous fashion, reaching the door and holding the opening bar with both hands, staring, waiting for me.

The noise in here is vast and sore on the ears, these men screaming their lungs off...

I walk quickly towards him and, last minute, I make a grab for the bag. I pull the handle, but, Jesus, Mary and Joseph, this is one heavy bag of father's. I heave once more and it comes out from below the table top, and then I have it – though I need to drag it more than lift it almost. It's impossible! How does father lift this?

I get some speed going and reach the doorway – *You'll need to help me lift this when we get out –*

WHAT? IT'S TOO LOUD HERE!

I SAID – never mind. Open the door. OPEN THE DOOR!

WE CAN'T LEAVE DADA.

BUT THIS IS HIS PLAN!

What plan it is I do not know. Him becoming raspberry jelly and us two becoming orphans.

The bar that keeps the door locked, well, it's not for children as Paul cannot muster the strength needed by himself. I put the case down and jump on to the bar myself, now using both our weight and strength and finally the thing clangs open, letting in a rush of cool air. I look round to see if anyone has noticed, but there's nothing – for the action in the ring seems to be heating up and I hope, hope, hope that father has told us the right thing to do, in getting out, but I cannot rightly ask him now, can I?

And then – and then – I see the following – I see father's fully thought-out plan.

I can only guess that father, for whatever reason, he must have been keeping an eye out. Or, maybe it was just a coincidence. Or maybe it was the orange glow of the outside street lights, breaking through this tiny wee doorway and shining through the gloom of the shed – but whatever, at that moment, father, I swear, looked over at us, at Paul and me. And maybe it was because he saw us here, almost out of the barn itself and certainly escaped from that wee caravan, or maybe he'd just had enough, but he raised his hands and shouted something our way – I have no idea what, for the noise was far too much to make it out – then he turned around and ran passed the big fatty, the giant he was *supposed* to be fighting, straight up quick to where that Fallon man was standing, and without warning, whacked his fist right down Fallon's throat, with Fallon dunking down to the floor in a second, like a dropped sack of flour.

32

THE PLACE ROARED. Bodies, leaping, screaming. The noise hooked up an extra tenfold. I was stunned by the sight, the event, the sound, until I heard a *JOSEPH! JOSEPH! JOSEPH!* from little Paul outside and quick as I could I turfed the suitcase over the lip of the door, following it quick myself and then slamming the tin door itself closed.

What happened?
It was… It was father – he walloped that dirty Fallon man –
Did he?
He did – it was…
Was it good?
It was, it was…

But there's a crashing and howling coming from inside, as though the crowd themselves have begun taking on each other and it is not an inviting sound and worse, it is surely approaching the door – *We have to go, help me with this bag, here –*

Ooft, how did Dada carry this then?
Because he's a grown-up…
But it's too…

And he drops it. *Ah come on, Paul…*

I lift it myself, all by myself this time and make a big show of carrying it single-handedly, but it's exhausting, I manage six, maybe seven steps into the gloom of the evening.

This won't work.
DADA can carry it…
No! We're meeting him in town, remember?
But… That's, that's… One hundred miles away!

It's not! It can't be that far — it only took ten minutes in that car, earlier.

But we were driving one hundred miles an hour, that's why...

We were not...

And there's a crash, as the tiny cabin door falls open and out falls some man into the open, a bloodied face on him, falling over straightaway, followed by another — but this one, this second man doesn't look injured, just angry and he's looking all around, until he quite easily sees us and shouts *HEY! THAT'S MY CASE, YOU LITTLE SHITS* and he's halfway on top of us until the bloodied man reaches out his foot and brings the big fellow to the floor, then scurries up his leg and begins to batter him on the ear.

We need to get out of here —

Look! Look!

And I wonder what it is now, but luckily, Paul is seeing sense, for just a throw further is a big three wheeled bike with a wooden basket on the front, reading *Brendan's Bakery.*

We can use that!

My head though, questions it — *But that's stealing...*

No, it's not — it's stopping that man on the floor there from stealing from us!

And I guess he's right and even if not, Paul now is practically on top of the bike and attempting to be riding away, I jump along beside him, wrestling with the gravity of this suitcase, pulling it in hops, then one massive *hurl* and it's up and into the baker's front basket.

Can you ride? Paul is asking me. *I'll fall off.*

I think he's gone a little daft as how could he fall off a three-legged bike, but then I hear the growl of the man chasing after our suitcase so I climb on around him and push down, but...

It's not moving... climb off and give me a push...

And with Paul no longer weighing us down but shoving away meatily on the back, slowly, slowly it begins its path and soon now Paul is almost running to keep up and then he jumps and is stood on the back wheels, his hands on my shoulders, still pushing us forward with one leg, as though on a scooter... I look back and there's gallons of fighting men now, squeezing though that little door and throwing their bodies at one another. Forwards once more and push the pedals as deep and often as I can, my legs quickly burning with the effort, then away, away from them all, the road getting darker, easier to hide in the gloom, the further away we get from lights at the scene of it all...

I guess the man who saw us with the bag has fallen back, he must have, but he'll still be on the lookout for us, and if he's got any sense, he's gone to get a car to scout around, or at least told his pals, can't relax, keep on going...

I need a wee.

I can't help you – we can't stop, Paul...

Last thing I need is Paul needing a wee, for God's sake.

My legs are burning through, and every push is getting worse and worse.

I need a wee! I need a wee!

Well! What can I do!?

Stop the bike! I'm going to wee...

Ah, Paul!

Ok, I'll pull over, wait, wait...

There's a shadow ahead, some scrub, perhaps, a messy old bush. That'll do – *I'm going to stop at those little trees, ok?*

Ok, ok, ok. Hurry!

I don't reply, I steer the vast iron handles just a little, and the baker's bike turns with me, up, off the road as it is and on to the rough grassed verge. The bike slows almost immediately with the traction of the grass and the softness of the ground, but I push ahead, and we almost make the bushes. I jump off the bike – *ok, go now and be quick and then we'll be off* – but as soon as I look back, I see the lights of a good half-dozen cars approaching, maybe more, maybe twenty and they're not far away. *Ah no! Help, Paul, help with the bike* – but he's peeing, of course, so he cannot.

I wrestle the bike forwards, bit by bit, but there's no way it'll make the bushes.

Damn it!

The cars are moments away, so I do all I can do, I grab father's case and jump in behind the bush, alongside Paul. He looks at me in surprise – *Do you need a wee?*

No! and Shhh! The cars...

As if they could hear us here, behind the bush...

Keep still!

As if they won't see the bike, abandoned there...

And the cars rush up, the first one ignoring us, then the second, then the third... Can they not see the bike?

I'm done...

What?

I've done my wee.

Shh! We have to... we have to bring that bike in here, behind the bush, as soon as there's a gap in the cars...

And there it is – a moment without a car upon us – *Now!* – and I'm out and yanking at the thing, bringing it forward, but going nowhere – and where's Paul!? – I turn around and he's looking up, up into the sky – *Look at the stars!*

What!? Forget the stars – give me a hand with this bike you eejit – and I hoik, I lift, I heave – *NOW!*

And then, THEN he's beside me, looking – *Give it a push! I'll pull, you push* – and now it moves, slowly, but creeping forwards and then into the bush, hopefully out of sight...

Are we waiting here?

Well – Yes. This is somebody's bike, remember? We need to keep it out of sight... at least until the most of these people have passed by – get back now – here's the next lot –

*

Car by car, truck, horse and cart... We're stuck there for a fair while, whilst that awful place empties out, more bikes, still... Was father

211

within one of these cars? I looked, but it was only shadows I saw, of course, shadows speeding past…

I'm hungry now.

Paul, you're always hungry! What can I do?

…Have you any food?

What!? Where would I have food? Don't be so daft… Shh – here's another cart –

We listen as the clap of the pony's hooves approaches, no lights on this one, comes right alongside us and then passes, pulling away in front.

I think we can go… It just seems to be people walking now – and we'll be faster than them, on the bike…

Will we take the bike?

We have to take the bike! We can't carry the suitcase, remember?

We must be some kind of weaklings…

We must!

Is father there?

Where?

Well… where we're going?

I do not know. We just need to go to the meeting place, remember? Father said! Now – come on… We're just going to get the bike and push it on to the road then you give me a kick start again and we'll be away…Understood? No mention of father, no mention of food, no mention of wees – just away. Ok?

Ok.

Good. And – There's some money in father's wallet. When we get into the town we can look for a roll or something.

Each?

What?

Will we have a roll each? And cheese?

What? I have no idea – come now – we have to go.

*

It's exhausting, but the repetition of the pushing is half the grind, so we swap, putting Paul up in the control seat for the long stretches, me behind the trike, arms outstretched, body flat and pushing away, Paul barely catching the pedals but doing his best, me occasionally feeling a fleeting help, but then the corners coming and us near crashing, so me back in the driver's seat, easier to use the handles when you can reach them after all, and my legs ache once more, but Paul, to his credit, is good at this bit and does his best to push us, the rattly old bike, the sad old suitcase, the raggedy children…

A car will pass, on occasion… at first we swerve to the side, but then we forget once and nothing happens so after that we just carry on… and I think, well although the baker man will know someone is on his bike it doesn't mean the Fallon man will and although this mighty jacket of father's isn't helping my movement, maybe it IS helping us look not like children, as I guess the size of it is puffing out and making me look like some sort of grown-up, albeit a grown-up with a massive fat body and very skinny legs, so maybe Fallon has ALREADY whizzed by us…

What would I know? Just that we have a long while of pushing and wheezing ahead before we rest.

There's a cold wind that mixes in with the sweat from the running and the pedalling and just the whole horribleness of the situation. I think of father and then I try not to think of father, for where is he and where he is not is something I can't control in any way, no, I just have to get Paul to the lightship and once we've done that we wait and if we wait too long and he's not there, well, we get a bus to Cork, and then to that Mary's, and then she can decide what happens next, and we will wait, wait again for father…

I cannot think of him being battered and bruised by Fallon or the meaty white-skinned monster who was on the other side of that boxing field or ring or whatever it was supposed to be. The boat, that's what it was. A boxing boat! *What a load of rubbish.* We shouldn't be here. We should be home. I don't care if we would be cold and hungry because we're cold and hungry here and now and we're wet too, from the exertions, and at least at home Paul and me could be on the steps playing with the flies, awaiting the cold to get so much that father may light a fire for the first time in the day...

So, I push and I push and I pedal and carry on the best I can and I wonder too about that roll because if there's anything I've learned from this little adventure it is that I don't want the money to all go and maybe we'd be better keeping everything we have for the bus, just to make sure we can get it all the way, because I do not want to be the man, the man making decisions, for what would I know to do other than beg again and surely that was the way we met this Fallon ruiner in the first place, was it not?

Is that a bridge? There are lights?

Where? I can't see...

There! Hang on, I'm pushing, are we close to it?

No... Not yet, but closer than we were...

I think I would be happy even to take that old nun back, at this moment, so long as we keep on getting the sandwich... I don't understand religion... but then, that priest let us stay in his church, well, he didn't let us stay, but he didn't call the guards now, did he? And father drank his wine and I can't help but smile at that and I wonder if I'll have the taste for wine when I am older? It looks better than the stout, the stout with that smell it puts out...

Another car pushes past us, a HONK from the horn...

Maybe it didn't see us –

Until the last minute –

Here, can we swap, I'm done with the pushing, let me steer –

Look, Joseph – I am sure it is a bridge not too far, either that or a long boat, all the way over the river...

I pull up, breathing heavy now from the effort of it all, my legs aching, my back crooked – I wipe my brow, the sweat, you know – and – it *is* a bridge.

Yes! Not far now, Paul.

Is that where we're going?

Well – no – not the bridge, but once we're over it, we'll be harder to find, surely? We'll almost be back… We'll be able to find that lightship and meet father…

Meet dada?

Yep, of course.

And then… we'll all go for food?

I shudder, I shudder at the thought of father not being there or being there with his face all cut up and bruised. Or being there waiting with that Fallon man and us all getting pulled away somewhere else…

That'd be up to father…

But it's tea-time! It's BEYOND tea-time…

I KNOW BUT THAT'D BE UP TO FATHER! DON'T BE STUPID!

And that quietens him, but only for a moment, a second perhaps, before he begins to sniff and to cry and the tears arrive again… *Can we go to Mrs Marra's maybe? She'll know where dada is…*

But she won't, she wouldn't know a thing, but how to tell the Fallon creature where we are.

We're going to get over that bridge. One thing at a time. You hear me, Paul?

He sniffs, he cries, audibly, whimpering, and I know it's not the food he's crying about but all the same – *I'm sure father will be hungry too, Paul. He'll want to eat. He'll find us and he'll hug us and take us for food…*

You think so?

Most definitely. I DEFINITELY think so. He'll be all over us with food and with hugs…

And will we stay with Mrs Marra?

Well, I wouldn't say so – I'd say she'd be busy, maybe, with this being a weekend, but father will find us somewhere, I'm sure of that…

Though I am equally sure that somewhere may just be the base of a statue or the doorway of a fishmonger's…

Ok, we're going to go over the bridge…

How?

Just as we are... We cannot climb underneath... and then, and then – look – there are little side snickets we can get into... then we can relax... Here – are you ok?

I am.

Have you stopped your crying?

A bit. A bit I have.

Don't you worry, we'll be home soon.

Home?

Well, not home, but, we'll be stopped. We can rest.

Good.

I hope.

Ok – let's just keep going, I'll keep pedalling, the road is evening up a bit, you just cling on and hang on and don't make a noise, you hear?

I do. Joseph?

A-ha?

I'm thinking about monkeys...

Are you?

I push at the pedals, keeping us going, keeping us moving.

I'm thinking about if there was monkeys swinging under the bridge. They'd get there faster than us...

They would, I'm sure...

This bridge is on a slight hill, it arches up the way, you know? To let the water under... It's killing me, this – *Push the bike a bit, will you?*

Will I?

Please...

And now he's running alongside me, chattering about monkeys, but not really pushing at all, just every so often tapping my shoulder...

And the monkeys could swing over and back in no time...

Good for them!

I tell you one thing, though, him being off the bike and running beside me helps a fair bit in itself, the bike being lighter, if only a bit. Not enough, though –

Please, Paul, push, push if you will, just until we're halfway over...

That does it, now he's behind and head down and my ride eases again, just a little, before we reach the top of the bridge, the flat the straight – *Now, jump on again!* – and he does, so we carry forward before reaching the slope down again and finally now I can ease off a little as gravity does the rest, easing us down to the other bank of the river.

We've escaped...

Well. Almost. Maybe.

*

Is it terribly further because I am very tired?.

I think we've broken the back of it.

We've what?

I think we're almost halfway or even more – in fact – look – is that the lightship there?

I... I think so. That's not far, is it?

Not too far now, no.

Can you see dada?

Of course, I have been looking, but there's not a soul there, not even someone I could mistake for father. Just a tree, but it is too bushy and tall and wide to be father. But no one else being there is a good thing too.

No. Not yet, but he may be there, hiding.

I hope so.

Yep, me too – hey – can we swap again? My legs are falling off...

*

We're yards away. A few dozen of them, maybe, but close. It looks like a strange old boat, this lightship. Painted rusted orange red colour with a big white ice-cream-cone-looking light on the top of it, lurching slightly to one side, but tied up, not moving or bobbing with the water...

We should hide this bike somewhere.

We slow, for we're in easy walking distance now.

Over there!

He points, but he's pointing to nothing, nowhere, just a bare wall, against the river.

What, just – leave it? Leave it against the wall?

Paul looks to me, for approval, to see if his suggestion was sound.

Let's… see if we can find someplace else, shall we?

There's an orange light up against the lightship, the light itself – the big one, on the back of the boat – that's nowhere near being on. As we arrive beside, almost, the whole ship looks as though it hasn't moved in a century.

Look at it!

It's abandoned, leaning to the wall of the river… we're not in a harbour, not in a boatyard, just halfway up or down a long, wide river. The rust, some of it is not rust at all, more a green sort of fungus or moss that's taken home on the side of this massive ship.

It's bigger than a house! We climb off the bike. The bike looks SO tiny compared to the boat that it'll never be noticed, just more bent metal, I give it a final push and it slows into the wall, the front forks turning slightly as it hits.

Can you see dada – DADA?

SHH!

But there's no one here – DADA!?

Shh!

I grab him – *We have to be quiet…*

But why? How will he find us?

Look… We have to keep hidden. In case.

In case what?

In case that Fallon man comes looking for us. He may be angry we left that caravan place…

Because dada hit him?

I smile – *He did, didn't he?*

He did. He knocked him over!

He fell down, didn't he?
With a bump!
With a bump. So – we have to hide.
Ok. Let's hide in here – and he leaps up to the side railings, throws his legs over then jumps straight from the quay on to the boat itself.

*

I'm aware of father's coat I'm wearing, of course I am. It's shaping my movement, cupping my hands, it has his smell, his shape... And Paul is sneaking a look at it – for comfort I'd say – I know he is. But what would father do now, in this situation? I don't know... No doubt Paul will start on about food again any minute, but there's nothing here, nothing with food in, anyhow... This side of the big river is just boarded-up buildings, small warehouses, probably nothing inside but rats... Over on the other bank, it looks more lively, but surely that's why father suggested we escape it and sure, we can hardly just pop over for a sandwich, can we? The distance alone... And as if we even had any money. If I look far enough, I think I can see Mrs Marra's place. We just have to wait. Wait for father or for morning, whichever comes first.

*

Look, Joseph, look –
I can't even see Paul, let alone see what he's on about. I climb over the bars and make the foot leap on to the boat. *Where are you?*
This way – Look –
Which way?
Then I see him, or the tuft of his hair any rate. The boat, once on it, seems secure and stable, I'm hardly feeling sea-sick walking down the narrow siding.
Someone is sleeping here, I think –
And he's right, for here, under the shelter of the great big light, the light that is looming above us like a white glass pineapple – well, there's an old sleeping bag, a blanket, a few boxes of rubbish,

scatterings of newspaper, paper cups, crunched and soiled…

It's sheltered. Non-visible from the roadside or the river – it would be a good place to sleep for sure, and therefore, maybe, a good place to hide… I'm hesitant, but I jump down and gingerly kick at the contents.

What if he comes back?

Who?

The man who is sleeping here, of course!

Yeah… Maybe we should try and find some other little place we could hide in?

Sure!

And he's off again, leaping around the boat, full of energy from somewhere…

I wonder how old all this rubbish is, but how can you tell the age of a dirty cup? It could be last year or last night. Or this afternoon. How long will we even be here? Would this little pile of soil be a good place for us? It looks… awful.

Here!… HERE!

I smile, little Paul so excited about this… *Hold on, I'm coming over…*

He's right by a door now. It's obviously not as good a place. For a start, there's no immediate cover overhead, but it's also very visible from the shore… *No, not this one…*

But look! – Look! – and slowly he leans over and pushes at the door, which itself creaks open.

*

Wow… Can we go in?

It smells. You go first…

I look down, and again, there's evidence of life around – the door itself seems to be stopping from swinging entirely open by a blanket. I look through the glass, but from this angle and with no light within, it's hard to see anything other than a smudged, greasy window.

Hello? Is… is anyone in there?

There's no one on this boat, I know that. There's no light or sound, just Paul and me creeping then leaping around, whispering then shouting, but we're drawing no attention, but…

…the thought of someone jumping out gives me the shivers. Especially some dirty man in a dirty mac with a filthy beard. A Fallon sort of man. A tramp. Smelling of wee…

Keep back, Paul…

I'm NOT going in there, Joseph, YOU are.

Me? How me?

Because you're the oldest and… There may be food in there.

There it is.

Are you mad? What food is going to be in there? An old apple or something? Some empty Taytos bags?

He looks at me, defeated. *Well then. You look and see. There MIGHT be. And MIGHT is better than WON'T.*

He's right, maybe.

I lean over and knock – *Excuse me? Excuse me?*

Nothing. I try the door again, and just as before, it slowly peels open, letting some of the remaining gloom and orange streetlight in. But there's little to be seen, just the blanket on the floor then – just a foot or so in – another door. This one without window and closed.

I think this outside one is just a storm door. Like our storm porch at home…

Do you think? Why would they have a storm door on a boat?

Well, why do you think, you eejit? For the PROPER storms, out at sea… Not like ours, which is just to sit in when it's raining…

Though the porch at home seemed more like a daddy long-legs sanctuary.

This door within a door on the boat looks completely sealed closed, rust and moss all the way around the circular handle, the edge of the door itself, to the extent that it'd make no sense me even trying to open it… Instead, and still a little wary, I give it a little kick.

Closed.

What! How do you know that?

It is – Look – and I kick it again.

You just kicked it!

I know – but it didn't move… for goodness sake, watch – and I go further in, slowly, and begin to push the door. Delicately at first, then stronger, and then a slight heave with my shoulder… and this time the inner door opens, just a splinter, but enough for me to be swamped by a terrible smell of old poo…

Oh no!

I jump back out –

It's a loo!

What? Whose loo is that?

I don't know whose! But someone has used it for a loo. It's awful. Deadly, even. Deadly smelly. And I'm going no further near it.

*

We settled down nearer the front of the boat. Just a cove, if a boat can have such a thing. It wasn't covered from the above, but we weren't for staying, were we? Not in our plans. For father would be back any minute, surely. We were sheltered from the wind, and that seemed enough at first.

Once Paul was settled, or sitting, at least, I went back to the butcher's bike and lifted father's suitcase. I looked all around, of course I did, but all I saw was a ginger cat, a good stone's throw away from where I was, and he was paying me no heed.

I'm hopeful that mother's ring is still inside this suitcase, for else it's been nothing but a weight around me. I push it through the bars of the boat, rest it there, then climb over myself and heave the case further on to the boat, making my way back to Paul.

He's asleep when I get there, I think, but then no, as his eyes peel open and he asks –

Any sign?

I shake my head. *No.* Then – *But don't worry. He'll come. Father will come back.*

I sit down then, put myself close to Paul, remove father's jacket – and straightaway miss the warmth this double layer had given me – and ease Paul forward, stretching the jacket around his shoulder, behind his back and then almost around me, though all it does for me, I find out, is provide a slight cushion against the cold steel of the boat. I place myself as close to Paul as I can, for his warmth, for the comfort he'll give me and I can maybe also give back. This time now, this pretend time, when we can pretend father is coming back, all fit and well, is not a time of comfort, for the worry is inside me and twisting my stomach in a way I do not know. And this is why Paul is not asking for food, for he will have the same worry, I am sure of that. I rest my head against his and before long I am in a stuttering sleep.

33

I HEAR THE *CLANG*, then a *cough* and I'm awake. I stiffen up, my eyes open and ears now alert, listening intently, deciphering, or trying to decipher, every scratch or movement I can make out.

Paul is still asleep, and I want to keep him there, for if he were to awaken and give away our place...

And there's a movement again, this time a sound I recognise, for it is the squeak of the handles of that bike. There is a man upon us, for sure. It can't be a cat, coughing and moving bikes...

Cough.

Again. A deep cough. I don't recognise it, as if a cough would have an individual voice, but I think it would, to an extent, and this does not sound like father coughing. It sounds as though the stomach is coughing, more than the lungs, the body itself, not some tickly throat from a bad swallow.

Ummghg.

Paul's awake now. His light snoring stops in an instant and his body becomes rigid next to mine. I clasp his hand, tight, then again, to tell him by some kind of code to *keep quiet.*

Urshern erf...

It's a whisper, this time, not a cough...

Urrgghf.

I am barely breathing now and my eyes have settled on the tiniest detail of the boat around me, the rusted head of a rivet, punched through two sheets of steel, holding them together. The remaining paintwork looking like some kind of map...

Foys... foys...

He's speaking – definitely –

It's father!

I shut him up, instantly, I sharply whisper – *QUIET!* – and squeeze his hand once more, listening...

Foys... Boys...

It is him, it has to be!

Wait here...

Why should I?

Oh!

But before we can move, before I can spy round a corner, this man looms above us, and this man's face is hard to make out, and not just because the orange buzz of the street light is all there is, bar the moon light itself, but because this man's face is a bloodied, pulped mess.

Boys! Are you – cough – *are you all right...?*

I cannot answer that though, because look at who's asking, it is my father yes but through a wringer. Paul holds his head back from the shock, bringing his knees up tight to his chest and whimpering. I take his hand, but my eyes are drawn to father's face, then repulsed, then back, over and over...

Father.

Joseph. Paul. Let me...

And he collapses down beside us, grappling at his own chest, swearing as he lands on his knees, coughing, dark spit coming from his mouth, on to the deck, the floor below. Paul retreats, pushing himself as far into the cold of the steel of the boat as he can do. I look to father and ask –

Are you... ok?

It is the devil's question for there is no way he is ok in any way, though he is here and he is not running from anyone and I am happy with both of those.

Sure... I just need... his body is aching down, aching him down to some kind of position, it couldn't be called comfortable, but down, resting, maybe?

What – what happened?

Heh! – and more coughing, longer this time, but coming to an end.

I took... I took a gamble.

He raises his left arm, the hand's fingers out, and tries to ruffle Paul's hair, but Paul pulls away further – of course he does, for father looks like an ogre, or a demon. Father's face... there's one eye completely closed, but the other... I see the pain of it when Paul recoils, and I instinctively reach my own hand out and place it on father's shoulder, looking straight into that eye and trying to tell him *everything*, how bad he looks, how worried we are, how tired we are, how we have been waiting, waiting... but within a second I cannot even focus on him, for my heart collapses and tears flood through my eyes, pushing again and again, and I try to squeeze the eyes shut, to push the tears back, but I cannot and soon father is doing the same – but just through that one eye, can you imagine – and soon Paul is with us, and leaning back towards father even, the three of us, as close as we can get, though it mostly being Paul and me in toward father now, for he must be in some pain, Paul then shifting his own body and kneeling almost on top of father, before him being scooped round so he can cuddle in from the side... I lift father's coat and place it over Paul and father, before taking the other side, if I can, if father's injuries will allow me, and slowly, he lifts his arm and I'm in and underneath it – and what warmth there is beneath his arm and the sliver of coat. My tears erupt further and soon the three of us are hurling our sadness from within us, over and over, my father coughing less, thank God, but sobbing like a child, us three as children now, wondering what on earth is what and what on earth is next within that.

Here – father – look –

And he turns his head, barely, to look at me –

We got your case...

He grunts in response, almost raising an eyebrow, but patting me on the shoulder, in thanks, or show of thanks, whichever it is.

Look –

I lean my body out from under him and heave the case over from beside where I had been sitting – only a yard away, if that.

It's heavy!

He twitches at that and replies, with a cough, of course – *Heavy?* Then, wishes it closer to him, gesturing weakly with a finger.

Open – cough – *Open it…*

I look to him in surprise – *Yeah?*

Yeah. It's empty – cough, then whispering – *Shouldn't be heavy…*

And I think, I think – *We should have looked.* Not for food, but that could have helped, I suppose, but maybe a hat or a blanket or anything we could throw away, lighten the load.

I click the clasp on the left easily enough, but the one on the right doesn't want to jump up, I push, again, but nothing. This is enough to stir Paul into action, though, this thought of a *device* not quite working, a latch he can try, a button to press. He leans over and quickly, lightly, flicks the top of the latch, causing it to jump up. Father laughs – *I knew… I knew you'd been watching me do it!* – before wheezing and coughing, over and over… I look to him and he slowly turns his head to the right, spitting a black gob on to the floor.

Lift it. Lift it now – go on.

I gently lift the top of the case, having to shake the base a little to get it to fall, despite the weight within. And when it opens, well, there's something there, but the light is so poor, it's hard to see just what it is…

Is that… here, pass me…

I lower my hand in, carefully and feel – newspaper? I pick a piece up, but no, it's not newspaper, unless it's all been cut up… I hand it to father and in that moment, myself and himself figure what it is, right away –

Money!

It's money, father!

And Paul – he leaps – *Money!? Are you sure? How much? How much is there…*

227

I'm looking at the small handful in father's hands, though his right hand is doing little indeed – *It's money... all right* – Joseph – *is it* *cough* *is it all money? Is it – full?*

I explore further, braver now, the more unlikely it is to be full of snakes or mousetraps *There's a load in here, father...*

Is it all... ones? All these...

He's lifting them, up to the little of the street glare that is reaching us...

All these... are ones...

I do the same, and yep, they all seem to be one, the spooky women on them shining through and staring down at me – no – no – *Here's a five!*

A five! Paul, excited there, though I doubt he knows what a five is.

I scurry through the rest, but father quietens me – *Boys... boys... close the case. Keep that five out... We have to go.*

I look to him, but I cannot read his face, for it is too swollen and mercifully, too dark.

Jesus! Where did you find the case? That... that will be the takings... for the fight.

It was just under a table...

A table? By the door?

A-ha.

He laughs then coughs, again, of course. *We... we have to leave. C'mon, boys...*

He tries to stand, but it's an almighty effort – *Joseph – give me – your hand* – So I stand first, and grip around his hand and wrist and on a count of three, I help pull him up to his feet. But it's like watching some dragon emerge from the gloom of a swamp, for in even the little light provided by the above it looks worse and worse for father and his face, his body, his shirt completely ripped, with markings of blood, surely, upon it. It reminds me a little of those soldiers we'd read about in the war comics who'd throw themselves on barbed wire so their comrades could run over the top...

But I don't let on. Or, I hope I don't. But maybe he can read it in my face…

C'mon, I don't look that bad, do I?

And I look to him, to examine, to look for some light, and whilst doing so, I notice the expression on his face is one of peace almost, and happiness, but something suddenly changes. His one eye that can still see, the one that isn't puffed up, catches sight of something behind me, to the left of me, and the expression on his face changes in an instant. He doesn't say anything, father, but he needs not, for I turn round and standing above us, glaring down and shaking his head, is Fallon.

34

*W*ELL. *I CANNOT believe you made it this far, McLeod.*

He twists and turns his head, counting – father, Joseph, me.

Ah well. Isn't this sweet? Everyone I need, in one little place. And is that... Is that my suitcase? Well now. Hasn't THAT worked out well? I thought that'd been taken by some... opportunist, in all the commotion...

He has a mighty swollen, obviously broken, blooded nose. That would have been father. I saw that, I saw that hit.

You did well to get out, McLeod, but did you think I wouldn't find you? Let me tell you, there are plenty of people in this city who owe me a favour. Plenty of eyes anxious to help me out...

Father, he tries to straighten up, then – *Have you come here by yourself, Fallon? That's taking a risk...*

Ha! What risk? A broken-down poet and some kids! There's no risk. Besides. Some affairs are best sorted without witnesses.

Fallon steps down further, shaking his head – *And God now – what are you doing on here? On this filthy old boat...*

Finally, one more step, and he's just above our level – *Now. McLeod. You're in trouble, McLeod. But what to do... What to do with you, eh? Look at the state of you – you couldn't fight again – you couldn't fight anyway, it seems – dancing around the ring, the way you were...*

Heh. I got you well enough... How's that face of yours, eh?

Father's speaking well, but it's an act, a show of defiance. I squeeze his hand, pull myself closer to his side. Paul though, has stayed down. I glance to him and he looks terrified. Of course he is.

Heh. Fair play, fair play, you did get me. For my guard was down. I

230

was watching your pathetic attempts at being a boxer – you were being battered senseless by that big fella you were up against! But I wouldn't get too cocky, McLeod. For the state of my face may just turn the course of your life. What were you thinking? He shakes his head, glancing out over the river – *I can never let things be now. You know that. It's not just economics now. No. It's pride, also. Come on. Come on out with you all.*

Father doesn't move. As much from the pain as the fear, I'd imagine. And, if he were to move, it'd show this Fallon just how injured he is.

I'll give you – but father breaks into a splutter, again – *I'll give you the suitcase – just… let us go. You won't see us again…*

The suitcase is mine already! Sure, I'll just reach down there in amongst the dirt and take it from you! What's stopping me? Look at you! You're crippled! Now. Come on. Out with you. Out with you all!

I look down at the case, then back at Fallon, who is glaring directly at me. He makes to climb down toward the case but I turn, grab it, then, using all my strength, quickly push it to the side of the boat, then further over the edge, half on, half off, balancing…

You little shit… You wouldn't dare.

I'LL DROP IT! I'LL DROP IT!

Paul then, joining in – *GET AWAY FROM US!*

I'LL DROP IT! I'LL DROP IT IN THE RIVER!

HE WILL! HE WILL!

And this does not please Fallon – *DON'T YOU DARE, YOU LITTLE SHIT.*

And Fallon lunges down, finally, he grabs into the throng of us, the threat of his body now upon us, and father, despite it all, he somehow stands and rams his shoulder straight into Fallon, I guess maybe the shoulder being the only part of father not hurting, for it connected solidly and knocked Fallon back, but at a cost for father, as he himself collapsed back down, wheezing…

FUCK OFF FUCK OFF, FILTHY MAN – Paul now, helping, holding on to the edge of the case, just keeping it upright and again – *FUCK OFF, FILTHY MAN*

I've had enough of this – and from the inside of one of the many gritted, oil-soaked coats he seems to be wearing, Fallon draws out what can only be a blade, for it is gleaming and shining back any light it is catching – *Pull that suitcase back in, boys, or I will kill your father right now in front of you both.*

And father, surely aware that this is the moment, begins another stagger at Fallon, but Fallon squeezes by him easily enough and reaches the suitcase. There's a struggle with Paul, for maybe half a second, before father reaches Fallon and simply begins to envelope him, to bear-hug him and then with a *heave!* Fallon is falling back and a moment later, father's sheer weight is forcing Fallon further off balance and the pair of them are soon collapsing over the railings toward the water, where they fall with a mighty *Whoompf.*

*

I stop. I'm not doing anything, but I stop. My heart stops. My hearing cuts off. My vision slows. I cannot move nor breathe, and I stay stunned, until just a split second later, Paul screams, loud, shrieking and long, high-pitched, involuntary screams. I look for him, but he's not on the boat –

He's overboard. *Paul's overboard.*

I run over to the side of the boat, to the spot where father last stood, the railing that father last grasped at.

There's no sign. There's no sign of anyone. The water is just black, a shining, tumbling, solid-looking black surface.

Then, there is.

I spy Paul, blustering in the water, and a moment later, there's a reverse crashing as two heads emerge from the water, spitting, coughing out water and whatever, huddled together as if one. They seem to want to destroy the other the instant they can, I see no knife glitter, but I can make out little more than that, which arm belongs to who, which face is taking the force of the other. Fallon is screeching with laughter and we have to presume he is on top and father defeated, until Paul, struggling perhaps in the water or from

232

watching the fight, Paul he cries, he cries out – *DADA* – and then he cries again, worse to hear this time – *MAMA* – and this, this cry of childhood, this deep memory, it must have stirred something in father, for we hear HIM cry this time, HIS voice, HIS anger erupt, erupt with the rage of all his life and another hand emerges from the water and begins to hammer again and over against the face of Fallon, the laughter stopping now, just a continued, repeating grunt as father brings his fist down and then his elbow, over and over until Fallon's grip has gone and he floats, slightly lowering, sinking, silently away.

Father turns his head and looks over at Paul, before he himself begins slowly drifting downstream, away from the boat.

Father!

Father's not responding. His head is laid back now, ears dipping in and under the water.

Father! – are you ok?

Paul! Are you ok? Can you see father? Can you reach him?

No! No!

Then come out, Paul! Come out – I'll help you…

And Paul swims to the side of the boat and begins to climb up some little side ladder. I reach over and grab at him, pulling him up, him now shivering and panicked. *Dada… Joseph… Dada.*

I can see father is drifting. Further from the boat. I have to jump in. I kick my shoes off, remove my coat and give it to Paul – *Try and keep warm, Paul!*

And I run to the edge, hesitate for a second, and jump in.

It's cold. Frozen cold, but I expected that from Paul, and I am used to that, forever swimming in loughs and the sea. The taste – there's little salt, though why that should register, I do not know – and Paul, he is screaming, screaming still – *Dada! Dada!* – but from the water, I cannot see father anywhere, or indeed take my bearings… I cry up to Paul – *Where? Where is he? Point him out!!*

Paul's slender grey arm, pointing out, randomly it seems, not in one straight line, one straight instruction, but somewhere – *there!*

There! – and I spy, I think, a slight bobbing on the water, father's head for sure, and swim straight toward him, the same current that is carrying him, helping me reach my goal. Head down, I go, to the area – and there he is, moved now, but closer than he was – head down again and toward him, looking out now, head above and reaching him, him floating, almost on his back, mouth and face sapping in and out of the water… *are you ok father* – and his head turning, slightly, towards me, letting me see he is alive, if not well, then submerging and up once more, over and over.

I pull behind him, using what strength I have to support his body, and it's all I can do to keep him up and out, my legs, my arms not affecting the direction of our journey in any way I can tell… I look back toward the lightship, it getting further away with each glance, I just hope, hope that Paul will know to follow, for I can hear him calling still, but fainter, of course – *Dada! Dada!* – and I am saying the same, of a sort, into his ear – *Father, father, you keep up, ok? Keep breathing, I'm going to find us to the shore, I promise you. I promise you.*

35

I HELP FATHER PULL himself out of the water, in amongst a low, muddy shore. First, it's just me, but within time, Paul finds us and grabs at father's arm, Paul slipping and heaving from the wet of the shore. All I could do really was encourage father, for he was conscious, and he too struggled his way out. I felt near frozen and half-drowned myself, make no mistake of that, for that Liffey water was not pleasing. Surely, if anyone had met ME on the shore now, in my state, they'd be coaxing me out, or lifting more like.

Father was spewing coloured water from his belly, from his lungs, never ending, thick and gloopy.

He's dying.

And I think Paul was right. I think.

He's dying right in front of us. From the water.

The water and the battering, of course. For he could have swam, no bother, if he wasn't half-drowned from the punches and hits and scrapes of that Fallon monster. Father was a good swimmer, though not good enough, we knew that.

We need to get him to a hospital –

Here –

And Paul thrusts his hand toward me, within a grasping of bank notes, but I shout at him, for what use are they, now, here? *And what can I do with that!?*

A taxi! For dada! We need a taxi.

*

And I'm out, running the streets, leaving Paul with father. *Keep him*

235

talking, I had told Paul, *Keep him out of the water, and talk to him. Keep him awake.*

There's no taxis though, not here, and why should there be, for there are no people, not at this time of night… I run up street after street, but the whole city seems as though in a sleepy orange streetlight gloop. Eventually, I spy a marked taxi cab, but its lights are off, I get beside it, as quick as I can, and find a man, a man in the seat, head down, covered with a flat cap –

Hey!

And then –

HEY!

And I knock, then rattle his door, causing him to jump, startled. He peers at me through the window, then points to where his taxi light should be –

What the fuck are ye doing? I'm sleeping – I'm aff…

I knock again – *My father, my father needs a lift to the hospital –*

He's looking at the state of me – *Fuck off. Get away. Can you no' see I'm… I'm not taking YOUR sort anywhere – now move it.*

He starts his engine and I panic – I jump to the front of the parking space, leaving little room for him to move his car round – *He's just – he's injured – he fell in the river…*

GET OUT OF MA WAY!

And he nudges into my knees and for one moment I'm worried he'll keep on going and plough into me, like you hear about what happens in the big cities and the films, but he draws back and I can see him, hauling his steering wheel all the way around to the right, then he's reversing again… This is my hope, and my hope is leaving – then – *I can give you this! Look! Look* – and I show him the five pound note – *We just need a lift! A lift to the hospital… My father is just round the corner – Look – please…*

I can see him, he's staring at the note, then looking all around him, all around the vehicle. He rolls the window down – *Show me* – and I leap round to his side – *He's just at the lightship, you know, just down a bit further* – he doesn't reply, but takes the note through

236

the crack of the window, then quickly pulls the car out and speeds away from me for maybe ten whole seconds.

Then he stops.

He waits. A good, long run away from where I am now, but still in sight. He's just sat there, engine running, at the end of the road. I stand where I am, he can see me, I'm sure of it. But there's no point me running to him, I'd never catch that…

I pat my pockets. There's three singles left, I know that. What to do now? I've got to get to the other side of the river. Find a phone box. Call someone. The police. An ambulance. The operator will know who. I cannot just run back to father and Paul, empty-handed, full of panic and soaked through. If I stop still I'll die in a moment myself from the cold.

Decision made.

I turn, face away from the cab and begin the run, for a run it must be, the run to the next bridge. I wonder what will Paul be doing, what he'll be saying to father, and I'm hoping father will be sat up, talking, comforting Paul, but I find it unlikely.

I shake my head, panic, fear, soaking wet and frozen cold, searching for something…

The steam from my breath, the cold of the night, reaching in with every deep inhale, scoring my lungs. I get into a rhythm, of sorts, head down, just continue and hope can I see a bridge, a bridge or a phone box… there are leaves, slippery leaves on this road, the trees overhead shedding, what with winter near, causing me to watch my footing, slow down, just another *thing* to put up with…

Behind me, there's a noise, a gruff diesel engine, a long way off, but enough to make me turn, turn and slow – and it's a taxi – *Would this one stop?* – I reach into my pockets for the notes, I arrange them in my hand like a fan, ready to show the man driving that I have money, for everyone wants money, right?

I look up, and as he approaches, a fear comes over. I squint my eyes, and spy – *it's the same driver*, the same man as before, *What's he after…?* I jump out of his way, thinking *the last thing I need to do is lose THIS money* – he reaches me in a moment, a handful of seconds, but I'm back on the path now, watching, curiously, but ready to sprint, keep on sprinting –

Hey. Is yer man really injured?

I nod, then, *He is. But I've no more money. And I can run. Quickly.*

Heh. I saw that. Don't you worry, I mean you no harm… Where is he then, this father of yours?

Back that way. On the riverbank. Just past the lighthouse boat. You know it?

Everyone knows it. Come on then. Get in. We'll go get him.

*

I had to be careful. Taxi drivers are seen as easy pickings, sometimes. But… I checked your money. It's good. And I saw you had no… others… waiting in the bushes to get me, you know? And my mother would never forgive me, if I left a boy stranded in the street…

It's good just to be sitting down. And the taxi has a warmth, out of the wind, though not a strong wind, but cold enough. I didn't miss it, that's for sure. My legs are slowly readjusting from the running, burning, then freezing, aching, slightly.

Where are you from, boy?

But I don't know the answer to that.

Cork. Scotland.

Cork, Scotland is it? I've never been, never been –

We pass the lightship, still now, no sign of the scuffle earlier, no sign of Fallon, somehow crawling back on board… I shiver.

Here is it, now?

It's just past down there – will you wait for me? I'll go and get him – and my brother…

Your brother? You never mentioned your brother…

He stiffens, anxious once more.

He's eight years old. You've nothing to worry from him… There! There they are, look…

Father doesn't look great, but he's almost sat up, he's laid against a post of some kind, a rotted wooden thing. Paul is holding his hand, but also looking all around, he's spied the taxi now and is watching us approach. I want to get the window down and shout to him and I would, but within seconds we're there, and the taxi driver announces our arrival with a *Holy Christ*. And I can see why, for as they approach us, they are both clearly as wet as me, and father is a hobbling, bloodied mess. Between them, they look like terrors from the deep.

*

There's no way he got in that state just falling in the water!

Father's eyes are puffed, bruised, but open. He's looking at me, keeping my eye, almost grinning. He reaches over a hand and I take it, but cannot lift him myself –

Will you give me a hand?

There's… there'll be blood all over the taxi… And water! And fish, maybe, even…

Paul, help me here, will you…

Hang on now, there's a sheet I keep for dogs in the boot. At least let me get the sheet from the boot…

We can but wait, as there is little chance Paul and me could lift a failing father.

It'll cost me more than five pounds just to clean the car!

And father, he leans over, whispers to me – *Don't forget the suitcase, Joseph* – and he nods, slightly, toward the driver – *You may need it* – before leaning his head back against the tree, stuttering and coughing.

We're similar.
We were similar.

Our worlds
just
Irish peat and Scottish clay.

Your soaking Atlantic mist, somehow more worn
and historic than
My own cold haar.

On a good day, when I walk these cliffs
the roar, the humbling,
I feel the tide
pushed you out and pulled me back.

36

I'M LAID OUT on the bed now, Paul in the bed beside me. We have
a twin room. Father is upstairs, in a different ward... Paul and
me, well, we were soaked, of course, so ended up being taken in to
be checked for pneumonia.

Where else could we have gone, anyway?

This is easily the most comfortable bed I've had for a long time.
We're in the maternity ward. Which is a bit odd, but then, I suppose
Paul is almost still a child...

Around us, there are new babies emerging the whole time,
screaming their lungs off for food... I get given a bowl with a
slippery peach in it. Paul too. Peaches are good food. I never knew
that.

The bed cover is itchy, bobbly brown wool, but the sheets, the
sheets – they're spotlessly white, though they smell... odd. They
smell like a pretend clean, if that makes sense... No wonder they
took our filthy clothes away, to wash them, keeping them away
from all this clean that surrounds us now.

We were made to have a bath. That was ok, it warmed me up.
And our hair needed washing from that filthy river water...

Our shoes are in the corner, underneath a blue painted wooden
chair. Which I guess is where the visitors would go, but we haven't
had any of those. I'm wearing pyjamas now. I can't say these are the
best, and, well, who knows who was wearing them before me? But
they're warm... I'm warm.

I hear the rain, a light smattering on the window.

The suitcase – father's suitcase – is beside the shoes. I was clinging
on to it, didn't let any of the hospital people near it. It became a

bit of a 'thing', I think, me not letting it go… In the end, they let me keep hold of it and I climbed into the bath holding it tight, but well, that wouldn't work, so I laid it at the side of the bath, and then, well, someone moved it to the corner, and here we are. I can still see it now, even though the light is off.

The cabbie waited around, for a bit. Until the *Garda* was mentioned, then he shot off, pretty-quick. I'm glad he did. Glad he waited, glad he left. He was still complaining about the mess, mind you. *And who'll pay for that?*

Paul is snoring. It's funny to hear him, nuzzling away. Poor wee Paul. I wonder if father is sleeping? Up there above, a whole floor away… I hope so.

*

Hello… Mary? Is that Mary?
  Who's this? Is that… young Joseph?
  It is, hello…
  …
  Well. And what is it you want? Why is this not Fraser? Why is this not Fraser on the phone?
  Well…
  Is your father after something, is that it? Has he ran out of money, then?
  We're in Dublin, he's…
  Sorry! – A man accidentally jolts me as he pushes past, on his way to wherever.
  Where are you? What's all that noise? Look – So could he not phone me himself, could he not? Is he not brave enough, is that it? I mean, I should have known…

The phone is black Bakelite, scored and scratched, too big for my head and smelling bad. The reek off the mouthpiece it is giving me a headache, just holding the thing, that and these starched clothes, edging into me… and Mary, Mary is rushing away, speaking new words before I can even think of a reply to the old words…
  It's… It's…

There's too much of a racket around me. Crying children, porters pushing beds, white-coated whoevers rushing past, whispering but somehow loudly… I'm exhausted myself, I've had little sleep, Paul woke crying…

We're in…

Is he too scared to talk to me himself, Joseph? Is this it, now?

And then the phone's beeping and I'm pushing in more change, plenty of change now, a pocketful from buying Paul and me some crisps and a Mars and a Coca-Cola in a tin for our breakfast.

Mary, can you hear me? We're in Dublin – We're in the hospital.

Dublin! What… what hospital?

Yes – I don't know who else to call…

What – what's the matter? Is it Paul?

And another *Excuse me!*, this time from a trolley, a trolley with a man lying down, being pushed from behind by one fellow and led from the front by another, but him not paying attention or little worry to me or maybe I should move further into the wall but these phones are hard enough to use as it is

No – no it's father. He's… had an accident. We need… The doctors say we need some place to go. To rest… or… Father said… to call you, to call you first…

Call me!? Joseph – What am I to do!? Have you any idea how far away Dublin is? And what kind of accident? – What's happened? Joseph?

He umm… He fell in the river…

In the river?

And with the word alone I freeze back to the hollow cold of the events and to make matters worse, every time I see a new arrival in this corridor, I fear it will be Fallon, out of the deep like some devil, or one of his henchmen, looking for him, but finding me…

In the river… He's –

Was he drunk?

Was he what?

Drunk?

Drunk.

No! He wasn't even drinking – he – um – he had a fight. And ended up in there. Listen, they want to…

Fighting?

Yes.

And he wasn't drinking?

No – he was sober.

Well… who was he fighting then, Joseph? People don't just fight one another – unless they've been drinking – and I can't have your father here simply as he's been off drinking and fighting people, do you think I need that? If he'd needed me, he should have called me before he was in hospital, not after… He should have called me the minute you arrived in Dublin, the minute you got somewhere to stay, not all these days later…

No – no – Listen, please, Mary, it was not father's fault. And he was talking of you, WE were talking of you. And here – we have some money now.

Money!? Did he sell those poems!

Well, yes, but… Mary we won't… we won't be a burden, I promise… But can you come? Please, can you come and get us? They're saying father's in no state to look after us and I think they are right and they are saying they'll call a children's home… and I can't go away with nuns, Mary, and I'm terrified they'll separate me from Paul. And I'm tired, Mary, and I don't know what else to do or who else to call. Will you come? Will you come, Mary?

*

Mary had a neighbour look after the bar as she drove up to Dublin. She knew the way, she said. She knew Dublin, had been there once before. She didn't look delighted to see us two waiting on her, even though our clothes were now fresh and washed and our hair clean too. Who knows what she thought we'd been up to.

She was looking around the ward, searching for father, and when she saw him first she walked straight by – I had to call her back – *Mary… this is father* – with the ward nurse watching on, curious. And once she'd seen father, in hospital, in that ward, in that terrible state, then she could see we really needed her. I heard her breathe in in shock, before slowly approaching father and staring at him, before turning to us – *Look. Here's fifty pence. Away and buy some sweets, boys. I need to see to your father.*

And that was a welcome enough distraction for Paul, and for me too.

As we reached the door to leave the ward, I turned and saw father holding his hand out to Mary. But she was far from the bed and made no move to take his hand back. At least, not when I was looking.

*

Sweets! Sweets! Sweets!

Paul, jumping around, almost colliding with a woman with her arm in a stookie.

For goodness sake, you two. Behave yourself. This is a hospital, you hear?

Sorry, sorry…

But thinking I knew full well it was a hospital, thank you very much. And as soon as we were past her, I made no effort to stop Paul, as he chimed up again –

Sweets! Sweets! Sweets!

*

When we returned with our haul, the ward nurse was with Mary, Mary telling her that *Yes, she was responsible for us…*

Mary saw us arriving, looked down and smiled, holding out her hand, which I took, although I'm not sure if it was for me or Paul.

And we were signed out, with father left in.

We said our goodbyes. Father whispering to me – *You look after Paul, you hear?* And I nodded, pulling my cheeks close in, to try and stop any tears. And then he told me, quietly – *And take the suitcase. But… Don't tell Mary – what's in it. You hear?*

But… why not?

She may not... may not understand. I'll sort it with her. When I come down. You hear?

I nod.

*

Paul was crying, father doing his best to calm him – *Sure, it'll only be a few days, and you LOVED it down at Mary's, no?*

But we didn't really. What we loved was father being there, and father being so happy. And leaving him here? Well, that's not the same at all. And I was thinking – *But what if that Fallon comes in? What if he's alive and finds out where father is?* Of course I was. But I couldn't tell Paul that.

On the journey home, in that cold, little car, I was sick with worry. Mary would see me upset and occasionally ask me details, distracting me maybe, but curious, too – *Tell me about the poems, Joseph. Tell me what happened.* And I'd struggle to remember, even though it was less than a week ago. Paul would help, kind of – *The man. He was fat and hairy.* And that would make Mary laugh.

Fat and hairy, eh? A man? Well I never.

And that would make us all laugh.

She'd made us sandwiches. And there was a large blanket, should we need to snuggle under. I didn't at first, of course not, but the journey seemed to last forever, and when eventually Paul crawled under, he looked so comfortable that I followed him.

I pretended to sleep, listening to the sounds of the road, the rain, and Mary talking away to herself. Whenever I opened my eyes, I'd see Paul, quiet but awake, squinting at her.

37

WHEN WE ARRIVED, in the dark, I didn't show her the money. When she opened the room up for Paul and me, I still didn't show her the money. I hid the suitcase behind my legs, even.

When she brought us some food, *a little supper*, I didn't show her the money. By then, I'd pushed the suitcase behind a stack of crisp boxes, almost.

The next day though, the next morning, when Paul and me were sat in the bar eating toast, well, she found the money herself. I heard her:

AND WHAT THE HOLY FUCK IS THIS?

I ran, I ran, the bedroom door open and me just standing there in the opening, looking in, looking in to her kneeling and, well, not counting, but rooting, sorting...

Joseph? For the love of God – Explain.

I wasn't sure what father had told her, but I knew he'd told me NOT to mention the money at all, so I mumbled something, something about the poems, something about them selling well and this maybe being an advance or something.

But she knew better.

I'm not a fool, Joseph. I read those poems. They didn't make much sense to me, but, well, they weren't good enough for a box full of money now, I know that... Is this something to do with that fight he had? The state that he is in?

And I began to cry, for I am no good at lying and who knows what father had told her, but maybe it was not only from that, maybe it was from the tension of everything and a fear of how father was and I was tired and it's not me to blame, this stack of money. I can only hope most of what father had told Mary was the truth and I'd only be filling in the gaps. I told her that Fallon had stolen our case and we'd taken it back, not knowing anything was in it. I told her it was father's money he deserved as that Fallon had promised. And I told her not to worry as the man who might want it back might not want it back at all as he'd fallen in the river and might well be in the Irish Sea by now.

Her face went grey. *He drowned?*

I don't know. But he was a rotten man.

But… Do you THINK he drowned?

I shake my head – *I don't know. I didn't see.*

Well, it may be for the best. Because what if he didn't drown? And what if he sees who signed you two out and comes looking, eh? What then…? Jesus Christ.

But he must have drowned. The number of hits father had got in on him!

He must have drowned.

*

She hid the suitcase and its contents in the loft. We kept quiet. Out of the way.

At lunch, she placed a plate of beans and soda bread down in front of us, not opening her mouth when doing so, except to say *You know where the tap is.*

And when she left the room, we poured ourselves some water.

And we heard her, next door, talking away to herself. We heard her say this –

They're not MY children!

Paul shovelled in his beans, and after a minute, I did the same. *We knew that.*

*

In the afternoon, Mary had us wiping tables and picking up nuts from the floor. I'm sure I saw Paul nibbling on one.

Don't eat that, it's disgusting!

And Mary, joining in –

Oh my goodness – Paul, are you eating nuts from the floor? Don't be so stupid…

She laid a full packet down for us soon after. And a lemonade, although only from that scooshy tap she had, not a real bottle. Paul looked on in wonder.

Imagine using that as a gun! A lemonade gun! Imagine. Teush – teush – teush!

I smile at the gun noise, but soon I'm back to thinking about father, how he is and when he'll get out.

*

We duck out. Tidy our little beds. I try to keep Paul quiet, you know. Quiet, but occupied. So as not to disturb Mary. She's downstairs, swearing at cardboard boxes.

Paul, he has a piece of wood. He's crunched over on the floor, pretending the wood is a car, and driving it over and over around the corner of the wall, *Vroom* noises and *Get away! He needs to get away! He needs to escape, and… he escapes!*

*

Come evening, the bar is busy. Mary sounds happier now, chatting away, distracted. We'd spent our afternoon outside, but the day had dragged, of course it had, and any time the phone had rung we'd rushed inside, but… No. No news.

We're sat now eating cheese sandwiches, with crisps for salt. Paul shoves the crisps into the sandwich itself, which seems daft, but soon I do the same and we're crunching away, laughing a little at the mess jumping out of the side of our mouths.

There's a clump outside the room, then the doorway flies open, and we're caught, surrounded by crumbs, mouths full.

Here. Is this him!? Is this the man?

Mary's holding, gripping a newspaper, *The Irish Press*, in front of me. I look up at her, to read her eyes, is she angry with the crisp mess? But she's pecking down toward the paper, jabbing a finger toward a tiny wee square of photograph, a speckled picture of a man, a man with short hair and a grin who perhaps could have been Fallon, one day, many years ago, maybe. He looks happy, as though he's smiling to a buddy just out of picture.

The caption reads: *DUBLIN GANGSTER FOUND DEAD*

Then, smaller: *POLICE SUSPECT GANGLAND TENSIONS*

I pull back. It's horrible seeing his face again, even if he is all neat and combed.

That's him. I think it is.

Paul though, he whimpers and jumps down into the corner, hiding his face.

Mary nods, eyes wide, but no smile – *It says he's been drowned.*

Yes.

She stares at it a moment longer, I dare to take a closer look, but she pulls it away – *Ah no, a newspaper like this is not for your eyes.*

*

Mary collected father, a day or so later. She'd got the call from the hospital, Paul and me, our ears sprang up from our activities – hiding at the top of the stairs, listening in to whatever was happening below – and we heard her, clearly – *Is he ready?* And then a list of *ah – a-ha – ah – ok – well – fine – ok – got ye – ok* – before the phone pinging down and Mary calling up – aware, I'd say, that we were listening, because of course we were.

He's ready. They're letting him out tomorrow morning. I'll go and fetch him. You boys will need to stay here. Your father and me – we need to talk.

And that suited me. It meant I could get ready. For whatever.

All I wanted was here.

And I thought,
blindly, perhaps,
once I had it,
I could keep it.

Then, shimmering,
your world took you back.
The beauty, the land you loved,
could not resist you.

Sometimes, that is truly what I believe.

And now, I must spend every moment
edging ever further away
from that quick, glancing smile, that kiss,
and that final touch.

Oh my darling, how I long for you.

38

IF YOU LEAVE through the rear door, there's the yard, a yard full of stinking, overflowing bins, full of broken glass, beer bottles, the like. The stickiness of the alcohol giving off a gloopy smell, a smell that just hangs around like an insult on the otherwise crisp and still early morning. It's quiet now, Mary has left to collect father. She's asked the neighbour, Freddie, I'm told, to come and open up for lunch time Guinness business, but he's not here yet... I don't like him, anyway. He's too thin. I can see the bones in his mouth and that thin beard he never removes looks like spider legs. Plus, when he talks, he has a whistle between the teeth.

Though I am not looking for flaws in the man.

Paul is asleep, I think, upstairs. He'd been awake most of the night, excitement about seeing *dada* and I didn't want to wake him.

And father will be back late this afternoon. What happens then? Do we leave? Do we stay?

It does feel safe here. Even though it's a main road and not much more. And those local children were ok, friendly even, after the beginning... Maybe we would have friends here...? I wonder where the school is. What it's like.

I think of home, of Creagh, I mean. At the bottom of our hill, at the foot of the mountain, there's the lough. And I know mother is not there, but she is, somehow... and that's where I feel we should be. Maybe father will want to sell that... and I don't think I could live with it. I cannot imagine leaving it. Selling it. My heart would break.

Mother certainly doesn't feel *here*, I know that... But father would be. And Paul.

38

IF YOU LEAVE through the rear door, there's the yard, a yard full of stinking, overflowing bins, full of broken glass, beer bottles, the like. The stickiness of the alcohol giving off a gloopy smell, a smell that just hangs around like an insult on the otherwise crisp and still early morning. It's quiet now, Mary has left to collect father. She's asked the neighbour, Freddie, I'm told, to come and open up for lunch time Guinness business, but he's not here yet... I don't like him, anyway. He's too thin. I can see the bones in his mouth and that thin beard he never removes looks like spider legs. Plus, when he talks, he has a whistle between the teeth.

Though I am not looking for flaws in the man.

Paul is asleep, I think, upstairs. He'd been awake most of the night, excitement about seeing *dada* and I didn't want to wake him.

And father will be back late this afternoon. What happens then? Do we leave? Do we stay?

It does feel safe here. Even though it's a main road and not much more. And those local children were ok, friendly even, after the beginning... Maybe we would have friends here...? I wonder where the school is. What it's like.

I think of home, of Creagh, I mean. At the bottom of our hill, at the foot of the mountain, there's the lough. And I know mother is not there, but she is, somehow... and that's where I feel we should be. Maybe father will want to sell that... and I don't think I could live with it. I cannot imagine leaving it. Selling it. My heart would break.

Mother certainly doesn't feel *here*, I know that... But father would be. And Paul.

All I wanted was here.

And I thought,
blindly, perhaps,
once I had it,
I could keep it.

Then, shimmering,
your world took you back.
The beauty, the land you loved,
could not resist you.

Sometimes, that is truly what I believe.

And now, I must spend every moment
edging ever further away
from that quick, glancing smile, that kiss,
and that final touch.

Oh my darling, how I long for you.

James would like to thank Oldcastle Books, Jim Gill
at United Agents, Domino Records, John Williams,
Walter Dexter O'Driscoll, Rodge Glass
and all the Bothy Heroes

●LDCASTLE BOOKS

POSSIBLY THE UK'S SMALLEST
INDEPENDENT PUBLISHING GROUP

Oldcastle Books is an independent publishing company formed in 1985 dedicated to providing an eclectic range of titles with a nod to the popular culture of the day.

Imprints vary from the award winning crime fiction list, NO EXIT PRESS, to lists about the film industry, KAMERA BOOKS & CREATIVE ESSENTIALS. We have dabbled in the classics, with PULP! THE CLASSICS, taken a punt on gambling books with HIGH STAKES, provided in-depth overviews with POCKET ESSENTIALS and covered a wide range in the eponymous OLDCASTLE BOOKS list. Most recently we have welcomed two new digital first sister imprints with THE CRIME & MYSTERY CLUB and VERVE, home to great, original, page-turning fiction.

oldcastlebooks.com

| OLDCASTLE BOOKS	| KAMERA BOOKS	| HIGHSTAKES PUBLISHING
| POCKET ESSENTIALS	| CREATIVE ESSENTIALS	| THE CRIME & MYSTERY CLUB
| NO EXIT PRESS	| PULP! THE CLASSICS	| VERVE BOOKS